The Dream of Hope Series:

THE BRETHREN
RISE

C. D. HULEN

© 2016

The Brethren Rise

All rights reserved. No part of this book may be reproduced or transmitted in any form or by any means without written permission from the author.

Trade Paperback ISBN 978-0-9988915-0-7
eBook ISBN 978-0-9988915-1-4

Copyright © 2016 by C. D. Hulen
Cover design by C. D. Hulen

Published in the United States by Hulen Publishing

www.thedreamofhope.com

In loving memory of Chris Landrum,
Your faith in our Savior Jesus Christ will never cease to encourage mine onward.

CONTENTS

	How Did We Come to This?	1
I.	A Town and a Fever	3
II.	Good Men Die	21
III.	The Good, the Bad, and the Broken	35
IV.	Caddarik	47
V.	Where We Will Go	59
VI.	A Darker Dawn	77
VII.	"Who will we be?"	89
VIII.	Doubt, Dread and Death	106
IX.	Varanus Descending	117
X.	Master of Those Who Serve Me	127
XI.	The Chink in my Armour	140
XII.	The Battle of Château de Dourdan	154
XIII.	Voice of the Past	162
XIV.	One War	168
XV.	The Man out of Time	179
XVI.	"Remember"	196
XVII.	Cold Reunion	205
XVIII.	Commander of Kings	220
XIX.	When Heroes Fall	231
XX.	Legacy of our brothers	242
XXI.	"We Stand as One!"	249
XXII.	The Brethren Rise	268
XXIII.	A Higher Calling	282
	The Future Torments	291

Foreword

I never knew the story of my father; how he became a legend – how he became a hero. He never told me how he became the greatest leader the Brethren ever knew. But I know now, I have seen it, now that I stand within the present. I know his story.

I know where my father began.

PROLOGUE

HOW DID WE COME TO THIS?

"I did what I had to do," I struggled to keep my voice calm amidst the sound of gunfire just beyond our door.

"There is always another way!" tears streaked Piper's face. "You did not have-"

"Not this time," I gritted my teeth to dispel the stone rising in my throat. "There is no other way," I clasped her hands in mine. "I am so sorry."

She nodded. "Promise me you will find him. No matter what the cost."

"Richard!" Edmond rushed into the back room before I could reply. "We are being slaughtered out there!" he yelled in desperation. "If we do not use-"

"No," I lamented turning from Piper and facing him. "We have lost too much, far too much. The Orbs will be used no more in this war. You have seen what their power can do. What it can do to us. Do you not remember our brothers? Tell me, do you not remember?"

"Then what are we going to do?" another man thundered from his place at the door of the room. "The Cardinal's army is overwhelming us," he motioned his hand for me to follow him out the door. Edmond, Piper and I walked out onto the rampart. I rested my hands upon the rail of the balcony and stared into the battle raging before me. Above us was the Castle of Northisle and the sky of seas.

Below was death and doom.

I gripped the railing harder. Every stone along the walls, every plank of wood on the floor, none of it lacked the deep red stain. The last remaining members of the Brethren fought desperately, darting around and about the dead bodies of their brothers, clashing swords and whistling arrows all about as they went. The booming of the cannon and crumbling of the walls, the sounds of steel on steel. Lead constantly tearing into flesh, gunpowder exploding each second, the screams of wounded and dying, the weeping of the children I could not save. The thud as yet another brother fell, and the constant drums of darkness. The railing began to crack as my fingers tightened around it.

The Brethren members were falling like trees in a storm and the forces of the darkness just as quickly. No hope remained for this age, nothing more could be done to stop them.

Over a hundred of the Brethren lay dead already, along with a hundred more of our enemies, who were constantly keeping in number with fresh troops as our people fell. Dozens of them poured into the fortress each second and would soon overwhelm us. I took a deep breath as I took in every detail of our downfall. A tear fell from my eye and dropped off the rampart, splashing down into the puddles of blood.

"How?" I stammered. My teeth clenched as I fixed my gaze on him. "How did we come to this?"

I

A TOWN AND A FEVER

1323

I opened the door to my home in London and breathed in the cool morning air. The sun had just begun to rise in the East, washing away the stars as it came. I brought my bag over to the wagon where my father was packing many of our possessions.

"Can I help you with anything Father?" I asked as I handed my bag to him.

"Nothing I can think of," Father answered, taking the bag and putting it into the wagon.

"What about your tools?" I asked.

"I have them here," he put his hand on a crate sitting next to an old anvil which had not been used nearly enough in the past six months. "Is there anyone you wish to say goodbye to? We will be leaving soon."

"No," I replied. 'Not many friends left here in London,' I thought to myself.

"What about, ah what is his name?" Father fumbled.

"Bennett?" I asked.

"Aye!" his face lit up. "Are you not friends with him?"

"Not really," I stuffed my hands in my pockets. "He is rather strange, well, no, more like hard to talk to."

"Strange and hard to talk to?"

"Well, you see, it is hard to get him to talk about something other than faith. Not that that is a bad thing, but you know, it is just hard to talk to him," now it was my turn to fumble over words. "I know, it is no good reason to avoid him."

"Well, that is where you are right Richard, that is no reason at all," Father admonished. "I understand how you are feeling, but you must remember, there is no such thing as too much faith."

"It is hard to explain," I grumbled and looked down. "I am sorry."

Father pushed a few of the bags further into the wagon. "Your Mother may need some help with the food and other bags," Father smiled down at me. I was instantly glad he changed the subject.

"Will we not have food there?" I asked. "In Shrewton?"

"Aye," Father laughed, "but you know Mother; she will not go an hour without having a meal within reach in case of a problem. Also, it will take a few days to get there."

"All right," I spun around and darted inside the house to where Mother was packing a bag of food. "Can I help you with anything Mother?" I asked.

"Oh yes," she replied, "could you bring that bag in the corner out to your..." she paused a moment in the middle of packing another sack.

"To Father?" I asked quizzically.

"Yes. Bring it to Father," she replied.

"Yes Mother," I said as I grasped the bag and darted back outside to where Father was working. "Here you are, Father," I said, handing him the bag.

"Thank you," he replied, grasping the sack and placing it into the wagon.

I turned and began walking back to the house.

"Richard," Father called after me.

I spun around to face him. "Aye?"

"Run over to the Hardwin's house and let him know that we are nearly ready to leave."

"Yes Father!" I shouted as I ran up the street. Before long, however, I found my breath too quick to sustain my small frame and therefore slowed to a steady walk as I clutched my side. I looked around at the houses and alleys one more time. None of it really mattered to me; I was born in London and had lived there eleven years, but sickness was never absent in the city and funerals were regular events. It was no home of mine. Something always drew us out of London; it was like a calling to my Father and Mother to return to Shrewton. I never understood why. All I knew was that wherever my parents were, that is what I will call home.

I rounded the last few blocks and strode fifty paces down one of the streets and came up to an old dirty house which I and my parents had visited so many times. I walked up to the door and knocked.

The door opened a moment later and Norwood Hardwin stood in the doorway - a young man of nearly twenty and even though he originally wanted to move to Durrington, he was more ready than I to leave London with his wife to start anew in Shrewton.

"Hello Richard," he ruffled my mop of hair. "Are you all ready?"

"Aye sir," I replied, "my Father sent me to tell you."

"Well then," said Norwood, "let me fetch Isabel and whatever she has gathered up - not that there is much to gather," he turned and shouted into the house. "Isabel! We are leaving!" he looked back at me. "Shrewton is a nice place - been there a few times myself."

"Nor, where is the money for the house?" Isabel shouted back.

"I paid for it already," Norwood reentered the house, followed by a loud indistinguishable conversation. I stepped away from the door and tried not to look embarrassed as a few neighbors turn their heads to see what was going on. Norwood and Isabel walked out a few minutes later. "Sometimes you are worse than that Wilson boy I used to know," Norwood laughed as he escorted Isabel from the house.

"Will your father allow us to put our bags in your wagon?" Isabel asked.

"I am sure that would be fine." I assured her, clasping my hands together and turning to walk back home.

"I have heard Shrewton is a lovely place." she said.

I nodded in reply before I realized that I was not a part of the couple's conversation.

"That it is darling. That it is," Norwood replied. "The Baron himself gave us a piece of land for a good bargain. Pays off to have relationships."

"Oh, so it is not just that Wilson boy you used to know?" Isabel laughed. "You speak of him so much, it would fool anyone!"

"Not as much as I speak of you," Norwood leaned down and kissed her forehead. "No one will ever take your place."

I rolled my eyes and picked up the pace.

We arrived at my family's house a short while later. I walked over and took the last bag from Mother while she and Father went to greet Norwood and Isabel, and placed the bag into the wagon.

After a few exchanges of small talk, salutations and the packing of the Hardwin's bags, Father announced. "So, we are all ready? What are we waiting for? We have a house waiting and a new life ahead!"

"Onward to Shrewton!" Norwood cried.

And so, it began.

***

Mother and Isabel each rode in the wagon while I walked with Norwood and Father, who led the horse. The road was long and rough but it was nothing we could not overcome. We covered a few miles of the journey on the first day, but stopped at nightfall. We continued our journey in the morning, well before daybreak.

We arrived in Shrewton on the evening of the tenth day. Father had lived there in Shrewton many years ago; he and Mother had left a few months before I was born. He had been friends with the Baron of the town and had many connections there; as a result, Father had already bought us a house when he and Norwood visited a few months before. Norwood also knew a woman there who sold him a small piece of land on which he had already built a small wooden house.

The reason my parents left Shrewton was something I never understood. Father always said that Mother was no longer at home there – that she was not comfortable with living in Shrewton and so they moved to London where Father felt that he could provide for his growing family.

I entered the town at my father's side and gazed up at the sun as it majestically fell into the western sky. I smiled as I remembered the good times in London, then let them fall with the sun as it began to set on my old life.

We emptied the wagon at our house and left Isabel and Mother behind as I, Father and Norwood walked to the center of town, where the Baron's house stood. We wanted to let the Baron know that we had arrived safely and that his old friends had returned.

We climbed the stairs to the porch and knocked on the door. An old man, the Baron's Butler, answered us.

"May I help you?" he asked.

"Phillip Armistead. Perhaps the Baron Aundray has spoken of my return?" Father motioned to me and Norwood. "This my son and my friend, Norwood Hardwin"

"Phillip!" the old man's eyes brightened as he embraced Father warmly. "My eyes must have deceived me, after all these years. It is good to have you back sir. How long has it been? Eleven years?" his smile gave me a warm, safe feeling. "Sir Aundray will be with you in a moment," he turned around and ran back into the house on his old hobbling legs and closed the door behind him.

A few moments later, after a bit of shouting in the house, the door opened and another man stepped out.

"Phillip, I see you made good time on your journey excellent time! I could hardly believe that you were already here," he smiled oddly at first, then regained his composure. "It is good to see you again. It is truly a pleasure to have you back in Shrewton."

"It is good to see you too Angus," Norwood said.

"I hope you all are comfortable in your new homes?" Angus asked.

"Well, considering that we just arrived, I cannot say," Father laughed. "But I am sure it will be lovely."

"Wonderful," Angus turned his gaze to me. "Hello," he smiled again in an odd yet loving way. "Richard, is it?"

"Aye sir," I replied. "How did you know my name?"

Angus shook my hand and smiled, "Phillip told me," he then turned back to Father, whose eyebrows were furrowed as if he were trying to remember something. "If you all would like," he said, "my wife, Annora and I would love to have your company on one night this week. We get so few visitors, by that I mean friends; we have far too many people here for business matters," he laughed aloud.

"Believe it or not, we are still using those silver knives your father-in-law made!"

"Is that so?" Father asked in disbelief. "Well, he always had a hand for fine smithing."

"That he did," Angus replied.

"I believe we will be able to dine with you though, even if we will be using twenty-year-old knives," Father nodded with a chuckle. "Norwood?"

"Absolutely!" declared Norwood, flashing a bright glad grin.

"Wonderful!" Angus exclaimed. "What day do you believe you will be able to come?"

"Well, I will have to talk to Mary and I will send word to you when I have a day," Father said.

"I will tell the Lady and we will see you whenever you deem right!" Angus smiled delightfully and reentered the house.

***

"Mary!" Father burst into our new house, startling Mother and Isabel. "We have been invited to dine with the Baron!"

Mother jumped up with a smile which soon crumbled. "When are we to dine?" she asked.

"We are to get settled in and then decide on a time," Norwood entered the house and strolled across the room to Isabel and lay his hand upon her shoulder. "Until then we have to get home."

"If you need any help with the final preparations of the house, I am always glad to help," Father embraced his friend.

"Thank you Phillip," Norwood smiled. "I am indebted to you, not only for the kindness you have shown me and friendship, but for being a brother to me."

Father lay his hand on Norwood's shoulder. "There is no debt now. This is a new beginning for all of us and kindness is a quality which must never be forgotten even in hard times."

"All the same," Isabel took Norwood by the hand and began walking out of the house, "we had best be going, it will be dark soon and we must sleep somewhere."

"Farewell!" Mother and Father both shouted as Norwood and Isabel walked toward the western edge of the town.

Father closed the door and took a seat at the table as Mother began frantically unpacking the bags.

"No need to do that now Mary," Father laughed, "we have only just arrived."

"The sooner we are unpacked and settled in the sooner we can dine with Angus and the sooner it is over!" Mother's tone bore a strain that I had never heard before. I raised my eyebrow, but then blamed it on moving into a new house.

"Mary, you mean to say you wish not to dine with them?" Father rose from the table and strolled over to Mother. "It is a great honor to be friends with the Baron and to dine with him. Why, you have known him well for some time, even longer than I have."

"It is not that I do not want to dine with him and his wife," Mother said defensively. "But times change, and so do relationships."

"Friendships do not change Mary," Phillip lay his hand on Mother's shoulder, pausing her frantic work. "I am sure you will feel better once we have dined and had a good laugh."

"You are probably right," Mother sighed.

Once I had determined that there was nothing more of interest they were speaking of, I scooped up my bag and a candle and brought it up to the room my father had chosen for me. It was small, however, just large enough to be breathable. I lay my bag upon the mattress in the middle of the room and the candle beside it. The light of the flame flickered off the walls and mixed with the pale light of the rising moon streaming through the window adjacent to the mattress.

I strode up to the window and rested my hands upon the frame. I smiled as I watched the stars appear one by one and the moon ascending higher into the heavens.

I jumped as the door creaked open. I spun around to see Father running his hands over the grain of the wood. "It is a fine house Father," I smiled.

"That it is Richard," Father turned to me and met me at the window. "I do believe we will be well here."

I nodded. "Is Mother all right?"

Father lay his hand on my shoulder. "She is only strained by leaving London, nothing more."

"It seems to be more than that," I chuckled.

Father forced a smile. "Nothing to worry about Richard,"

I wrapped my arms around him and rested my head upon his chest as his strong arms surrounded me. "Goodnight Father," I sighed.

"I love you Richard," and I remembered no more of that night.

***

Father, Mother, Norwood, Isabel and I, all dined with Angus and Annora Aundray when that day of anticipation finally dawned. The Aundray Manor was quite large and well furnished. There were many shelves on the wall lined with books, more than I had ever seen in one place. Where there were no shelves, paintings filled the wall space.

We sat down at a long table in the dining room as the first course was served. This consisted of many types of breads and some cakes all perfectly baked, and a taste that I could not remember lest I fall into wondrous dreams. The second course consisted of many fruits all ripe and sweet. And the third course, all kinds of meats such of which I thought to be only at a King's table and wines redder than blood.

After the meal, and much discourse of which I was too full to remember, Angus stood up holding high his goblet while running his fingers through his black hair and said: "I would like to thank you all for coming back to my humble town. Newcomers are few yet always welcomed here and I dearly hope that in the future we may grow to become even closer friends than we were in the past. And that we would be of one accord always!"

"Let these things be so!" Norwood stood up smiling and holding up his goblet of wine.

"Aye," Father took in a deep breath, "so shall it be."

"Now with all respect rightfully due," Angus said, laying a hand on Lady Annora, "my wife grows weary."

"No Angus," she whispered softly. "I will be fine. Let them stay a bit longer."

"Annora you must rest. Think of the baby. You need rest," Angus whispered back, then turned and addressed us. "It was quite delightful dining with you tonight," he continued. "And I wish to do so more often, but for now my wife must rest, for she is with child. Farewell to you all and good evening."

"Thank you Sir Aundray," Father said as he stood up. "And my gracious congratulations to you and Annora. You will be in my prayers for health and safety."

"Thank you Phillip," Angus replied clandestinely and I felt a tension rise in the room that I could not explain.

Angus then shook hands with Father and Norwood and knelt down beside me right before I followed my parents out the door.

"You have great things ahead of you Richard," he smiled so kindly that I felt as if it had melted my heart. "Never let anyone tell you otherwise."

"Why are you telling me this?" I asked.

"Because I do not want you to forget that you are loved. Too many people do and it leads them onto the wrong path."

"Richard!" Father called back into the house.

"Thank you Sir," I turned and ran out of the house after Father and Mother who had said goodbye to Hardwins and were now waiting for me.

"Farewell my friends!" Angus called to us with a wave as he wrapped his arm lovingly around Annora's shoulder.

Father waved his farewell and we all began our trek back to our new home.

"He is so young," Mother spoke as we walked, "still."

"Aye. These years have passed him well." Father replied. "How old would he be now?"

"Thirty-eight." Mother answered swiftly.

"Aye. He still looks so young," Father sighed. "Ah, but I have something far better than youth," he put an arm around Mother's shoulder. "I have a beautiful wife and son."

Mother looked down with a smile and a long sigh. "Is his father well?"

"His father passed away five years ago," Father replied.

"How did he die?" Mother asked in anticipation.

"Ergotism I think. A nasty affliction," Father told her. "He was a good man. It is a pity he is no longer with us."

"And what of his mother?"

"When old Aundray died," Father replied, "Angus' mother left for reasons unknown except that his father told her a secret when he died. The last she was seen was in London so I hear. Angus has been the Baron ever since."

"Why did he not speak of it?" Mother's voice rose as her eyebrows lowered.

"I suppose he simply forgot to mention it. Maybe? Well, no, he knows what happened, but I guess his infatuation with Annora has drowned out the pain of his father's death and his mother's abandonment."

"Infatuation?" mother gasped defensively. "What do you

mean?" I listened closely as we walked.

"He seems overly concerned and attentive. He is very protective of her as he was this evening and has been on my prior visits," Father looked down at Mother. "You seem very interested in the affairs of the Aundrays. Why is that?"

"Never mind that. Is his infatuation the reason he said she must rest?" Mother asked, trying to avoid Father's question.

"Most likely," Father replied as we came up to our new house. "Here we are," he opened the door to bid us enter.

***

The thud of my father's hammer upon the glowing blade sparked my thoughts back into motion.

"Yes Father?" I blinked rapidly in the smoke which billowed about my father's shop. "What was your question?"

"Well, we have been here three months, and still you claim to have no friends," Father turned the sword over and examined the blade. He looked up and peered into my soul. "Are you all right?"

"Well, they do not like me, and I do not like them," I scowled at the thought of the other boys of the town.

"Why?" he lay the sword on the anvil and strode over to a counter covered with tools and the like.

"I do not know, they are just," I thought for a moment, "well, simple minded. They only care about themselves and who caught the biggest fish."

Father pulled a cloth out of the pile of tools and returned to the sword. "And talking about fish is bad? Christ said be fishers of men." he began wiping a few places on the sword.

"Well they are not fishing for men!" I exclaimed.

Father tossed the rag aside and lay the sword in the flames. "Is there anyone that you find even slightly interesting besides your mother, the Hardwins and me?"

"Angus is interesting," I replied. "And kind, and smart."

"Well then, we are getting somewhere," Father chuckled. "Why do you find him interesting?"

"Just how kind he is. Just a month ago, he popped into the church and began building pews with the other workers!" I smiled at the thought. "Or another time I was walking by and he was handing out money, quite freely, to the homeless. And he actually talks to me, like really talks! Not just all the simple jabber!"

"Oh?"

"Yes, about many things. History and science and more," I sighed. "But the truly amazing trait is just how much he loves, not just his wife, but everyone around him!"

Father nodded as he drew the sword from the fire and lay it upon the anvil. "So you are at home here?"

I shrugged. "I do not know, I just do not quite feel at home yet," I remembered Angus and smiled. "Yet."

Father nodded once more.

"What about you? Are you well here?" I asked.

"I am," Father replied. "I have you and your mother here with me. But I may not be well if you are not at home here."

"What about Mother?" I inquired.

Father's hammer clanged against the steel. "Your mother is fine too," he replied.

"Fine?" I raised my eyebrows.

"She is well," he smiled. "As I told you, leaving London has put a strain on her, nothing more."

"She just does not seem happy," I replied.

"Give her time Richard, she will come around."

I bit my lower lip, furrowed my brow and after a moment of silence my attention span was exhausted.

***

Summer was drawing to an end, when Father came running into the house several weeks after our discourse in the shop. His blonde hair was a tousled soot-blackened mop and his blackened face was streaked from sweat. "Mary!" he cried. "Mary!"

"What is it?" Mother strode into the room, wiping flour off onto her apron.

Black and white! I laughed to myself as I glanced up at them from my table full of metal trinkets. However, my smile dropped as Father began guiding Mother into the back room of the house.

The few trinkets I held in my hands clattered onto the floor as I stood up. Going into the back room always meant something either very good or very bad and I was never one to miss out on interesting information. I ran over to the door of the room and pressing my ear against it, listened as my parents talked:

"Mary," Father said, "now I need you to stay strong and above all to stay calm."

"What is it Phillip?" Mother stuttered.

"A plague has come to Shrewton," I heard Mother collapse into a chair at these words and surprisingly let out a sigh of relief. "I have been hearing of it for quite a while now. It started in London and has slowly made its way down."

"Oh Phillip. How bad is it?" Mother asked.

"A long painful sleep – then death."

My heart nearly stopped beating. Mother began to cry.

"The good news is that there are some that seem to be unaffected; only a few people from each town so we might be safe!"

"Who has it now in Shrewton?" Mother asked further.

"One of Angus' guards has it. And the younger butler has been dead now for nearly a week."

"And where did he get it?" Mother asked.

"A merchant from Birmingham." Father replied. "The slave trade."

"What are we to do?"

"All we can do is pray for God's healing and protection."

I opened the door.

"How long have you –" Mother stammered.

"I heard," I replied.

Father beckoned me to sit down with him. "God will keep us from harm," We then closed our eyes and pleaded for Christ's protection.

***

The days passed slowly as everyone waited to see what would become of the guard—not even his family saw him again.

Then one day it came. A day Shrewton doubted would ever happen. A day they all dreaded bringing death by way of a messenger bursting through our door.

"Sir Armistead!" he cried.

"Aye," Father stood up. "What is wrong?"

"Lady Aundray!" he gasped. "She is ill and Angus has requested your company!"

Mother and I caught our breath.

"I am on my way." Father threw down his work, ran outside, mounted his horse and rode quickly to the Aundray Manor.

Mother stumbled a little and ran her hand along the back of a chair, then collapsed into it and put her head in her hands.

"Mother?" I said as I lay my hand on her shoulder. "Mother what is wrong? She will be healed will she not?"

"He deserves better than this!" Mother wept. "Angus is a good man!"

I sat down in another chair. I felt bad for Angus but not enough to cry, or perhaps it was because every emotion seemed frozen in time and every feeling blurred into blindness. The only change that showed us that time had passed was the sun in the sky moving slowly from the southern sky and finally falling in glimmering brightness into the west.

I left the house after sunset and went into Father's shop to see what he had been making. Nothing much in the works: a lot of nails, a couple of horseshoes, I saw a few other farm tools but could not identify them. I lit a lamp and explored the shop further to see if anything needed to be done. I tried to forget the plague and Lady Aundray and even the butler who had been so kind to my parents. I took the sword my father had been working on a few weeks before and held it out.

"True Armistead craftsmanship," I smiled looking at the razor-like blade and eventually put it back then wandered around a while longer. Finally, I went out around to the garden with the lamp and scared a few rats away. After I finished, I went back into the house and fixed some supper for Mother and me.

After I ate, I cleaned up, leaving a morsel of food for Father when he returned, and went up to my room.

I lay on my bed in silence, hoping that all would turn out alright. Lady Aundray is such a kind woman, I thought. And Angus such a kind man. They accepted us without contempt or hesitation and they welcomed us into their home. They do not deserve this plague. Lord please. Hear me. If it is your will for her to be healed so be it! At least let her baby be well, I closed my eyes and clenched my teeth. Agonizingly long minutes passed and hours longer still. Night fell and darkness surrounded the house, but not just the dark of night.

The moon shone dimly through my window and the night grew cold. The wind outside sounded like a screaming child.

The door opened downstairs and I heard Mother get up for the first time since Father had left. I bit my lip in anticipation. Mother opened the door and footsteps resounded in the room.

"Where were you?" Mother cried. "You have been gone all day!" she paused. "What happened?"

"Sit down Mary," Father's voice shook.

The scratching of chairs on the floor and creaking of the legs made me cringe as I crept out to the foot of the stairs.

"Philip?"

Father put his head in his hands then ran his fingers through his hair. He drew in a deep breath and exhaled heavily. "I - I do not know what to say," his eyes glistened and his jaw shook as he stared down at the floor.

Mother's breath quickened. "What is it?"

Father clasped mother's hands in his and looked up into her face. "She's gone,"

I slapped my hand quickly over my mouth to muffle the sound of a loud gasp.

"No! He has been so kind! He deserved her!" Mother wept. "And she was too young Phillip! What of the baby?"

Father shook his head as a tear fell from his eye. "We tried."

Mother wiped another tear away as it fell down her cheek. "He did not deserve it."

"Neither did she."

"Was there anything you could do?"

"That is not the half of it," Father clenched his teeth.

I could almost see Mother's distraught tears streaking her face.

"The doctor is dead too!" Father blurted out, half yelling in furious rage and half weeping in sorrow.

"How?" Mother stumbled over her words. "Does not the fever take time to infect people?"

"It is not the plague that killed him." he shuddered. I moved closer down the stairs to hear better but still out of sight. "It is the broken back and crushed throat that killed him!"

Mother caught her breath.

"What? Who?" Mother trembled as sadness gave way to horror.

"Angus murdered him after Annora died," he caught his breath. "And would have killed me too!"

"Why?" Mother gushed. "Why would he murder the Doctor! And then try to do the same to you?"

"He blames us!" Father yelled. "He blames the Doctor for not saving her - thus killing her! And blames me for bringing the plague here! He might not be far from the truth!"

"What do you mean Phillip?"

"The plague started in London and came here the exact same route we did!" Father paused. "No one else has come to Shrewton since we have been here," he sighed.

Mother fell silent.

I clambered back to my bed with my heart nearly beating out of my chest. I closed my eyes, trying to believe it was all a dream. I heard no more talking after that.

The horror of Annora's death gripped the town in sadness and, for the few who knew of Angus' murderous actions, clutched us in fear ever more so.

After the death of Lady Aundray, Shrewton was never the same again. Over the next few months, things got steadily worse. No one knew why or how - all we knew was that doubt was in our hearts, dread chilled our souls - and death was coming.

II

GOOD MEN DIE

Mother, Father and I huddled together by the fire that January of 1323. The winter was one of the coldest I had ever experienced, and we did our best to keep warm, but nothing seemed to keep out the piercing cold.

I jumped as a sudden pound came upon the door. Father rose and opened it as Norwood nearly fell inside.

"Norwood! What in the name of England are you doing out in such cold?" Father exclaimed.

"I need work," Norwood stammered, "Isabel and I have nothing left. I need work Phillip. Can you give me a job? I will do anything. Please Phillip."

"I have no work but you and Isabel are welcome to stay with us until you find a job."

"No," Norwood stumbled back out into the cold, shivering and breathing heavily. "I cannot. I left London to find a better life and I will not take charity to get there. You must provide for your own family. I will find some way to provide that does not take a toll on you."

"Do not let pride stand in your way, Norwood!" Father yelled as Norwood staggered out along the road. "Please Norwood. Come in. You are always welcome here!"

"Do not worry. We will be fine. I will find a way," Norwood shouted back. "I always have and I always will!"

Father closed the door slowly and began layering on more clothes.

"What are you doing?" I asked.

"Stay here," he opened the door.

"Wait Father. I am going with you," I hoisted on my coat and tried to get as warm as possible.

We ventured out of the house into the wind and needle-like cold. Thankfully, it was not snowing so we could see fairly well, but that was such a small comfort when compared to the cold.

We followed Norwood's tracks through the town and after a half hour, Father's countenance dropped into a grim stare toward the center of town.

"Father," I shivered. "I think he is headed toward..."

"I know. The Aundray Manor," Father interrupted.

"Why?"

"Necessity," Father pulled his coat on tighter and stared off into the wind. "It is the only place to go to in such a time."

"Why?" I asked. "Certainly there could be another place?" I shivered. "Can we go home?"

"I do not know," Father took a look around and felt the chilling wind. "Not just yet. Can you run?" he turned to me, his eyes once more ablaze.

"Why not?" I asked again, desiring to return home.

"I cannot let you go alone in this cold, and we cannot leave Norwood."

"Where to?" I stood tall trying in vain to show my father that I was happy to come.

"The Aundray Manor," he replied as he knelt down in front of me. "We cannot let Norwood go there."

"Why not?" I raised an eyebrow. "Angus will give him a job, it will be all right again!"

"Trust me Richard," he stood up. "Come."

"Yes Father," I broke out into a sprint, but Father was much faster and quickly outpaced me. The road was slick and hard to run on, so that I lost my footing many times.

Finally, the Aundray Manor came into sight. The lights were lit in only one window and the silhouette of a man stood in it. Norwood climbed the ice covered stairs to the door and knocked four times. Father was less than a hundred yards away and tried to shout for Norwood to stop, but even I, being closer to Father, could hardly hear him because of the now raging wind. Several more times Father shouted in vain.

The silhouette disappeared from the window, and the door was opened by Angus' old butler. Norwood entered the house and walked into the lighted room. The door slammed shut just as Father reached the stoop.

"Norwood!" Father thundered as he collapsed on the steps. He struck the wooden step with such force that I was surprised it did not splinter.

I reached the steps as Father ascended them and began to pound upon the door, over and over, until he had no strength left.

There Father sat, propped up against the door until finally it opened and a guard emerged from behind it.

"Where is Norwood?" Father asked.

"Norwood is fine, go home Phillip," he replied.

"Where is Norwood?" Father repeated.

The guard placed his hand on the hilt of his sword and looked Father in the eyes. "Go home and take Richard with you."

"Where is Norwood?" Father shook the guard viciously until a fist met his jaw and sent him down the stairs.

"Go home Phillip," The guard rubbed his hands together to regain feeling and he returned to the house without another word. Father stood up and wiped blood away from his mouth, and began walking home.

"Is that it?" I asked. "We are just walking away?"

"There is nothing we can do Richard," Father scolded. "The moment we set foot in that house we are outside the law, and Angus possesses the power to imprison and kill any of us! I will not let that happen to you or your mother."

"Fine, but Father, why did we try to stop him? There is nothing amiss, Angus will give him a job."

Father froze in his tracks and turned back to me. "I do not know," he replied. "But there is something dark in this town, and I cannot see it."

After a silent walk home, we entered the house and startled Mother who was preparing supper. "What happened?" she turned instantly from her work and stared at Father in anticipation. "Where is Norwood?"

Father silently walked into the house and seated himself at the table. "He went to Angus," Father breathed deeply.

"Angus?" Mother echoed.

Father ran his hands through his hair. "I could not stop him," he said as his hands rested on his head and he stared aimlessly at the floor.

Mother quietly went back to making supper.

"What are we going to do?" I asked.

"There is nothing we can do," Father stood up abruptly with his face set like flint.

"I am sure he is fine," Mother forced a smile. "Angus probably just has a job for him."

"We can hope," Father replied. "We will go first thing

tomorrow to the Hardwin house to make sure of that."

"I will bake them some cakes and bread for you to bring," Mother said.

I looked on in confusion and tried to understand, but I could not. I could not understand why they were worried about Norwood or Isabel or even Angus. For all I knew, all was well.

***

The next day Father and I went out with the cakes and bread mother had made, and went quickly to the Hardwin home on the far western edge of Shrewton.

We strode up to the doorstep, knocked several times and waited for several minutes. The door did not open nor was there any sign that it would. We then heard something scratching and a loud crash.

"Hardwin!" Father exclaimed. "Are you well?" Father gripped the handle of the door and pushed as hard as he could, but it was blocked.

"Could we try the window?" I ran around to the north side of the house to a side window. The shutters were rent into splinters on the ground. To my right, footprints led back to Shrewton. Chills ran down my spine as I thought about who, or what, made the prints.

"Father?" I turned his attention to the window.

"Let me go first." Father said, climbing into the house and helping me in after him.

It was very dark. As our eyes adjusted, we saw the table and chairs overturned and in pieces. Nearly everything was torn apart or bore signs of destruction and violence.

"What happened Father?" I whispered, gazing around the room. The sound of movement rustled behind us. "What was that?" I spun around in shock. "Who is there?"

A feeble form sat huddled in the corner.

"What is that!" I stammered reaching for Father as my heart began to race.

The head of the figure slowly turned toward us.

"Father!" I cried.

The figure moved into the light of the window revealing a pale, clammy face with bloodshot eyes filled with fear and rage.

"Isabel?" Father asked slowly as I clutched his arm in terror.

"The doubt!" she cried aloud.

"What happened to her?" my voice shook.

"Isabel. What has happened? Where is Norwood?" Father demanded.

"Dread," sweat dripped down her face, and her hair was tangled and matted. "So much dread!" she shuddered. "It is coming for us all!" She screamed gazing blindly at the ceiling.

"Isabel answer me!" Father yelled. "What is wrong?"

"It is coming!" she screamed again.

"What is coming?" Father asked in confusion.

She stiffly moved her head to face Father. Her eyes blazed with gruesome fear, and her face was covered in black oval shapes.

"Death!" she stood up quaking terribly. "Let me out!" she threw herself on the door "It is coming for me!" She scratched at the door like an animal. "It is coming!"

"Calm down Isabel!" Father tried to restrain her in vain. "It is me, Phillip, death is not upon you!"

"Yes," she shuddered and pointed toward the town, "it is!" she gagged out black liquid and collapsed onto the floor. She whispered something else neither of us heard and breathed no more.

"Father?" I gasped.

"Get out!" he hoisted me out the window as quickly as he could and he himself followed like a bolt of lightening behind me.

"What was wrong with her?" I stared at Father as he hurried me away from the house, and stopped suddenly when he found a clear footprint.

"I do not know," he knelt down examining the print in the snow leading away from the house. "Someone did this to her," he stood up.

"Who?" I asked.

"I do not know," his fingers curled around into fists, "and I do not care. I have had enough. If he gave her such suffering, I will not rest until the LORD grants justice! I want you to go home, Richard. Keep Mother safe for me."

"I want to help you!"

"Whatever happened to Isabel could easily happen to you. Now go home!" Father commanded.

"And what about you? Could it not happen to you?" A lump began rising in my throat.

"Listen," he cradled my head in his hands and wiped away my tear with his thumb. "You take care of your mother, you hear? Do that for me."

"Where are you going?" I sniffled.

He cast his gaze toward the town. "I need Angus," he gritted his teeth, "I need to know who did this to them. I need his help. You go home."

"Why?"

"I am going to find whoever did this," he turned to me with an anger I had never seen in him before. "And I will make him pay for killing her"

"Oh Father!" I said but never finished as he waved me away and I began to run home.

As I ran, I passed by many others who showed the same signs as

Isabel. Many more who were doomed to die.

I burst through the door startling Mother and slammed the door behind me shouting, "To the back room!"

"What is going on Richard? What has happened?" Mother asked quickly. "Where is Phillip?"

"Mother, there is a new plague, or something terrible, Isabel is gone, everything is falling-" I choked through the tears attempting to relate to Mother all that had happened.

"Slow down Richard," Mother lay her hands on my shoulders and looked me in the eye. "Where is Phillip?"

"Father went to Angus to ask for help, to end this new plague," my teeth chattered. The image of Isabel was still engrained in my mind. "I am scared."

"Richard," Mother wrapped her arms around me. "Everything is going to be all right. Phillip and Angus are both strong and wise" she smiled. "God is with them, they will find a way to end this plague."

I sniffled in reply.

An hour passed with no sound from inside the house, but outside, chaos reigned. Nothing broke the sound until the door of the house opened and footsteps entered. Mother and I peered out of the back room and ran into Father's arms as Angus forced a smile.

"What is going on Phillip?" Mother asked as she pulled away.

Father nodded to Angus who replied, "The plague has infected the town. Dozens are already dead. The only way to stop it is to quarantine the infected."

"How many are infected? And how?" I asked. "When we went to Isabel, everyone was fine!"

"It spread into the town," Father replied. "I do not know how but there are too many who are already showing the same signs."

"Can we not just abandon this cursed town?" Mother pleaded as she stared at both Father and Angus.

"No one leaves," Angus retorted. "We cannot let this spread more than it already has."

"I want to go back to London," Mother met Angus' eyes and then Father's. "I want to go home."

"No one leaves. I cannot let this spread more Mary!" Angus' voice rose in passion.

"The only thing we can do now is try to save this town," Father spoke.

"Just promise me you will come back," Mother cast her gaze to the floor. "Just promise me that."

Father gently placed one hand on her shoulder and the other on her cheek. "I promise. Mary, I promise!" He drew her into his arms. "No matter what."

***

Within a week, the quarantine worked and the plague was quelled – but the price was paid. Every one of Angus' guards was lost. No one survived in his manor except the Baron himself.

The prison was sealed off and it was ordered that it should never be opened again, lest the plague return and bring havoc with it.

Upon the evening of the last day of the second week, as the sun was setting, Mother and I received word that Father was coming home. The prison was sealed and all remnants of the plague were gone.

We prepared the house and cooked with whatever remained in the cupboard. We had not seen Father for several weeks and we were ready for him to return.

I sat on a stool in front of the fireplace coaxing the smoldering coals into a flame. Meanwhile, Mother paced the floor looking out at the sun, then outside, then drinking a cup of water, then continuing again.

I nearly jumped out of my seat when a great slam came against the door. Mother and I ran to see if it was Father and pulled the door open once we had seen it was him.

Father looked up from behind the door. "I promised you I would come back-" a bloody cough cut off his voice as he stumbled into the house and collapsed into a chair, grasping his side as blood spilled out quickly from a gash upon it.

"What happened?" Mother exclaimed rushing to his side.

He lifted his hand revealing a deep gash. "Someone is out there," he coughed again.

"Who?" Mother asked.

I came over with a bowl of warm water and a clean cloth. Mother began to clean Father's wound.

"Mary there was something there! There was someone there!" he gritted his teeth through the pain. "I tried to run. I tried!"

"Slow down Phillip," Mother's voice quivered as she began treating the wound. "Where were you? Where did he come from?"

Father winced. "I was at the Aundray Manor, with Angus – I saw things there."

"What did you see?" I asked.

"I saw where the darkness hides-" he gritted his teeth and screamed as more blood spilled from his wound.

"Needle and thread Richard!" Mother demanded as she tried harder than ever not to lose herself in the horror.

I entered my parents' room and searched around for what Mother had asked for. I returned to Mother and Father a few minutes later with the needle and thread in hand.

"A man?" Mother exclaimed. "Who was it?"

"Who was who?" I asked as I handed Mother the supplies.

"He was sent to kill me, Mary, for what I have seen," Father winced as Mother began sewing up the wound. "I need you to take Richard and run!"

"All of those in the Aundray Manor are dead! Who could have been in there?" Mother interrupted again. "There is no one he could send!"

"You are wrong Mary," Father stared at the door and listened to the silence. "I need you to run! Go now. Leave me – you and Richard..."

"But Phillip who?" Mother interrupted.

"There is one man who it may have been," he shuffled in his chair, still staring at the door. "One man."

"Who?" Mother and I asked at the same time with equal anticipation. "Who was it?" Mother continued.

He stood up shaking. "The man at the door!" Father stumbled to the mantle and grabbed his sword hanging above it.

The door crashed to the floor and a man in a dark cloak entered the house. "Run Mary, take Richard!" Father cried as he bore his sword down upon the intruder. The man dodged the sword with ease. Mother and I stood frozen in surprise and horror. "Run, the man in the capsule is-" Father's voice was cut off suddenly. The hilt of a knife protruded from his chest as he stumbled back, dropping his sword as he fell into the corner. His earlier wound reopened and he began bleeding more profusely on the floor.

Mother screamed in horror as she ran to Father's side. The man walked toward them. "Mary!" Father gasped. "Run Mary. Run!" The man grabbed Mother's arm. He yanked her up so hard that her arm was dislodged. He then spoke these words with a horrid fury like nothing I had ever heard.

"You want to know who I am?" he pulled out another knife from his belt.

"No..." Father said weakly. "It is me Angus wants. Let them live! Let them go! Take me instead."

"Angus is dead!" he thundered as he sunk the dagger into Mother's back. "And they will all be dead!"

"Run Richard!" Father tried to yell in vain through the blood and pain. "Run!"

The man threw my mother's body aside and gripped Father's bloodstained shirt, lifting him several feet from the floor. "I bring doubt!" he thundered as he pulled the knife out of Father's chest. "I bri--"

I turned and ran out of the house as fast as I could. Out into the muddy, cold streets, I ran through the town to the western end. I ran as fast as I could until I struck something on the road and fell back down into the mud. A man stood before me.

"Sir Aundray!" I screamed and clung to his cloak "He said you were dead!" tears poured from my eyes. "He killed them!" I sobbed. "In front of me! He murdered my mother and father!"

"It is all as it should be Richard," Angus knelt down and embraced me. "Everything will be fine," his strong arms held me.

"I do not believe it! It can't be true!" I wept.

"Some things Richard," his voice comforted me as the last person I knew to be alive, "we just cannot stop. We cannot prevent them."

"You do not understand," I sobbed.

"Yes Richard. I do," he pushed me away and looked straight into my eyes, "I lost my father to a sickness and my mother abandoned me. I lived alone for years until," he paused as if he decided not to say something. "Until I found Annora. She was the one bright star in my life, the one thing which kept me going, and now she is gone too, lost to a plague," A tear streaked his face. "Your father and mother were the only friends I had left. I knew them since I was a child when they lived here in Shrewton and when I heard they were coming back I was more assured of greater joy! It seemed as if perfection had finally come to me. Then they too died. Richard, I know what you are feeling and it is all right. I have felt it all too many times," he paused again and grimaced with a glint of hatred in his eyes. "Too many times."

"It is okay?" I cried. "Then why does it hurt so much?"

"Because we are human," he embraced me once more. "Pain defines us Richard. It forms us into who we are and decides what we are capable of. It shows us light and throws us into shadows. It makes great men rise and turns angels into demons. It is the pain of a man, which makes mountains fall and cities crumble! Makes empires rise and tyrants write themselves into the pages of history! But even through the pain and suffering we still have a choice to what we become."

"And what will become of me?"

"Shrewton is no home for you now Richard. It never was," he stood up and took my hand. "Shrewton's time is closing now. New days are dawning, dark days, and I will not be able to protect you when they come. Not yet. But after dark days comes triumph."

"Then what am I to do?" I swallowed my sadness. "Where can I go?"

He put his hand on my shoulder. "Durrington is not far off and it is not a bad place to start over."

"Alright," I clenched my fists. "What do I do?"

"Always doubt," he said. "Do not trust anyone. Do not love anything. Those who love lose the most. I know because I have lost," he removed his hand. "Remember Richard, and let it burn. Let the pain fester and embrace the longing for justice. It is what gives you strength and what makes you able to stand through anything, for through the passion you will always know why you stand. You will always know what you fight for and if you always know that, then you will never be defeated. You will never be cast down. Remember this, my dear Richard, and be on your way."

III

THE GOOD, THE BAD, AND THE BROKEN

I ran out of Shrewton, out of my old life, out of myself. I ran harder than I had ever run before. I felt no fatigue or pain. Rain poured, as did the tears from my eyes, falling behind me as my rage stood ahead of me. I ran until I collapsed, feeling numb with fear and cold. All I felt was my faith being crushed by sorrow and sadness. I knelt in the mud and put my head in my hands. Drops of tears and rain dripped between my fingers and landed in the freezing mud. I closed my eyes as tightly as I could, forcing out the stinging droplets. Instantly I saw again the face of the man who killed them. I saw my parents' screaming faces as his knife entered into their bodies.

I tore my hands from my face and slammed them into the ground. "Why?" I clenched my teeth. "You let them die," sadness and anger began to fuse together. It burned. "You could have saved them!" I stood up screaming. "Why?" I ran forward and threw myself on the ground and beat it, hoping it would shatter, and be destroyed along with me. And there I lay as the hour passed.

Finally, I stood up and looked around. I could feel myself changing. I could feel myself burning; like my skin was being transformed, revealing a new body and every layer of it wanted to destroy my parents' killer. It blazed like nothing I had ever felt before, taking the place of every emotion: sadness, anger, sorrow, happiness, joy and pain - nearly drowning them out completely. A new emotion; a dark feeling, the feeling that nothing mattered except revenge, and nothing could stop me from obtaining it. That revenge was right, and that I was going to have it no matter the cost. It was hatred - and I gave into it.

I closed my eyes once more and saw the murderer's dead body. "Let it burn."

I opened my eyes and saw a light shining dimly through the rain. I began slowly advancing toward the light with each step like a blow on the embers of hatred - enticing it into flame.

Slowly the light grew brighter as I came closer. A massive stone ring unfolded before me. Within a few more minutes I could make out the form of a man walking among five great stone structures making up the ring. He studied the stones as if they were made of diamond.

"Hello there," he looked over at me, his dark hair matted by the rain. "Now what is a lad like you doing at this time of night? And in such weather?" he smiled brightly. He looked to be in his thirties.

"Does it matter?" I replied "Nothing does anymore," I turned and continued walking toward Durrington. 'Except his dead body.' I told myself bitterly.

"Wait!" he ran over to me. "Listen, it matters. No matter how bad it gets, it matters."

"That sir, is where you are wrong," I turned on him in anger. "You are dead wrong!"

"Are you sure?" he asked. "I know I do not know who you are, why you are out here, or even why you are so downcast, but there is always hope, there is always a reason."

"I just watched my parents murdered," I revealed my new found hatred as though it had always been a part of me. "Tell me there is a reason now? Go on then! What is the reason?" I gnashed my teeth at him.

He bit the inside of his cheek for a moment and sighed, "Where are you going?"

'That is what I thought!' I screamed inside myself. "Durrington I think," I said aloud. "A friend told me it was a good place."

"I live there. You can stay a while with me if you have no other place to go."

"I will make it on my own," I replied.

"Each and every person in this world suffers. But you do not have to do it alone. If you try," he paused for a moment, as if contemplating what to say next, "bad things come of it."

I looked up at him. "And do you know what bad things are?"

"I lost my wife and son," I raised my eyebrow in surprise. "Everyone has lost something dear to them, some more than others, but no one lives without pain. But you have to let it go."

"I can never let it go," I scowled.

"Not alone," He placed his hand on my shoulder. "So let me show you how."

"What is your name?" I asked.

"Andrew Freeman."

"Freeman? Good for you," I jabbed at him.

"I was not always," Andrew replied. "What is your name?"

"Richard Armistead."

"Well then Richard," he smiled. "Come. You are soaked to the bone and look more beaten than a soldier from the front."

"Thank you sir," I replied under my breath.

He smiled, "Let the little children come," his eyes blazed in such a vibrant blue that even the midday sky looked dark in comparison. "For unto them belongs the kingdom of heaven."

I scowled, "And when they are old," I said under my breath, "a knife in the chest," the killer's face returned to my mind.

I followed Andrew to the west side of the ring of stone where he had a wagon. He helped me up and asked me to lay down in the back.

"What about all those things you were working on?" I asked "Are you not going to retrieve them?"

"You need to get warmed up," he smiled. "By the time I finished cleaning up, you would have been long gone. Wet and cold do not mix well," he laughed.

"But sir..."

"To save one person's life is far more important than chasing legends," he chuckled and turned the wagon toward Durrington. I looked back at the ring to see the silhouette of a man staring back at me then disappearing behind the stones. I quickly turned my face to the town and tried to rest.

After an hour of attempted sleep in the back of the wagon, and restless nightmares of the killer, a loud thud threw my mind back into reality.

I shot upright, arms flailing for something to destroy.

Andrew hopped into the back of the wagon, grabbed my arms firmly and stared into my eyes, "It is all right," he smiled warmly, "we just hit a rut."

"I cannot do this," I tore my arms away from him and curled up in the far corner.

The wagon creaked slightly as Andrew maneuvered himself and plopped down next to me. "You will get through this Richard, trust me. It just takes time."

"What do you know?" I yelled. "Why are you helping me?"

He sighed. "I saw a boy alone in the rain and in his tears. I could not leave."

"I want to die," I clenched my teeth.

He nodded slowly. "Someone already died," he stood up and hopped from the wagon, "and He did it for you," he then went around to the wheel that had sunk into the rut and began pulling the icy mud away.

"If He saved me, why did He not save my parents?" I remained huddled in the corner.

"That I do not know – yet."

I peered over the side of the wagon. "Yet? Well, that is a foolish thing to say!" I grimaced.

He looked up at me. "Richard, I do not know you, and you do not know me. But there is one thing I know and I told you before, there is a reason."

I scorned his kindness and sat back in my place as he worked, but eventually grew bored and decided that I would help him.

After nearly an hour of heaving, digging and shivering, we were able to shove the wagon free. On top of that, the horse protested the whole time as it fidgeted in the cold rain.

Andrew climbed back onto the wagon and I next to him.

"You do not want to rest?" he asked.

"I cannot," I retorted as I stared forward into the night. I was just about to make another degrading comment when I noticed a rider ahead of us, galloping hard.

"Did he pass by us?" I asked pointing to the man on the horse.

"Probably. Nothing to worry about though," Andrew smiled. "Looks like he has his own business to attend to, at least by the way he is pushing that horse."

"Aye, he sure is going hard," I replied. "How much further to Durrington?"

"Not far. Not more than three miles."

***

It was well past midnight when we came into Durrington. It was not large in comparison to London, however, it was larger than Shrewton.

The rain which had poured since I left Shrewton finally subsided.

We came to a small house not far from the southern edge of town. The peace of the town was a welcome sight compared to what I had seen over the past few weeks.

Andrew pulled the wagon up next to the house. "Here we are," he leapt out and helped me back onto the solid ground.

He walked to the door with me following close behind, pulled out a set of keys and unlocked it. The door swung open with a creak revealing a ransacked house.

"Biscuit's blood!" Andrew exclaimed as he walked into the torn up house.

"What?"

"Oh no," he ran to the far end of the room to an open cupboard. "No. No. No!" he struck the broken cupboard. "It is gone!"

"What is?"

"It doesn't matter. I will write it down again."

"What?"

"Have you ever heard of the Alignment?" he asked then chuckled. "Well, at least that is what I call it."

"No," I replied.

"I have not truly either, but what I have found has been amazing!"

"What is it?"

"Power they say. Unlimited power."

"Unlimited power will corrupt you," I said. "Are you sure finding it is a good idea?"

"Power like that in the hands of a good man would change the world. Imagine wars ended without the loss of life. Imagine food for the hungry, and hope for the hopeless."

"My parents were murdered by the power of one man," hatred engulfed me once more. "One man's power ruins a family, unlimited power ruins the world."

"Or saves it. Your parents could have been saved by that power. My family too, if that power was in the right hands. But enough of that tonight, it is late."

"Thank you for allowing me to stay. I will do my best not to disturb you."

"But are you disturbed?"

"I will be fine."

He nodded, showed me where to sleep and there left me for the night.

I tightened my eyes as tears forced their way out and stung my face as they fell. "Why?" I clenched my teeth as the rage began to boil. "Why?"

***

The next morning I stumbled out of the bed and into the main room of the house.

"Have a seat," Andrew said, nodding to the table. "Breakfast will be ready soon."

"You do not have to do this," I said taking a seat at the table. "I know a few trades, I can make my way."

"You do not have to though," he replied.

"And you do not have to help me."

"You are right," he stopped "However, I could not leave you out there."

"Why not?"

"Because as a father, it is just something I cannot do."

"Where is your family anyway?"

He froze. I contemplated if I should have asked, however, concluded that I did not care.

"My wife died when my son was born," he sighed and lowered

his head. "I got low. Left my son with a friend and-" he bit his lip. "a flood destroyed his house – washed them away."

I nodded.

"I tracked them down to the northern side of London, in the middle of the woods. My friend was dead, and my son was gone."

"How did you cope?"

"I have faith that one day my son and I will be reunited," he wiped his eyes. "I know he is alive," he laughed. "Nineteen years; could be married by now," he put some stew into two bowls, sat down at the table and gave grace.

"So," I began, in an attempt to lighten the mood. "you used a very strange phrase last night."

"Oh?" Andrew looked up from his meal.

"'Biscuit's blood' I believe it was," I said.

"Oh yes! Biscuit's blood is our personal family exclamation," Andrew said happily.

"Aye, it is quite strange."

"Aye, but the story is a silly one."

"What happened?"

He paused a moment in what I assumed to be an attempt to recall the story and with a smile, he began. "Well, it was my grandmother on my mother's side. She was dining with my father before she let him marry my Mum," he laughed. "So, she told my father to make her a meal fit for a King."

"Oh no," I chuckled.

"Oh and a meal it was!" Andrew grinned. "My Mum always said it was the hardest thing my father ever had to do. But anyway, it was amazing. Well, that is until the final course. Now you must know that my grandmother's favorite fruit was strawberries. So my father with this in mind decided to give her a big surprise. He filled biscuit dough with the ripest strawberries he could find and baked them for, well, I believe it was ten minutes; then he fried them and baked them once more; so that by this time the outer layer of the biscuit was tough and hard to break. He then served them to my grandmother," Andrew's grin widened. "My grandmother tried to pull it apart, but that did nothing, so she tried to cut it, but even that would not work. So she resorted to her final option. Not wanting to be rude and leave it untasted, she picked that biscuit up and chomped on it as hard as she could, but nothing happened, until she yanked back and tore the thick crust in two sending the red juices out all over her and the table and the floor as she screamed the words, 'Biscuit's blood!' in utter shock and horror!"

"Hah!" I laughed. "Sounds like you have quite the heritage!"

"Oh yes, my family has been yelling it ever since!" he laughed.

"Aye, ever since." We finished the food and leaned back in our chairs. "So," Andrew stated, "you said that you knew a few trades?"

"Aye."

"What would they be?"

"Well, my father was a great blacksmith so I know almost everything there is to know about the trade."

"Well then," he said, "quite a lot for a boy your age. It just so happens that I also am a blacksmith..." Andrew was interrupted by a loud knock at the door. Andrew strode over and opened it. "Edmond! Did you find any of my things back at the ring?"

I stood up and came to the door. "The ring?"

"Oh," Andrew exclaimed. "Pardon my manners, this is Edmond Caddarik," he gestured to the boy at the door. "And Edmond this is Richard. I sent Edmond to where we met last night to retrieve my research."

Edmond shook my hand and smiled, "Hello Richard."

"So, Edmond, did you find anything?" Andrew asked.

"No sir. Everything was gone," Edmond replied. "All I found was this," he handed a folded piece of paper to Andrew who opened it eagerly. On it was written the word, "Doubt."

He stared down at the paper, motionless and expressionless. Edmond and I fixed our gaze upon him in anticipation.

Andrew looked up from the paper, "Doubt."

"Doubt? What does that mean?" I asked.

"I do not know. That is besides the meaning of the word," Andrew replied. "Are you sure there was nothing else there? Any of my notes?"

"No sir," Edmond replied.

Andrew sighed. "Thank you Edmond, you did your job well." Andrew pulled a few coins out of his belt and placed them into Edmond's hand.

Edmond stared at the coins and offered them back to Andrew. "I cannot accept these," he said with authority.

"The farm has not faired well these past few years. You know that more than I," Andrew pushed Edmond's outstretched hand back. "If anything I should give you more."

Edmond smiled uncomfortably, something it seemed he was not accustomed to, though his eyes were sober and kind. "My mother thanks you, as do I and my brother."

"There is no need for thanks," Andrew smiled and ruffled Edmond's dark hair. Edmond turned with a more comfortable smile, and ran down the road heading south through the town.

Andrew closed the door and we seated once more at the table.

"Why did you give him so much?" I asked. "Pardon my saying, but you do not seem to be rich."

"Edmond's family is in need, and I cannot stand by watching them suffer," Andrew replied.

"Why are they in such need?"

"Edmond's father, Baldwin Caddarik left twelve years ago to fight in Scotland. He left right after Edmond was born and fought as a soldier in the English army. He told his wife that it was his duty to fight for his country. Ever since, Edmond's family has been struggling to survive. Edmond and his brother have been working to provide on the farm, and through many odd jobs wherever they can find a commission. They have even sold portions of the farm to stay alive."

"I see," I replied. The possibility of Edmond's father being dead should have helped me relate to him; however, it was drowned out by my own feelings of revenge. With each passing second my passion grew stronger and I could sense that Andrew knew it.

***

Over the next six years, Durrington served me well and Andrew selflessly cared for me – though I had no inclination to serve in return. It was a fine town and full of kind people – many like Andrew. I lived with Andrew for quite a while and learned many things from him, from his blacksmithing, to his surprising talent with the sword, to his study of the Alignment, which I learned was an aligning of the sun and moon on opposite sides of the earth. It was hard to learn, but once the foundations were laid, I found the Alignment easy to understand - or so I thought. Andrew was like a father to me, but I never accepted it. Edmond became like a brother to me, but I never valued it.

Through those years I learned more blacksmithing and metal work from Andrew than I ever thought possible. His skill was unmatched by even my own father. He never ceased to surprise me in how many things he knew. His skill with the sword was far greater than any man I had ever seen, except Edmond, whom he had trained along with me and who had by this time surpassed the teacher. But all his skill and wit was drowned out by his unending joy and the light in his eyes, which left me wondering – how is it that this man who has lost so much, can still carry a smile?

IV

CADDARIK

It was November of 1328 and I was working in my shop, on yet another sword, when a man and a boy rode up. The boy was slightly younger than me, and the man was old and rough. One glance told me that the man was a sailor, but no ordinary sailor or deck hand. This man was a soldier. The reigns of his horse rested in one hand, and the other hand on the hilt of a sword of such splendor that it surpassed any I had ever seen. Nothing I, my father, or even Andrew had ever made could compare with the majesty of even the pommel. Simple though it was.

The man dismounted and handed the reigns to the boy. I parted my gaze from them and focused on my work, desperately hoping they would not come to me and ask some dumb question - as so many visitors were inclined to do. To my dismay, the man strode over to my shop and spoke in a firm, raspy voice, "Certainly a blacksmith knows many people in this town? Or perhaps your master?"

I looked up from my work, trying to keep my eyes from rolling in annoyance. "I know a few," I replied.

"So you have started your trade young? Wise, very wise," he smiled.

"Perhaps. Who are you?" I was not in the mood for conversation.

"My name is Lawrence Forwin, this is my son Henry," he motioned to the boy on the horse. "I have business here in Durrington and was hoping that you could help me find the family I am seeking."

I shook Lawrence's hand. "Richard Armistead," I forced a smile as I returned to my work, away from Lawrence, and placed the sword into the fire. "And who are you looking for?" I asked as I watched the sword give way to a glowing red.

"The Caddarik family," Lawrence replied. "Do you know them?"

My attention was sparked. "Well, you have come to the right place," I looked over my shoulder at the man. "What do you want with the Caddariks?" I asked. I turned back to the sword as the red began to brighten into a vibrant orange.

"I bear something that belonged to their family – their father specifically."

I froze and forgot about the sword in the flames. 'Baldwin Caddarik?' I thought. 'He has been gone for over fifteen years!'

"Can you help me?" Lawrence asked.

I blinked wildly to regain my composure, and wrenched the sword from the fire as it began shooting sparks of molten metal.

I thrust the ruined sword into a bucket of iron-blackened water and turned to Lawrence. "I will bring you to a man who will be able to help you," I forced another smile.

"Thank you," Lawrence replied.

"Wait here," I told him, as I spread out the coals of the fire. "I will be back soon," I brushed past him and briskly ran east toward Andrew's house. I knocked on the door and entered. "Andrew?" I yelled as I closed the door behind me.

Andrew appeared from around the corner. "What is it Richard?" he asked.

"There is someone looking for the Caddarik family and I have never seen him before. I thought you might know him? I did not want to bring some stranger just in case..."

He nodded in reply.

I spun around and left the house with Andrew following. Within a few minutes, we arrived at the shop and found the man and his son waiting.

Andrew stopped and stared hard first at Henry, then his gaze locked onto Lawrence and searched him from his tarnished silver hairs down to the leather boots on his feet. Suddenly, Andrew's eyes lost their ever-joyous gleam and fell into sorrow. He looked back into Lawrence's grey eyes.

Andrew struggled to keep his composure as he spoke. "Was it with honor?" he asked.

Lawrence gravely nodded. Henry's eyes showed that his confusion was as great as mine.

Andrew nodded and looked down toward the ground. "And I suppose you are here to deliver the sword to them?"

"Those were his final instructions to me," Lawrence replied. "He was a good man."

I began to understand their discussion – Baldwin was dead. The idea did not strike me hard at first, but then I realized the impact it would have on the Caddarik family. The hope of his return was what kept them tirelessly working to keep their land; now that their hope was gone, despair would take its place and its toll.

"Follow me," Andrew turned to face the direction of the Caddarik dwelling, and walked at a steady pace until we arrived at the familiar run down wooden house on the edge of town. Andrew bid our new friends to stay behind while he and I covered the remaining distance to the house. I knocked on the door and was soon answered by Edmond's mother, Margaret and elder brother Thomas.

"Oh Andrew, what a surprise!" exclaimed Margaret with a smile. But her smile faded as she noticed Henry and Lawrence standing beside their horses and a sheathed sword in Lawrence's hand.

"Who are they?" Margaret asked cautiously.

"Your husband," and that was all Andrew had to say to send Margaret into Thomas' arms.

"What about my father?" asked Thomas.

"Your father was killed," Andrew blinked a tear away from his eye and sighed.

"Who are they?" asked Thomas. He swallowed hard and tried to keep his eyes upon Andrew. The result was a scowl.

"They have brought back your father's sword," Andrew replied.

Thomas glared at Lawrence for a moment, then looked back at Andrew. "I do not want it, and neither does my mother. He ran off to play soldier. I do not want the thing he used to kill other men. I do not want to live with that in my family."

"Your father fought for his king, country and God," Andrew replied. "Though he was unable to raise you as a father desires, he wanted you to have this final gift from him. Do not deny it."

"My son does not want it and neither do I," Margaret looked up at Andrew with tears in her eyes.

"Perhaps Edmond will?" I asked.

Thomas grimaced and Margaret said, "I cannot live with losing another to war. If you give it to Edmond, I will hold you accountable for his death."

"I am not accountable for your son's actions," Andrew said. "But I know that a boy should honor his father."

"And mother!" Thomas snapped.

"Let the boy decide," Andrew replied. "And whatever he chooses will be the will of God. Giving a boy a sword will not make him a soldier."

"No, your training did that," Thomas gritted his teeth. "And now with the sword, he will run off just like Father did. My brother is a fool. You know that he will choose to keep it!"

"Let Edmond decide," Margaret wiped her eyes and ran back into the house. Thomas glared at Andrew with a scowl.

"Where do we find him?" Andrew asked, but Thomas slammed the door on him.

"I can find him," I told Andrew.

Andrew nodded. "Not much like his brother," he raised an eyebrow as he looked at me. "But all the same, it is better that we asked his mother first."

Andrew and I turned and walked back to Lawrence and Henry. "What happened?" Lawrence asked.

"They refused to accept it," Andrew replied, "however they agreed that their younger son, Edmond, should be allowed to accept it if he wishes. Richard is going to fetch him."

"Henry will go with you," Lawrence addressed me. "I will take your horse," he took the reins of Henry's horse and the boy dismounted.

"Meet us back at my home Richard," Andrew said.

I nodded and went off with Henry.

"Where are we going?" the boy spoke for the first time after we rounded the bend.

I looked at Henry carefully. He was nearly as tall as I if you counted his blond hair which curled up and made him look a bit taller.

"Edmond is at the market and most likely in a fight," I replied as if it was a normal occurrence.

"Do you believe Edmond will take the sword?" Henry asked.

The question was simple, yet it was enough to get me thinking.

'What if he refused for the sake of his mother? What if he refuses it to keep peace in his family?' I thought through it and replied, "I do not know."

We walked in silence for a while, but the quiet soon became uncomfortable. "So, your father is a soldier?" I asked.

"Aye, and a sailor as well. He fought in Scotland alongside Master Caddarik," Henry replied.

"Well," I tried to think of another question, "when did your father return?"

"At the beginning of this year," replied Henry.

"Why has it taken so long for him to return Baldwin's sword?" I asked.

"My father was barely alive when he returned. He was starved from his sail from Scotland and wounded badly."

"The war ended well before this year did it not?" I asked in confusion.

"Aye."

"Then why did your father wait until this year to return?"

"He was captured for a while, I know that much," Henry said. "I have also heard that he stayed in Scotland of his own will."

I would have continued the conversation further, but we came upon a great disturbance in the crowd, and my attention was redirected.

I pushed my way in, followed by Henry. The people were all gathered around two young men beating each other to pieces. I broke through the bystanders and stared at the bloody mess. It seemed as if Edmond had found his match in the miller's son, a tall lean boy of eighteen. 'What has he done now?' I thought as I watched Edmond plow his broad shoulders into his opponent's chest, sending the latter tumbling to the ground.

"I told you the price is fair!" the miller's son hollered as he hoisted himself to his feet, clasping his chest in pain.

"You paid twice that much for the same amount of grain last week!" Edmond yelled. "You cheat!" he gripped the boy's shirt and pulled the miller's son toward him. "Do not try to cheat me," Edmond gritted his teeth. "Now tell me the truth."

The miller's boy scowled in reply.

Edmond let go of the boy's shirt, allowing him to collapse to the ground. "Come on John, it does not have to get any worse. Tell the truth."

The boy grimaced and pushed himself up. "Fine!" he spat. "I paid you less because I am sick of you and your family!"

Edmond scooped up a sack of grain in one arm and tossed it to the miller's son, nearly toppling him over. "Now pay me right."

The miller's son hauled the sack into the mill and came out handing the money reluctantly to Edmond. Edmond smiled and walked into the crowd. I pushed through the crowd and made my way toward him.

"Edmond!" I shouted above the crowd. He turned his bloodied face to me.

"Hello Richard," he smiled. "What are you doing here? And who is your friend?"

"This is Henry, he and his father have something for you," I replied.

"Do they?" Edmond wiped the blood from his nose and shook Henry's hand then returned his attention back to me. "And what would that be?"

"I think it would be better if you came to see for yourself," Henry said, wiping Edmond's blood off on his own shirt.

Edmond shifted from one foot to the other, "I must take the money back home," he said, "mother will be wanting it."

"I think your mother will understand if you bring it once this errand is completed," Edmond raised an eyebrow, knowing something was amiss.

"Where is this gift?" Edmond asked Henry, raising an eyebrow.

"Lawrence, Henry's father is waiting for you at Andrew's house," I replied. Henry smiled in agreement.

Edmond nodded and we began to walk. "Could you not have settled it without a fight? Just this once?" I asked Edmond.

"Oh you know John, he is always looking to get more money into his own pocket, and usually gets it too," Edmond scowled at the thought of the miller's son. "He has deserved a beating for a while now."

"On that we agree, but you did not have to knock out another tooth!"

"He hit me first," Edmond laughed, "Or at least tried to!"

I laughed as well and turned to Henry, who was staring silently at something behind us.

"So," I regained my composure and addressed Henry, "You said your father was captured?"

Henry's head snapped back and looked at me, "Aye," was his only reply.

"Do you know who captured him?" I asked.

"And where was he?" Edmond added, trying to understand.

"I know they were not Scotsmen," replied Henry. "Father said they could have been Khanite marauders," his voice trailed off as he gazed over his shoulder. I looked back as well, but seeing only the marketplace, returned my gaze to what was before me.

"Khanite?" Edmond said thoughtfully. Henry looked ahead once more.

"That is what father said," Henry replied. "They were the remnant of the empire of Genghis Khan."

An eery feeling entered my gut as I thought about the conqueror, but I could not understand why. I awakened from my thoughts to find Henry once more staring behind us.

"What are you looking at?" I blurted.

Henry slowly turned to me and nodded in the direction which lay ahead. His face contorted into a dreadful expression.

"What is wrong?" Edmond asked.

"Do not look back. I have already revealed us for sure," Henry whispered so that only I and Edmond heard. "A man has been following us since we left the market."

The urge to look back was unbearable. "What does he look like?" I managed to say.

"Tall," replied Henry, "and big. Very big. In a red tunic. With black hair and a big beard."

"Enlighten me," Edmond spoke, "how big is 'very big'?"

"Over six feet and he has a sword," Henry replied.

I could resist the urge no longer. I spun myself around and stared into the crowd. A tall man stood out more than anyone. He was as Henry described. Our eyes locked for a moment; a grin crept across his face. A familiar fear entered my heart and beckoned for me to run. I tripped suddenly and fell to the ground. "Run!" I yelled as I scrambled to my feet. "Run!" I broke into a sprint with Edmond and Henry following close behind.

I glanced over my shoulder, but the man simply stood in his place watching us. I turned into an alleyway, ran to another road and turned south, roughly in the direction of Andrew's house.

We ran for a few more minutes and stopped to catch our breath.

"Who is that?" Henry gasped. "Why did you run?"

I could not speak because of my fear.

"Whoever he is," Edmond said, "we had better keep moving before he catches us."

I nodded in agreement and we began running once more.

***

Edmond stared at the sword laying upon the table in Andrew's house. His eyes filled with pain and sorrow. "How did it happen?" he asked without taking his eyes off the sword.

Andrew looked up at Lawrence, from the corner of the room, as if to say, "no," for he had already heard what had happened. Our attention was fixed upon Lawrence as he began his tale:

"I left my wife and children fifteen years ago to fight the war in Scotland. There I met your father, Baldwin, and we became friends. We fought for a year together until the Battle of Brannokburn. There we were both wounded and separated from the army. And upon the fields of battle, we lay until we gathered enough strength to drag ourselves south. After another day or more, we were captured by a band of Khanite warriors. We knew not what they wanted, nor why they were there, but we realized soon that these men were chasing a fantasy, an evil force which they had conceived themselves." Andrew's gazed relaxed.

"The Battle of Brannokburn was years ago," Edmond clenched his teeth, "Did it truly take fourteen years to come home?"

Andrew returned his gaze upon Lawrence, who in turn kept silent.

Edmond jumped up and slammed his hands upon the table, "What happened to my father!"

Lawrence continued. "The Khans were an order. A secret order."

"What does that matter?" I asked.

"They were looking for power, power like the Alignment," replied Andrew, seeing that Edmond would have to hear the story in full.

"Yes, but what does that matter?" Edmond was obviously beginning to lose patience.

"We became intrigued by these men and convinced them that we could help them find this power," Lawrence's expression was grave, "And after thirteen years we found it."

"What does my father have to do with this?" Edmond asked impatiently.

"Your father saved my life," Lawrence's voice grew heavy. "He did the right thing, even when the choice was impossible."

"What happened?" Edmond asked.

Lawrence wiped a tear from his eye. We found that power, but the first engagement was a disaster. The Khanites called together all the remnant that they had scattered around Europe, hundreds of men. Then he came. One man. Tall and dark. The servant of the pure darkness they sought to destroy. He gave the Khanites over to a plague. Half of them were killed and the others were left beaten and broken. Once the plague subsided, I tried to get your father to leave with me, but he refused. He told me that he was doing it for you, Edmond, to protect you.

"When the man saw that the plague had finished its course, he began to cut the rest down with the sword. Many fled, but your father and the last and bravest of the Khanites stayed, they were determined to complete their goal. To destroy that cursed darkness!"

"And that is where my father died?" asked Edmond. "Fighting for a cause that was not his own? Fighting for a people who were not his own?"

"Your father sacrificed himself to save me and all the survivors," Lawrence let out a sigh, "He did what was right when no one could."

Edmond sat back down and rested his head in his hands. I thought back on my father's death. I knew what he was feeling. Guilt. Anger. Sorrow. But as he looked up, one thing was absent – there was no sign of hate.

Edmond reached out and laid his hand upon the shimmering hilt of the sword and closed his eyes. All the pain seemed to drift away, all his sorrow no longer mattered. He stood up once more and pulled the sword free from the bondage of its sheath and stared at it as the light reflected off of it onto all corners of the room.

"Your father's last words were to give it to you or your brother. He said that you would know what to do when the time comes," Lawrence spoke.

"The honor of wielding his sword is not mine to take. But as his death was a sacrifice to save your life," his jaw set, "I shall wield this blade to save others," his eyes peeled away from the sword and rested upon Lawrence as he rose from his chair. "As surely as I live, no matter what cost it brings me," his fingers tightened around the gilded hilt of the majestic blade. "I accept my father's sword."

V

WHERE WE WILL GO

A week after Edmond accepted the sword, Lawrence and Henry went on their way back to Folkstone.

As the year 1329 dawned, I practiced blacksmithing more and more, and enriched my skill in the trade. Many of my jobs were tedious at first, however, it soon became known that I was developing new techniques in weaponry and swordsmithing. By February I had attracted more valuable customers from the neighboring towns.

Halfway through the year 1329, I sat with Edmond and Andrew in Andrew's house. It was all too familiar with all its memories, both good and bad. The week prior to our meeting had resulted in Edmond's mother taking dreadfully ill and leaving for London with Thomas. Upon that, we received word that Henry's father, Lawrence, had died and left Henry, his mother and five younger siblings to fend for themselves. The three of us pitched in and sent the Forwin family as much money as we could muster, as well as our sincere condolences.

Thus, the three of us sat around the table at Andrew's house and the shadow of silence stood with us for the first hour.

"Massacre in Ireland last month," I started, trying to bring up a meaningful conversation.

"Truly, was that necessary?" Edmond replied condescendingly.

"Well, I just thought...maybe we could..." My voice trailed off as I thought of how limited we were.

We were only a farmer and two blacksmiths, one with an obsession with God and science. What difference could we make?

"Could what?" asked Andrew.

"If only we could stop it," I replied quickly as the grin of the killer entered my heart. The night had never left me, no matter how hard I tried to push it away. "All the pain and suffering in this world. If we could end the wars – all the fighting and loss."

"That is impossible," retorted Edmond. "The wars will not end until the Peace comes."

"The Alignment is on its way and if we could harness the power from it, we could perhaps..." Andrew was cut off.

"You have been saying that since I was a lad, and there is no proof," Edmond said. "I am not saying it will never happen, just do not count on it."

"I have proof that it will happen!" Andrew countered.

"When?" I asked. "I think it is time we do something with our lives and stop relying on hope of the impossible. And that goes for both of you."

"You think I am crazy?" Andrew eyed the two of us.

"No," Edmond reassured him, "You are in perfect control of your faculties! But no man can predict the abilities or the effect of harnessing that power," he leaned back in his chair. "So, I am with Richard. We need something more than armies and Kings. Something that stands not for just England or France, but for all mankind."

"What are you suggesting?" Andrew asked.

"I am not sure yet," Edmond replied.

"Edmond is right," I said. "We cannot just stand for one nation."

"Allegiances like these have been formed before, and they have not changed anything," Andrew said. "Remember the Khanites in

Scotland? The problem is something we cannot fix because as men, we are the problem. We spread our sins as abominations."

"Andrew, we could be so much more than the Khanites ever were," I replied. "We could stop the abominations that others spread. Stop the war and pain."

"You do not see though," Andrew protested. "We cannot stop it. Sin will run its course until the appointed time of destruction."

"We are not 'sin' Andrew," I met his gaze, searching his eyes for some explanation. "We are men. You yourself have said that we are made in the image of your God."

"And yet we defile that image with all our pride and selfishness," Andrew replied. "Man is not sin itself, but he carries it through this world. And that is why all these federations fall. They spend out their lives in the lie that they can achieve perfection."

"But we will not fall!" I proclaimed. "We are better than them. We know what pain is. We know what suffering is, therefore we will be able to see its rise and stop it," I leaned back in my chair. "We may not be perfect, but we are the best there is."

"We are not what this world needs!" Andrew exclaimed. "We cannot offer salvation."

"Why do you not support me?" I asked. "Here I am trying to make the world a better place. I want to end wars and stop pain! I want to stop that murdering wretch from hurting anyone else, and you are discouraging it! Is that not what you always taught me? Is this not what your God would want? Helping others?"

"I am not discouraging making the world a better place," Andrew countered. "I am trying to show you that we cannot achieve perfection until perfection comes again."

"Where was your God when my parents were killed?" I gritted my teeth.

"I want to help the world. I want to help people. But I cannot save it," Andrew sighed. "And neither can you."

"Then maybe we can do it together," Edmond spoke.

I fell silent.

"We can make this brotherhood," Edmond continued, "and it will change the world. It will make a better tomorrow," his eyes filled with passion. "But it will never be good unless we listen to Andrew."

I stared at him in confusion. "You just said-"

"Richard," Edmond interrupted, "you have the idea and the passion to carry it through, but Andrew speaks the truth and righteousness. His faith will hold us together! And if we do not have that, we will fall into pride and destruction. If He is for us, no one can come against us."

"You can have your faith," I scowled. "Mine died with my parents."

"Your faith did not die, Richard," Andrew spoke forcefully.

"Then what did it do?" I yelled.

"You were not ready for it."

"Ready for faith?" I fumed. "I was not ready for faith? Then why were my parents ripped away? Why were they taken if I was not ready to do it on my own?"

"Because faith has nothing to do with doing it on your own."

"Yes," I jeered. "But you have faith. So did my father, and my mother and Norwood and Isabel and almost everyone who died in Shrewton! They all died! Lawrence and Baldwin had faith too! And look at where they are – all dead!"

"There is always a..." Andrew tried to speak.

"No there is not! There was no reason they died and there was no reason those hundred and sixty people had to die in Ireland!" I took a deep breath. "That is why we need this. We need to end these wars and holocausts before they start. And I will do it alone if I have to."

"You are not alone, Richard," Andrew stood up. "I will help you form this brotherhood under two conditions."

"And what are those?" I glared at him.

"First and foremost, that it is honorable to Christ. And second, that it is secret. No man can know who we are, lest they give us credit and reason for pride. There will be no personal gain."

"Fine," I relented. "Keep your foolish beliefs. Go ahead, believe in a God who lets his followers die by the sword!"

"Richard..." Andrew began.

"Believe in a God who lets children grow up fatherless and sends them running into the night! Go on Andrew!" I slammed my hands on the table. "Believe in that."

"His work is perfect, for all His ways are good and just," Andrew replied calmly.

"Andrew is right," Edmond chimed it. "There will be no unity without faith."

I grimaced.

Edmond stood up. "Well then," his eyes beamed, "a brotherhood it is."

"A Brethren," announced Andrew. "Founded on the principles of God's word and His divine instruction – The Brethren."

"Brethren?" I grimaced again.

"Aye," Edmond smiled.

Andrew stood up and scrambled about the house and returned with a blank sheet of parchment and lay it on the table. He then walked over to a shelf and brought back a bottle of ink and a quill. He sat down, dipped the pen into the ink and began to write. As he did, he spoke the words which set the course of my life.

"On my honor, in union with the Brethren," his voice was as

strong as the sea and yet calm as a cloudless sky. "I hereby pledge to do God's will in all my power. To Heal all Offenses," he dipped the pen into the ink again and continued. "To help all those in need," he spoke with passion and hope as he continued to write the commission. "And to Protect the Earth and those in it from whatever perils should come," he lay down the pen and blew on the wet ink to dry it quickly.

"Sign it," Andrew said, holding out the pen.

I drew in a deep breath.

"The Brethren is established," Edmond declared as he snatched the pen and scratched out his name in bold, powerful letters below the pledge. He handed the pen back to Andrew, who proceeded to sign it in a much finer, calmer fashion. He leaned back a moment, staring at the parchment, then handed the pen to me.

"Go ahead," he said, "for Christ, and for His people."

"I cannot," doubt filled me.

"You wanted this," he continued "I will not let you back out now."

"I cannot make that promise!" I stood up and turned my back to them. "I cannot promise that I will heal them all," I ran my fingers through my hair. "I cannot make the promise to do the will of the One who allowed everything to be taken from me!"

Andrew strode over and put his hand on my shoulder, "Evil and corruption took them, not God."

"And you say God is all good and powerful - so how did he let them die?"

"That problem was resolved at the cross. The one good man who ever lived, the Son of God was beaten, stripped and nailed to a tree. Is there anything more evil? Yet God used that evil deed, to save all mankind from eternal judgment," I had never heard Andrew speak with such power. "So instead of dwelling on what was taken from you," he held out the pen to me, "why not try to stop it from being taken from others? Christ's life was taken from Him to give you a new life, so why not give it back to Him?"

I took the pen in my hand 'I will never give it to him,' I thought.

The pen felt heavier than it should have, like a weight was on one end pulling it from my hand. I stiffly walked to the table. I read silently over and over again taking in everything. I lifted the pen to a place below the pledge. My heart sped up. I wrote the first letter of my name.

'Regret,' an echo filled my head.

I stopped and looked around "Did you hear something?" I asked.

Edmond and Andrew shook their heads. "No. I did not hear anything," Edmond said.

I shrugged and continued with the 'I'

'Iniquity,' reverberated through me.

"You did not hear that?" I asked again.

"The only sound is your slow writing," Edmond smiled. "Are you well, Richard?"

"I am fine," I continued to write.

'Contemptuous, Hopeless, Abhorred, Renounced,' the words pulled at me from every direction, and yet came from nowhere.

I stopped writing for a moment and took a deep breath and wrote the last letter.

'D'?' I thought to myself 'What does that mean-' my thoughts were interrupted by a strike at the door.

Edmond hastily opened it.

A knife was sunk into a piece of paper with one word. 'Doubt'

Edmond tore the paper from the knife and lay it on the table. "Doubt," he said. "Again, doubt."

"Doubt what?" Andrew asked. "What are we to doubt?"

"I do not know," I said as I walked over to the window and

gazed out at the surrounding streets.

The moon shone brightly and lit up the road. The torches too were burning in several places. It hardly looked dark. All except one place. Across the street to the left, in the darkness of the shadows stood a man. His eyes beamed with fire and his presence brought a familiar sense of dread. And then he was gone. I quickly closed the window and turned back to Andrew and Edmond, "I do not know."

***

Four years passed and the Brethren took shape as we gathered forty men who were willing to fight for the cause. However our goal was unclear and the more sacrifices we gave, the more doubt rose in our minds and hearts. Doubt that maybe we were doing it all wrong.

***

It was a cold December day in 1332. I sat with Andrew and Edmond in Andrew's house, as we huddled next to the fire. We stared at the coals as they glowed brighter and brighter. None of us felt like speaking, for after a warm meal and now before the blazing fire, all we wanted to do was sleep. But that would have to wait, for there was a knock.

I turned and looked at Edmond longing not to have to get up. But his distracted gaze forced me away from the warmth of the fire and toward the door.

The icy cold air and snow flew in as I opened the door, and with the cold, three men, who looked more like bundles than people stood upon the threshold.

I hastily let the men inside. "Whatever are you three doing out in such weather?"

Edmond and Andrew stood up to greet the men, as the tallest of them spoke in a voice I knew better than any other. The one voice which comforted me more than Andrew's, for it was the first to do so.

The voice of Angus Aundray.

"Lord Aundray?" I gasped in disbelief.

The man lifted his hood and revealed the rough, clever face of my father's former friend. His countenance was grave and his dark eyes blazed. My parents were right to say that the years served him well, for he did not look a day older than when I left Shrewton. Neither was there any silver upon his wild black hair.

He drew in the warm air of the house through his tall, pointed nose. "Hello Richard," his lips curled into a smile.

"Why-why?" I paused.

"I beg your pardon Richard, but who are these men in my home?" Andrew asked as he walked and crossed his arms uncharacteristically.

"Andrew!" I exclaimed. "This is the Lord Angus Aundray, The Baron of Shrewton. He is the man who sent me here!"

"Hello Andrew," Angus extended his hand to Andrew, "I am truly sorry for the intrusion, but I could wait no longer to see Richard again. It has been far too long," he said as his eyes met mine.

"That it has!" I embraced Angus. It was comforting to feel his strong arms around me. I broke away a little. "That it has."

"And who are your friends?" Andrew asked inquisitively.

"I am Roger Wilson, of Birmingham. Son of Sir William of London, the head of the Anglo-African Trade company," Roger extended his hand to me first and then to Andrew and Edmond.

"And you?" Andrew's eyes shifted toward the third man.

"My name is Bennet Burnell," he smiled as he removed his hood, spilling snow upon the floor.

My memory sparked at the name. I stared into the man's bright green eyes, "Bennet of London? Bennet Burnell!"

He laughed. "Do you really think that I would leave you alone after you left London?" The feeling of joy upon seeing my old friend was new and unfamiliar to me.

"What has brought you here to my home?" asked Andrew to Angus. "Or have you only come upon chance?"

"It is rather a long story," Angus replied, "and chance has as much to do with it as anything. My primary objective though, was to find Richard."

"As was mine," Bennet replied.

"Well, you are my guests. Please take a place by the fire and we shall hear your story," Andrew smiled and gestured the three men to the fire. Roger and Angus rested themselves in two of the chairs, Bennet, however, said that he was more comfortable standing and insisted that Andrew sit. Andrew looked at Bennet curiously and then seated himself. Bennet stood near to the fire, beside Edmond and me, and warmed himself.

Angus began, "It all started with the death of Roger Mortimer, the King's Regent. I was glad to have a new king on the throne, and Edward seemed to be the right man. However, I was as shocked as anyone by the execution of Lord Mortimer – a man I knew well. After his death, I feared for my own life and hoped that Edward would overlook my relationship with him. However, as I waited for the king's troops to show up at my doorstep, I realized that though Edward's reign began with blood, very little blood had been spilled since," he paused and adjusted himself to get closer to the flames. "I thought to myself, 'Is there any way that this King could become peaceful after all that has happened?' The answer was no. Men do not change their nature. Therefore, I believed that there was something else happening behind the scenes. And then came the Battle of Dupplin Moor, and several other fights, where bodies were found without emblem nor rank nor weapons. That is when I became curious."

"How do you know this?" Edmond asked.

"Any good Baron will have friends to tell him which side to

choose if war should arise," replied Angus.

"Please continue your story, sir," Andrew pressed.

"After the battle, I was determined to find who those three men were. I needed to know how they did it. How they brought peace in a land of war," Angus smiled.

"How did you know they brought peace?" I asked.

"Because I heard a witness. His account was that those men fought and died to bring peace," I nodded and he continued. "After finding the bodies, I found Roger Wilson. I told him of my quest and he was determined to join me and find this group of men.

"After more searching, we discerned a name; the Brethren. And later the motivation and pledge – to save the world."

"That is when I joined the quest in earnest," Roger chimed in. "I had to find these men with such a noble purpose who would risk everything for the world they love."

Angus nodded in agreement. "So we took up our search with more vigor, asking nearly every man we knew if they had heard of the Brethren. Finally, we ran into Bennet."

Bennet smiled, "No really, he ran into me when I was visiting Shrewton, looking for you actually," he looked at me. "Ah, but that is a story for another time!"

"Oh do tell," I said anxious to hear the story. "Why would you be looking for me?"

Bennet's face contorted as if he were trying to remember something. "Well, it was more of a hunch, as if I remembered something."

"Remembered something?" Edmond asked before I could.

"Aye, but now it is gone," he smiled. "I will be sure to let you know when it comes back to me."

"Back to the story then," Angus continued. "Bennet opened my eyes to many things, which he probably does not remember now. But most important to this story, when he came asking about you, I remembered your resolve Richard."

"Resolve?" I asked.

"Aye. If any man would want to end a war before it starts, or would want to save people, it would be you. After what you have lost, you know what it is like to feel pain," my face was downcast as I remembered the brutal murder of my parents. "And so, here we are," Angus smiled, "sitting with the men, destined to change the world."

"Well, you have told me how you got here but not what I truly must know," Andrew stated. "Sir Aundray, why are you here? Besides finding Richard, for you said that you were on a quest to find the Brethren. Why?"

"Roger Wilson is here to join the Brethren," Angus replied.

"And me too," Bennet smiled. His eyes sparkled with excitement, looking greener than a lush blade of grass.

Andrew seemed to stop breathing. For more than a minute he stared at both Roger and Bennet. He appeared to take in every detail, from Roger's waving hair, to Bennet's shifting from one foot to the other. And then to Angus. The two men's eyes locked upon each other. Both had minds that could be matched only by the other, both had loyalty beyond comprehension and both would do anything for those they loved. They even resembled one another, but the two could not have been more different. "You tracked us down to join us?" Andrew asked. "Why?"

Roger stood up. "Sir, I wish to clear my conscience of the sins I have committed and free my soul from torment."

Andrew raised an eyebrow.

"My father was a slave trader. I saw their blood and washed my hands in it," Roger's eyes blazed with passion. "You do not know what that does to a man."

Andrew nodded and turned to Bennet. "And you?" he asked.

"All I ever wanted to do was serve Christ, my Savior. And here I see a way I can let His light shine, and save the world as well," he smiled. "I cannot think of any better way to spend my life."

"And what about you Angus?" Andrew asked.

Angus smiled. "I am here to help you. Not to join you, for my duty is to the people of Shrewton, but to help you when I can."

Andrew nodded and looked toward Roger. "What brought you to the conclusion that you had done wrong?"

Roger seated himself once more and ran his fingers through his brown hair. After catching his breath he began. "The brutality which is used upon those poor souls," he drew in deeply. "Sir," he addressed Andrew, "I took part in those beatings. I took part in causing them pain. It is something I can never forgive myself for. As the knights of old fought in the Holy Land, I beseech you to permit me to crusade in my home land, for my own soul."

"So, you wish to clear your conscience of this by joining us?" Andrew asked, and Roger nodded. "Remember this Roger Wilson, He is the only one who can forgive you," Roger nodded once more and Andrew turned to Bennet. "Bennet your words are pure and I can see that you long for your heart to be at peace. But you refuse to sit in another man's home, not so that he may rest himself, but because you are running and cannot rest."

"Running's what I do best," he swallowed. "I always have."

"But what are you running from?" Andrew asked.

"Sir," Bennet replied. "I can neither remember my father's face, nor how I came to live in London. All I know is my name, what my father did, and why I'm here."

"And why are you here?" I asked.

"The dream of hope will come," his eyes brightened. "That had something to do with why I was looking for you – but I can't remember," he sighed and set his chin on his chest. "I'm sorry."

"Do not apologize, Bennet," Andrew smiled as he stood up and addressed Roger and Bennet. "If you pledge yourself to the Brethren and most of all to God, then we accept you into this brotherhood."

Angus stood up as well and embraced Andrew. "Thank you, these men will doubtless serve you well. I trust them with my life."

Andrew nodded. "Your word, Baron, will not sway me either way, but your trust in them is a thing I shall never forget."

Angus smiled and said, "Never is a long time," he shook Andrew's hand. "Well then, I thank you for your hospitality, but it is late, and I must be going. I have stacks of letters back in Shrewton that I must attend to."

"Thank you for coming," I embraced Angus once more and he was off before anyone could say another goodbye.

"Well then," Bennet exclaimed. "Where to begin?"

***

By the year 1335, the Brethren spread from Scotland to France. Roger became a leading member, and Bennet the head messenger. Henry also joined us and helped lead. In November 1335, we were all seated in Edmond's house in Durrington. The house was neither nice, nor messy but rugged – the home of a warrior.

"Well," Roger spoke, "as we come into our seventh year, I believe the Brethren is ready to expand to Ireland and Spain at least," he laughed, "perhaps even into Germany!"

"Now you hold on their Mr. Wilson," Bennet laughed. "I'm dead tired from running up and down from France to Scotland!"

"Aye," Henry replied. "But your running has saved many

lives."

"Not those at Halidon Hill," I threw in. "No one could have stopped that."

Henry nodded. "But if you remember Richard, the men who fell at Halidon Hill served as a call to arms for the Brethren. Our numbers increased tremendously!"

"Henry is right," Andrew commented. "The suffering of the fallen along with their sacrifice has made us stronger."

"All the same, we cannot expand so quickly," I replied. "We have been spread thin before and every time lives were lost. None of those men deserved to die. If we spread ourselves too thin we will only repeat our errors and more people will die."

"We are already spread thin," Henry commented. "Yet not thin enough to be broken with ease."

Edmond nodded. "Spoken true."

"But we are not spread far enough. We could do so much more," Roger countered. "Lives were lost then, on that we agree, but look how many were saved. Our numbers have risen seven times our strength three years ago. In just this past year our numbers doubled. There are five hundred of us!"

"Keep in mind, Roger, that it is not our doing that makes the Brethren's number rise, it is the LORD'S, and you will remember well to leave the census to Him," Andrew's position was as unchanged as ever.

"Aye," Edmond said, "Andrew speaks the truth. However, the Brethren needs to expand or else our presence will diminish in France.

"You see, even Edmond agrees!" Roger exclaimed.

"Edmond doesn't run up and down the coast of England," Bennet objected and Edmond nodded once more.

"Roger, surely you have enough to do with the Brethren in

France already?" Henry spoke. "Is that not enough for you now?"

"But that is what has driven me to this conclusion," Roger announced. "Look at how England has prospered, look at how many lives we have saved! I want not only France, but all nations to see days as peaceful as England!"

"And someday we hope it will," Andrew replied. "But not now. It is too early."

"Seven years and we have England's peace," Roger stared in astonishment at Andrew. "How many more will it take for you to see that the Brethren is rising to a higher calling?"

"As many as patience and rest dictate," retorted Andrew. "And the calling is neither higher nor lower on the account of nations."

Bennet raised an eyebrow and nodded in agreement with Andrew.

"And how many is that?" Roger demanded. "How many more years will it take?"

Andrew answered without faltering. "As many as it takes for you to see your lust for power clearly," All of us were taken back by the power and poignancy of his words.

"I do not lust for power," he began to stumble over his words as Andrew's rebuke set in. "I-I just want to free the world."

"As do we," I said, "but it is too soon."

"Fine," Roger stood up from the table and strode quickly to the door.

"Roger wait," Andrew rose from his seat at the table. "Know why you fight and who you fight for."

"I know you well, Andrew." Roger replied with a grimace, "do not think I do not know why you refuse to move on. Your son would be ashamed if he finds out who you are!" he turned and went outside, slamming the door behind him.

Andrew took a seat once more in silence. Evidence lay within the heaviness of his eyes that Roger's words pierced his heart.

"I believe Roger needs some time alone," Henry stood up solemnly and placed a comforting hand upon Andrew's shoulder. "And I also believe he needs to know who he fights for," he paused for a moment. "And who you fight for."

"Do you think he will be all right?" I asked Henry.

"Aye," Bennet agreed, "what do you think?"

Henry replied. "Roger is a man of power, and he lusts for it. He will not stop until he gets it. And with this passion, he can be a wonderful friend, or a formidable enemy. He needs time or else he will become the latter."

"Spoken true," Andrew commended, still shaken by Roger's harsh words. "He is beginning to lose sight of our calling."

"Aye," replied Henry. "Thank you Edmond for having us tonight," he shook Edmond's hand, gave Andrew a warm smile and left the house.

Bennet rose up and nodded to Edmond. "Thanks Edmond," he smiled. "I'll be off now though. I've got a message that I need to get to London, so," he said his goodbyes and left the three of us.

"Well then," I said, "the Alignment?"

"Not now Richard," Andrew replied.

"Soon though?"

"Aye," he answered.

I stood up, said my farewells, and left Edmond and Andrew to talk further.

I walked out into the middle of the street pulling my cloak tight to fight the chill of the wind. I took a deep breath, turned to the left and began walking toward my house.

It was late when I finally arrived. The wind howled. It felt like frost was forming on my face as I reached for the door and pushed it open.

I immediately started a fire and soon had one blazing. I sat back and enjoyed the warmth for a bit, then stood up and walked quietly to the end of the one roomed house. As I did, something caught my eye. A piece of paper was attached to the door.

"Not another!" I thought aloud. I pulled the paper off the door and read. 'Doubt'

"Who are you?" I asked myself staring at the paper and flipping it over several times to see if I missed something. "What do you want?" I looked up and out the window, then threw the paper into the fire and went to sleep. The face of the killer always in my mind, day in and day out, just as it had been for thirteen years.

VI

A DARKER DAWN

February 27th, 1336.

It was cold and wet on that fateful night as the wind howled outside my house in Durrington. I sat near the fireplace staring at the embers of a dying fire. One thought weighed on my heart and shot through my head like a flaming arrow, burning out all other thoughts. The world seemed to revolve around it. Revenge! Revenge and hatred were what ignited that arrow coursing through my mind. The face of my parents' murderer always stood as the arrow passed. Each day I imagined his death. I nearly felt it. Each day my hatred became stronger and my visions more vivid of how I would make him pay. I dwelt on this for quite some time. My eyes closed. I fingered the blade that I had fashioned that day. It was made of a metal that Andrew and I created, Valinium, and nearly covered my forearm. The gauntlet was fastened to my arm with leather straps which had been reinforced with the metal. A two-foot blade was concealed within the gauntlet and could be released atop the dorsal side of my hand. It made for a formidable hidden weapon, and with such a weapon I fully intended to destroy my parents' killer.

I stood up suddenly and opened my eyes. His face was out of my mind for a brief moment. I walked over to the end of the house. A mattress lay in one corner on which I slept, and a dingy old pillow on top of it. One door on the left side of the room lead out into the street, another door stood on the right, and led to my blacksmith shop. A few shelves lined the walls with several books and other necessities. The remaining walls were covered with weapons of my fashioning and of the greatest secret. However, it was not the weapons themselves that were the secret, but what I fashioned them from. Only Andrew and I knew how the weapons were made, for we alone possessed the secret to making them.

I walked over to a small stack of wood in the corner and threw another log on the fire. I returned to my seat before the hearth and watched as the log smoked, slowly blackened and was consumed by flames.

I sat alone in silence for what seemed like hours before it was broken by a loud knock on the door. I stumbled to the door and opened it. Two very familiar faces came in from the street. Andrew and Edmond.

Andrew had aged well over the past thirteen years, his eyes were wiser though and the many years did nothing to dim his wit. His once brown hair however had given way to a shimmering silver.

Edmond's jet black hair sharply contrasted Andrew's, and only seemed to get darker as Andrew's gave way to more silver. And as if his hair was not enough to contrast Andrew, his eyes were shimmering brown, like chestnut, as opposed to Andrew's deep blue. And as his arms were nearing the thickness of tree trunks, Andrew's grew lean with age.

The two men could not have been more different, even in tactical thinking to wiley strategy that differed in every way, save for the one – their faith, rooted in deep belief.

The two of them entered the house and we all seated ourselves around the table in the center of the room.

"So, what brings you two here?" I asked as I sat down at my place.

"You know Richard, desperate times, desperate measures," Andrew chuckled. "Truly though, it is not good."

Edmond simply nodded in agreement.

"How so?" I inquired.

"This," stated Andrew, as he pulled a folded piece of paper out of his cloak and handed it to me.

"What is it?" I asked as I unfolded the paper.

"A letter from the far east, from the Khans," retorted Edmond. "A dark shadow that has befallen us."

"The Grand Emperor's chief Ambassador to the Monarchs of Europe. All peace and friendly greetings to thee.

A war passes through our land. The Khan of Kipchak, the finest Empire of the world, is falling to these barbarians. A war has started without any end except our destruction. The armies, of origin we know not, have descended upon us with more brutality than any that we have ever seen before. All the great cities have fallen to their hand and our armies are beyond repair. Every day we watch the innocent perish without hope. Beware, they are coming to you. It is too late for our people to be victorious over them, but perhaps humanity will not die in these days. Assemble your armies, we beseech thee, and guard your lands and your people! They bring Doubt..."

A stain of blood covered the rest of the writing. I rapidly refolded the paper. As if the final word had been a battle cry, the face of the murderer came vividly back into my head with a river of my darkest memories.

"Where did you get this?" I clenched my fist and lay the letter stiffly onto the table.

"It is a long story," Edmond replied.

"We have time," I gritted my teeth in order to keep myself steady.

"I was in Liverpool several weeks back supporting our brothers.

Once I received this, I then tried to spread a word of warning of what is coming," he took a sip of a drink at the table. "Like what I was doing in France," he paused. "Well, that and trying to keep France and England away from open war. Believe me, war is on its way between the two."

"What about the letter?" I asked.

"Well, you see that is the strange part," Edmond said. "I had hardly been there a week when it came. It was a strange looking man, he looked sick as a dog, when it has been…"

"Edmond," I interrupted, "I do not care what he looked like. I want to know who he was!"

"The enemy of someone," Edmond retorted. "I believe he said he was the enemy of someone."

"Do you know who?" I asked.

"Nay, nor could I tell where the man was from."

"Was he from Khan Kipchak?"

"I do not know," Edmond thoughtfully said.

"Have you ever seen a man from Khan Kipchak?" I asked.

"No."

"Well, that is why," Andrew spoke.

"Aye, but those confounded dogs!" Edmond, even in anger spoke dryly. "Do they think that they can simply attack the rest of the world and not reap the whirlwind?"

"Not to come on too strong—" Andrew tried to speak.

"This is the worst that's happened since the crusades!" yelled Edmond suddenly realizing what we were being led into. "Biscuit's blood! How did I not see that before?"

"Would you shut it Edmond!" my voice rose, then fell to a calmer tone. "This is more than the Brethren alone. We are too weak to stop this threat. Has the King been notified?"

"No, he is away in France on diplomatic matters. France and England are pressing towards war as Edmond said," Andrew replied. "On top of that, the King has ordered tranquility, no visitors whatsoever. Trust me, we already tried to send our messenger, Bennet, but he came back saying that he was not able to get into the castle."

"There must be a way to get this to him," I sighed holding up the letter. "There has got to be a way!"

"There is," said Edmond.

"What is it?" I asked.

"Aye," echoed Andrew. "And why did you not say so sooner?"

"I just thought of it," Edmond dryly replied. "He is at the Castle of Château de Dourdan am I correct?"

"Yes, why do you ask?" I inquired.

"Under the castle are a series of escape tunnels built for the inhabitants. I saw them when I visited there a few years ago when I was finding the new recruits. We can use them to get in and out again."

"Do you know where the tunnels let out?" I asked.

"If I did not, I wouldn't be telling you about it," Edmond smirked.

"What did you have in mind?" I returned.

"We go down to Château de Dourdan with as many of the Brethren as we can rally. The King will be there, and he will be having banquets in his honor. We sneak in, midnight, after the parties. The tunnels will bring us to the kitchens. The cooks will be asleep after the long evening. The halls will be poorly guarded at that time. In any case, we should go in directly before the changing of the posts. We sneak into the King's chamber, give him the letter and get out before they even notice that we were there."

"Well done Edmond," I commended. "We must assemble the Brethren."

"I will ride down to Folkestone for Henry," stated Edmond.

"Then I shall go to Birmingham for Roger," I declared. "Would you, Andrew find us a ship and assemble the brothers? Heaven knows we may come to war."

"It will be my pleasure. I will send Bennet to find and ready the Brethren. He is in Durrington now and free to help us," Andrew continued, "I also know a young man down at Portsmouth who can help us. Once you two get Henry and Roger, come down to Portsmouth and meet me there at the docks. I will be waiting."

"Well then," I said, "do we set out tonight or wait to go in the morning?"

"Tonight," Edmond replied. "Such things need not wait. War is upon us, and the enemy waits not for our sleep."

"Very well then," I said. "Andrew to Portsmouth, you to Folkestone, and me," I stood up from the table, "to Birmingham."

By around eleven o'clock that night we were all on our way to our destinations. I rode on my only horse Acheron.

I galloped out towards Birmingham, over a hundred miles to the North. After several hours of riding at a fast pace, Acheron was tired, and I rode him at a slower pace from then on. It was much more pleasant going slower; however, my thoughts more easily drifted back to the murderer.

The moon lit the sky as though it were dusk, and large trees grew on either side of the dirt road, their leafless branches creeping overhead reaching out to the sky.

The man's face came into my mind many times as I rode. Suddenly, Acheron reared up in terror.

"What is wrong boy?" I asked as I steadied myself on his deep ginger back. I looked up and around at the silhouetted trees. "There is no one—" I stopped, and the form of a man on a great black horse was suddenly running ahead of me on the road. "Come on!" I yelled at Acheron. The air grew colder and the moon fell behind a cloud.

The rider drew farther and farther away as the shadow grew stronger. Then, just as quickly as he had appeared, he fell from my sight.

"We lost him Acheron." I gasped. The moon slowly returned and we rode again at our slower pace.

I came into Birmingham on the morning of the third day, after several stops for nourishment. The town was rather large compared to Durrington. I rode into the center of the town in the early morning. The stars were fading into the darkness of the sky and the moon began hiding itself from sight, then I proceeded to the Northern most part of the city where Roger resided. His house was quite large and rather ostentatious for my taste. It reminded me a bit of the Aundray manor.

The sun began coming up in shimmering brilliance, but even so, a cold, bitter wind came from the north, driving clouds before it like a flock blocking out the brightness of day. I patrolled slowly up the cobblestone path towards the house. Acheron's breath quickened.

"What is it, boy?" I asked looking around at the surrounding terrain. Suddenly, the black horse darted from the shadow of the trees.

"Stop!" I yelled turning Acheron in his direction. The rider stopped for a moment, then turned and began to advance toward me.

He drew a great black sword yelling. "And so it begins!"

I released my blades and prepared to engage him. The last twenty yards closed faster than an arrow flying from a bow. His sword came down like a hammer on heated steel. I raised my blades into a Cross and blocked the blow, but was thrown from Acheron. Pain shot through my back as I struck the cobblestone street. The man dismounted his black stallion and strode over to me, spinning his sword in his hand. "So pathetic," he smiled from beneath his hooded face, "your resistance!" he raised his sword and chuckled.

"I thought it would be more pleasurable," he sneered victoriously then suddenly reeled back and tumbled to the earth. An arrow stuck out from his back. His horse reared up and galloped back into the southern woods. I stood up in astonishment and looked toward the house. One of Roger's servants came running down the path with a bow in his hand.

"Master Armistead!" he yelled as he ran over to me. "Master Armistead! Are you injured sir?" he exclaimed.

"I think I will be fine," I stammered. "Who in the name of England was that?"

"I do not know, sir," he grabbed Acheron's halter and led him and me towards the house. "What brings you to Birmingham?"

"I have information for Sir Wilson and the Brethren."

"Very well sir," he answered.

We soon came to the house where the servant tied Acheron to a post and I ventured indoors. A young girl met me inside. She led me to the center staircase and up to the next floor. The house was very large and slightly familiar. On the upper floor, there was a long hall with several doors. I was led to the far door and told to wait as the girl entered. There was much noise coming from the room as I waited.

Finally, the door opened and I was bid to enter. The room was very large and cluttered. Books were stacked everywhere and papers littered the floor. In the middle of the room there stood a large oak desk where Roger sat. He was around twenty-eight years of age, and his hair being still quite dark proved that he was still in his prime. He was tall and evenly proportioned and his eyes burned with passion like a forest of flaming trees. He stood up. "Richard," he said in a slight surprise. "I was not expecting you."

"Neither was I expecting to come," I answered while seating myself in front of his desk.

"What seems to be the problem?" he asked.

"'Seems' is quite an understatement," I chuckled. "We do not quite know yet." I took out a copy of the letter and handed it to Roger.

He took it and began to read.

He collapsed back into his chair with an expression of dread and anger on his face.

"Who else knows about this?" Roger questioned.

"I, Edmond, Andrew, and by this time Henry and perhaps a few other men Andrew has selected," I replied. "Why do you ask?"

"No matter," he said, getting up and walking toward the window.

"No matter what?" I inquired.

He froze in his tracks. He stood there for a moment. "No matter what we do," his voice was shaking, "We cannot stop this," his face went pale. "We cannot stop them."

"Are you well?" I asked.

"I am fine!" he snapped

"We are going to France," I said.

"We?" he looked at me. "Oh, I never said I would go."

"It is your duty to go—"

"My duty is to protect what is mine!" he thundered. "Not to go into the middle of a war."

"But is that not why the Brethren was formed?" his anger began to aggravate me. "To end the wars before they start. To protect the world from things such as these."

"It was never said in the Brethren's Pledge that we are here to stop war," he protested.

"No, but it does say that we are to protect the world from whatsoever should come against it."

"Then protect it," to my astonishment, his eyes changed from passion to hate. "Do not lead it to worldwide war."

"How then will it be stopped!" my anger began to unleash.

"Are we to sit by and watch as the world we protect and love is torn apart by this enemy? Whatever it is."

"If that is what must be done."

"So you would watch as innocent people are murdered?" I stared at him, surprised and all the more enraged. "Think of the women and children, think of your family!"

"No man is innocent!" his rage seemed to heat the room. "My family left me and yours is dead."

"If no man is innocent," the night of the murder returned to my mind and rage nearly overcame me. "What then is to stop me from killing you?"

"Nothing."

"Even so..." My voice trailed off.

"I know," something burned within him as he spoke. "I will think about your offer," he walked toward me and began guiding me out of the room.

"It is not an offer," I gritted my teeth in defiance, "it is an order."

"You are not authorized to give orders alone Armistead," he drew in a cold breath. "Come now," he hustled me out of the room.

"I was sent by Andrew and Edmond," I stood in the hallway facing him. "Even if Henry was in accord with you, you would still have to come."

"And if I leave the Brethren?" his voice shook, yet still was cold.

"Do you hear yourself?" I whispered sharply. "You came to the Brethren, you committed your life. You cannot back out now!"

"If my life was owned by the Brethren," he hissed and moved closer to my ear. "I would rather die."

"Who is this man speaking?" my heart burned inside of me.

"For certainly it is not Roger Wilson, with whom we formed this brotherhood?"

"And do you know Roger Wilson?" he raised an eyebrow as he reentered his study and began closing the door.

"I thought I did," I placed my foot in between the door and frame. "What is wrong?"

Roger peered through the crack of the door. His eyes were dead and cold. "Get out of my house," the door slammed shut.

I walked out to Acheron, mounted and prepared to set off. The sun had just begun its journey to the south. I gazed at the house for a moment, then turned my face to the sun and rode off. I looked back one more time at the house, the silhouette of a man stood in the window. I quickly turned away and rode a bit faster southward.

Time flew like the wind in my face. The sun reached its peak in the heavens. The dust from the dirt road made a cloud following us like a bounty hunter on his prey. I cast my eyes to the cloudless sky.

"Why?" my voice crashed through the rhythmic beat of Acheron's hooves on the road. "Why does he refuse to come with us?" Tears, bitter with anger fought their way from my eyes. "He made an oath," I quieted myself as I heard another rider come from behind me. I looked back and saw a white rider on a white horse.

"You are angry Richard?" the white rider said.

"How do you know my name?" I clenched my teeth.

"I am," His voice was calm and strong.

"Who?"

The rider was silent.

"What do you want sir?"

"I want you to seek me," He said. "Seek me with your whole heart, then your anger, and your want for revenge shall cease."

"I have no want of revenge," my voice quivered.

"You will only go deeper into separation with those words."

"You know nothing about me!"

"No," He put His hands over my eyes. "There is nothing I do not know about you. You will see me again. And you will hear my words. What you fight for is not wrong, it is why you fight."

A feeling within me wanted to break down in tears, but my pride prevailed.

"I know," I felt His warm smile as He lifted his hands and was gone. I looked around for Him, but no sign was left. The landscape changed as well. I was no longer on a dirt road, but a cobblestone street leading to a town on the shores of the sea.

"I am in Portsmouth!" my astonishment overtook my anger as I rode calmly to the wharf.

VII

"WHO WILL WE BE?"

The ships rose and fell as the waves sloshed against them. Many rode low in the cold sea of blue, being weighed down with their cargo.

I strode briskly through the town, searching for a stable to keep Acheron while I was away. Passing by bustling merchants and locals huddled within their booths, looking overwhelmed by the throng, yet still offering a hospitable place to tour.

Once I had found a place to lodge Acheron, I swiftly made my way to the nearest tavern. There I ate and was on my way to the docks.

Each dock was about ten feet wide and stretched thirty feet into the water. The pilings were made of cedar and new looking oak planks made up the decking. Old Roman symbols were inlaid in tarnished bronze on each of the pilings, most of which had a wooden eagle carved on the top looking like mighty sentries guarding the sea.

At the end of the dock, a young man stood waiting. He was dressed in a long black armoured cloak, which appeared to be made of iron plates attached to thick leather. Not much for combat, but it was an adequate defense in shadowy districts. The man's hair was brown and shoulder length with the beginnings of a beard on his face. The moment I noticed him, our eyes met and with a friendly smile, he walked toward me. His eyes were a grass green and he had more facial hair than I saw before. Under his beard was a face that bore the weight of life on the sea.

"Are you Richard Armistead?" he asked as I drew nearer.

"I may be," I parried.

He lifted a small round medallion with the Brethren emblem upon it. "I do believe you know what this is," he said.

"Who are you?" I asked.

"The name is Captain Feargal Elmsbirch," he smiled, "Captain of the Silver Star."

"And where did you get that?" I pointed at the medallion.

"Andrew Freeman," he smiled again. "Come on, he is waiting for you."

"No," I answered sharply. "I know not who you are or how you came by that emblem! For all I know you could have murdered someone to get it!"

"Now just hold on! I assure you, Sir Armistead I am a man of my word!" he replied.

"So said the killer in the court," I countered.

"Richard!" a voice came from behind me.

"Roger," I turned to him in disgust.

"You!" said Roger to Feargal. "What do you think you are doing?"

"I am doing what Andrew told me to do." answered Feargal.

"And how do you know that name?" asked Roger.

"I told him," a loud voice came from the deck of one of the ships next to us.

"Andrew!" I yelled, looking up at him.

"Who else?" he said, "I see you have met our captain."

I looked at Feargal whose smile touched both ears. "My apologies, Captain…Elmsbirch was it not?" I said shaking his hand. "You did your job well."

"Yours as well," he said. "I see you are the cautious one of the lot?"

"Perhaps a bit too cautious," smirked Roger.

"That is impossible," I said under my breath as we walked up the gangplank onto the Silver Star.

The ship was clean and ready to sail. It was larger than a Cog vessel, yet not so large as a Hulk.

As I looked around the ship, Andrew caught my eye, beckoning me to follow him into the cabin in which we were to stay, and closed the door behind us.

"How was Roger when you went to him?" Andrew asked. "You seemed angry at him."

"I would rather not talk about it at the moment," I answered, unpacking my few belongings.

"What happened?"

"I do not exactly know," I leaned up against the wooden wall of the room. "It is like he was afraid of something."

"Well," said Andrew, "we are entering a war."

"Aye," I answered, "it was probably that. How are our calculations on the Alignment?" I asked, trying to change the subject.

"Very well. It should happen in the next fortnight. But there is something else I found."

"What is that?" I asked.

"The Alignment is to happen at the ring of stone at Salisbury Plain!"

"How can that be?" I asked.

"The Alignment has happened before, nearly one thousand years ago," his voice was calm yet extremely serious and excited at the same time. "In the year 336, during the reign of Emperor Constantine, it was said that a great beam of light fell from the heavens, and landed upon that location directly in the ring of stone. My guess is that the stones were erected after the first Alignment, but," he began to get more visually excited, "do you remember those Egyptian lights we obtained when Bennet journeyed to Paris?"

"Yes," I answered at the edge of my seat.

"Then you remember that we were able to light them using the Egyptian arts."

"Yes," I answered.

"I passed the ring with one of the lights a few weeks ago," he sounded more excited than a peasant welcomed to a feast. "It lit up! Brighter than anything the Egyptian method ever did. Not only that, but it—" The door opened. Roger stepped in.

"What is going on?" he asked. "Is there a party and I was not invited?" he laughed.

"Nothing," I answered with contempt creeping back into my voice.

"Well certainly something," he continued his verbal assault, "or else there would be no reason to be hiding in an enclosed room."

"Or maybe it is business that you have no right knowing," pronounced Andrew.

"Fine," retorted Roger. "Keep secrets from the rest of the Brethren," he fixed his eyes upon me. "You have no need to protect me from the secrets of this world," he turned and strode stiffly from the room. Muttering under his breath. "I know how it burns," Andrew gave me a suspicious look, which I promptly ignored.

"Is there anything else you know about the Alignment?" I asked turning back to Andrew.

"Not here," he replied. "Please sit down."

We each took a chair and sat down at the table in the corner of the room. "What happened?" Andrew pleaded.

"I told you," I answered, "I do not know what happened. He was cold and defiant."

"If you did know, you would tell me, would you not?"

"I would tell you and the rest of the Brethren, if I knew anything to be wrong," I said. "I assure you, if I find out anything about Roger, I will not keep it to myself."

"Let this be so when the time comes."

"And until then?"

"We pray," he said solemnly.

"If I must," I said. "But I will hold out as long as possible."

We sat in silence for a while as Andrew bowed his head. The quiet however, was soon dispelled by a firm knock on the door.

"Who is there?" I yelled out.

"Let me in Richard," Edmond's voice blew like a cool breeze to my burning heart.

I stood up and walked to the door. "It is unlocked,"

I opened the door and pulled Edmond in, then closed it again. "Roger's allegiance may be changing," I informed Edmond as we seated ourselves.

"Pardon me?" Edmond looked at me confused. "What do you mean by changing?"

"We do not know yet," Andrew said, "Just keep your eyes on him."

"That I will," he replied, still sounding quite confused as he rested his hand upon the hilt of his gallant sword.

The Silver Star and two other ships under the Brethren's command set sail the next day at 9:00am. We brought with us over two hundred well trained soldiers of the Brethren. Captain Feargal also brought another hundred sailors.

The day we set out was cloudy, and the wind cold as we sailed to the shores of France. A shadow seemed to have befallen our world. All that I had grown to know now seemed blurred. I stood on the bow of the ship staring aimlessly into the rolling waves.

'Why? Why me?' I thought as my eyes left the sea and gazed up to the heavens. 'Why have you chosen me?' Anger and fear rode like horsemen through my heart and mind. 'I cannot do this,' I trembled 'I cannot protect the people around me! Neither can I forget what he has taken from me' I paused a moment; the face returned 'Why did you let him kill them? Why did you let them die! You could have saved them!' I shuddered. 'You seem to be there, but why can I not believe it? Please end this silence!'

My thoughts were interrupted by footsteps coming from behind me. "Fair enough," I said through clenched teeth as I turned to see Andrew slowly walking toward me. He took one glance at me and sensed something was wrong.

"What are you not telling me?" his calm shimmering eyes pierced through my soul.

"What if," I stammered.

"What if what?" he interrupted.

"I do not know," I mumbled.

"What is stopping you?" he passionately spoke. "Why are you troubled? If Roger is no longer with us, then this is the will of God. What then do we have to lose?"

"Everything!" I shouted. Several crew members glanced suspiciously. I lowered my voice to a whisper. "We fail and we lose everything. Our lives, our homes, our friends. The Brethren itself will dissolve!"

"What does it matter? This world is not ours," he stared hard into my eyes and his lips pressed hard against each other. "If we die, so be it. And if by God's mercy we live, so be it. All is God's will. And we will fight and die in the name of His Son and no other!" he pointed toward everyone on the ship. "Do not look at anyone here as if they have it better. I know you lost your parents, and yes I know how much pain and anger you felt, but we all have lost something. For all we know, we could die tomorrow. And then again, the LORD may very well grant us victory! Take heart for He has overcome this world."

"How do you know that all that is true?" I interrupted his speech.

"I do not know, I have faith. What is this world if not a place to display our faith?" Andrew spoke with passion. "Just as God will show his power through the glory of the Alignment, so should we show our faith through our actions, and how we deal with the pain and suffering."

"Why?" I asked. "I want to believe it is true, but why?"

"What more is there to ask?" he said as his voice softened and his countenance relaxed. "There is always a reason."

"The old man is right," said Edmond walking across the deck. "Life is like a meal."

"Pardon?" I asked looking at him inquisitively. "A meal?"

"Aye," said Edmond. "We can make all we want to give to God at the last day, but without His salt, what good is it?"

"Salt?" I questioned. "What in the name of England are you talking about?"

"I believe what he means to say is that a life without Christ, is like an unseasoned meal, it is dull and dead, without flavor. As Christ said, 'you are the salt of the earth'," Andrew continued. "Look," he hesitated, "I know this is hard to hear, but we need you to become the man you were meant to be."

"And who is that?" I questioned. "Who am I to be?" I shook him off as he tried to comfort me. "I have waited thirteen years to find out what I am supposed to do!" I fumed. "How much longer must I wait before I will know?"

"Do not doubt the power of God!" Andrew thundered again.

"Power?" I pointed back to England. "He let my parents die in a pool of their own blood!"

"But you lived," Edmond countered.

"I lived in misery for thirteen years," I yelled. "If you call that life," my voice became little more than a whisper, "I want to die," I turned back to the sea.

We sailed on, without word or sound except for the salty water hitting the bow of the ship. The wind blew hard, but I could see nothing except the darkness which stood in a great cloud before me. I lay down on the deck and attempted to sleep, but alas, all my efforts were in vain.

My thoughts soon began to drift and drown out all else, and bringing the doubt, and dread, making everything terribly silent.

'Is this what I was made for? Fighting a war to save the world? Why me? Why did you bring the letter to us? A lowly group of warriors! Why was it not brought to Angus, or my Father? They could have done so much more!' tears formed once again in my eyes as I thought of my parents.

'You will pay!' I told myself in my rage. I had walked through it in my head many times. The way the murderer would be brought to justice. I had dreamed it – nearly seen and felt it. I imagined him tall, with dark hair and a slight beard, almost the same as how he looked that night. His heart was always evil and his eyes burned with murderous hate. I saw his dark form in my mind. He stood there with his back toward me, as always, he stood right outside the ring of stones. It stood imposingly on a small muddy hill, like a beacon for the sun to align above it. The sky was black with clouds and rain poured like a river. The only light was a beam that extended from the sky down into the ring.

'You have come,' he would say turning and drawing his black

sword.

'Your time has come,' I would reply in my rage, drawing a sword that was unknown to me.

We would fight, for hours until either I or he lay dead.

I lay there for a while, with my eyes closed and my mind dwelling on what I wished I could be: a strong leader like Edmond, an emblem of hope and life like Andrew. Yet more than anything, torn between becoming something more and longing for revenge.

They were more than friends, Edmond and Andrew. Andrew was like a father and teacher to me. My father and mother meant more to me than anything, but Andrew was always there.

Edmond was like a brother, nay, far more than just a brother. Although he didn't show his emotions often, somehow I knew he loved me.

I was suddenly awakened by a hand on my shoulder. I looked, it was Andrew 'Well maybe he doesn't care.' I thought smiling.

"It seems a man cannot get any rest around here," I said in jest.

"Aye," he answered. "But you will rest enough when you are dead," he smiled warmly.

"You always can shine a bit of light in darkness." I stated.

"Aye," he answered. "We need all the light we can get now."

"Yes," I replied. "Even if the light does not come though, I would be content with justice."

"What do you mean?" Andrew asked.

"I search for him," I replied.

"Richard," Andrew said, "search, deep down, I think you will find that you are not truly looking for revenge, you are looking for salvation."

"Andrew I know! I know what you are going to say, you always do. And I do believe. I do believe it."

"Perhaps, but the question is, what do you believe?" he paused.

"I know I did not know you before you lost your parents, and I know you are angry—"

"Well, would you not be?" I yelled. "If everything and everyone you loved was gone in one night?"

"Aye, but now is not the time to be lingering on such personal concerns. What matters now is that we make it to the King. We must put down our wants and needs. Now is the time to do our duty. To God and country, Savior and King. No matter what the cost," he stood up, pulling me up with him. He looked at me as passion beamed in his eyes, yet still, his voice was composed. "These are the times that define who we are and how we live," he sighed. "I know who I am and whose I am, and I pray that you would too."

"Quite the speech," interrupted Edmond. "Could you show me how to get into his thick head?"

"Takes a lot to do it," Andrew said to Edmond with a slight smirk then turned back to me. "Do not let these moments pass. The world could end tomorrow, and I want you to be on the right side when it does."

"Thank you, but my father's faith got him a knife through the chest. If that is the side you are on, I do not need faith helping me get there," I proclaimed.

"That is only the price that must be paid," Andrew replied.

"And it will be worth it when the time comes," Edmond assured me.

"Somehow I doubt that death is worth so much," I countered.

Andrew put his hand on my shoulder, "And that is where your path is leading,"

Andrew let go beckoning Edmond to follow close behind to another part of the ship, leaving me with my thoughts.

All was silent for a while as the shadow grew deeper. Fear crept into our hearts like a serpent trying to wrench the life from its prey. I stood motionless on the bow of the ship. The wind itself brought bitter fear.

"Richard. The Brethren have assembled," Bennet's voice called out.

"Where?" I asked.

"In the captain's cabin," he replied. "They await your company."

"Thank you," I said turning to him. "Tell them that I am on my way."

"Aye," Bennet replied as he turned and began walking away, singing an old tune under his breath. "When shadows mark the line and five stars rise..." The words trailed off as he walked away.

"Bennet!" I called after him.

He stopped and turned back to me. "Richard!" he grinned and walked back to me. "Did I miss something?" he asked.

"No," I assured him. "I have a question for you."

"Make it quick," he continued smiling. "First mate challenged me to a wrestling match."

"That man is an ox!" I exclaimed. "You are a mad man, you know that? What goes on in your head?"

"Aye, best not make him wait long," he laughed, "But I doubt your question was about what goes on in my head."

"Aye, on that we agree," I shifted my weight and asked. "Do you remember what happened to your father?"

His smile disappeared. "No."

"How do you deal with it? How do you deal with never knowing your own father?" I sighed. "How do you not hate him for it?"

He slapped my shoulder, "The same way Andrew lives without

knowing his son," he turned on his heel and began walking away.

"And how is that?"

He stopped again, turned his face to me, and smiled. "I have faith that Christ will come again."

I nodded and he walked off toward the giant waiting for him.

I looked down at the water. 'Who will I be?' I thought and then scowled. 'At least the hoping of His return is worth something, I guess?' I turned and began walking toward the captain's cabin. The ship itself rose and fell in sequence with my drifting thoughts.

I opened the door to Captain Elmsbirch's cabin and ventured into the lamp-lit room. In the far right corner of the room, sat a desk and stool, where Captain Elmsbirch sat, and on the desk there lay a large map and an ink pen. In the opposite corner there was a suit of leather armour and a two handed Scottish sword next to it. In the middle there was a large rectangular table at which sat four men. Edmond and Andrew were among them. The others at the table were Roger Wilson and Henry Forwin . I found the last open chair and seated myself at the table.

A few trivial matters were discussed before the situation at hand overwhelmed our thoughts.

"May I see the letter again?" asked Roger.

Andrew hesitantly handed the folded paper to him and he read over it once again.

"So," Roger finally spoke out, "why then is the whole Brethren here?"

"What?" I said as we all stared at him in disbelief. "I thought this called for a full scale call to arms!"

"Yes it does," said Henry trying to break up the tension. "But I think what he means is what are we to do?"

"We meet the King and assemble the armies of Europe and stop this plague of invaders." said Edmond.

"Aye!" interrupted Roger. "However, where is the King? 'Tis that not the question at hand?"

"He is at Château de Dourdan, in France," I answered. A long pause afterward ensued.

"A funny thing," said Edmond breaking the silence.

"What?" asked Henry inquisitively.

"The Alignment is happening right as we receive word of the attack upon the Khans," Edmond said.

"Along that line of thought, what more do we know of the Alignment?" asked Henry with an intrigued look on his face.

Andrew pulled an old, brown tinted map of the world from his cloak and placed it on the table.

"It is round?" said Roger, "Is not the world flat?"

"Nay, that was my first thought, however after further study of the scriptures and of the earth's rotation, I have come to realize that it is round," said Andrew. "It is the only way life could work right you see? When you consider the pull of the earth..." he stopped seeing that Roger had no intention of listening. Andrew then flattened out the map and prepared his speech.

"Carry on Andrew," said Edmond.

"These are my predictions, though slightly changed since the first time I told you. On the 14th day of March, this year, the sun and moon will cross on opposite sides of the earth," he motioned his hands to show how it would happen. "In the southern part of England, within Salisbury Plain, the sun will shine upon the earth and by design of the ring of stone, the light will pass through the earth and strike the moon on the other side. That beam of light will then be reflected off the moon and return to the sun. I know not how this happens, but if we could harness this power," he began to get excited, "the options are almost limitless. This however only happens once every one thousand years, and by my calculations, the next Alignment will happen as I told you on the fourteenth day of March."

"And if these are your predictions," said Roger in an awkward tone, "why does our enemy choose to attack now? Does it not seem strange? Were not these kept in secret?"

"We do not even know who or what it is we are fighting," I said. "Let alone what they are capable of."

"Well then," Henry announced. "What are we to do? Moreover, what can we do?"

"That my friend is why we are here," Edmond broke in "We must gather as large an army as possible, or at least a capable one, to go out and face them before it is too late."

"How?" asked Roger.

"We are going to King Edward to ask – no – to implore him to come to the aid of his people and the rest of the world," Edmond continued, "To unite the Kingdoms of Europe into one army, under one banner and save whatever is left."

"Are we all going to implore the King or are some of us staying behind to await further orders?" Roger asked impudently.

"I am glad you asked Roger," declared Edmond, "Richard and I are going to find the King, bringing with us twenty men. The rest of you will stay here and await the King's commands."

"I am going with you," proclaimed Feargal stepping up from his desk in the corner.

"No," said Edmond, "you belong on the sea. Heaven knows who will be needed to defend England if worse comes to worst."

Feargal looked at Edmond with fiery eyes. "I said I was going with you! I would rather die trying to find the King then perish in a hopeless cause."

"Let him come," I interrupted.

"Fine," answered Edmond.

"So," Roger asked, "what now?"

"We wait," Edmond replied standing up and laying his hand on his sword. "A time comes where all men will stand, not only for themselves, but each will see the need for unity and strive towards it."

All fell silent at Edmond's words.

***

The ship rocked violently that night as I tried to rest. Soon however, I found it impossible to sleep. I gazed up at the ceiling of the room. All was dark, not a pinch of light could be seen through the panels of the ship. I attempted to sleep once again, closing my eyes as the darkness encompassed me.

The ring of stone stood on a hill in front of me. I looked around. The sky was dark and grim. Rain poured from the heavens looking like the sky itself wept over a broken world. The man once again stood at the top of the hill. I drew my sword and ran at him. Same as always, he attacked as well. I slipped in the mud and began to sink. He stood over me with his sword raised. I gripped his foot and pulled him down. We struggled in the mire for a time and eventually I came out on top with my sword poised.

"Would you surrender yourself to the hate, and become the very thing you long to destroy?" he said through curling lips.

"I will never be like you!" I yelled out and ran my sword through him as he had done to my parents. My eyes peeled open. "It is only a dream," I clenched my teeth. "It is only a dream!" my arms flailed searching for something to destroy.

I looked around the room, breathing heavily. All seemed the same, it was dark and filled with a putrid smell. But all the disdainful smells and dark was wiped away when I saw a slight movement in the corner. I strained to see what it was. Slowly a form appeared. A man in a dark cloak staring straight at me. It looked more like a black phantom than a man for I could not distinguish his face, but he seemed familiar.

"Who are you?" I demanded.

He gave a devious, hateful smile.

Everything else in the room melted away into a sea of swirling blackness.

His eyes shot out like the red coals of a fire. "Beware," he spoke like the north wind, "For soon comes the night!" he spoke with both warning and fear. I could not tell if he was fearful himself or trying to frighten me, but whatever the case, dreadful fear was overpowering me. "The shadows will assemble."

I looked away. His words pierced through me like a blade of ice. Doubt crept into my frozen soul. Sweat fell in a continual stream off my forehead. My heart nearly stopped. I looked back at him trying to sound unafraid, "Who are you?" And in a moment, he was right in front of me grasping my throat. His eyes stared deep into mine full of pain and sorrow. "I am doubt," he thundered, "I am dread," his voice like a stinging wind, "I am death!" he fumed in a voice like a tempest of rage and pain, and his eyes seemed to burn the darkness into death. My eyes flew open in terror.

"Leave me alone!" I yelled, nearly in tears.

Edmond was right next to me and tried in vain to hold me down as I convulsed rapidly.

"What is wrong?" he said in a calm powerful voice.

"It is all wrong!" I stammered coming out of the horror. "Everything! I cannot sleep without wandering into that night. To those horrid shadows!"

He stuttered trying to find the right thing to say, "I know how you are feeling, no honestly, I do not know, but I can help you."

"How?" I whispered coldly. "How can anyone help me?"

"I do not know," said Edmond, "all I know is that He can,

somehow."

"Who?"

"Chri-"

"No! He left me when everyone else did. He left," my voice trembled with rage as I thought back again on that night. "I still see their faces and hear my mother's cries!"

"I know you are hurting, and I know that you are angry," Edmond said, "but someday you need to let it go, to let go of your hate and anger. Only then can you move on and live."

"I cannot! Every time I close my eyes I see either my parents or that murderer who took their lives! I have not had peace in thirteen years because of him!" I looked away from Edmond and stumbled over to the dark corner where the second man had stood moments before. "I want him dead," I spoke through teeth clenched so hard my jaw nearly shattered. I looked back at Edmond, my eyes burning with hate. "Biscuit's blood! I want him dead!"

VIII

DOUBT, DREAD AND DEATH

The tunnels were dark and smelled like death itself. The floor looked the same as it smelled, and was covered by a foot of stagnate water, littered with decaying animal corpses. The walls, curved into a circular shape, were made of large eroded stones covered in a putrid slime. I had two of my gauntlets with me, and we each wore a set of leather armour of my fashioning. The main body of the armour was laced together with leather cord and was reinforced with tiny pieces of Valinium. Edmond could not convince me to wear a helmet; I could never find one that fit. Edmond never understood nor did he approve. Edmond had one gauntlet and a set of the reinforced armour, also without a helmet; the reason for which was merely his competitive nature.

Edmond also carried with him the usual extension of his left side – an 8-pound broadsword the beauty of which stood unsurpassed among the weapons of war. Its simple yet breathtaking blade was made of a strange shimmering metal which Edmond would never disclose to me. I began to think he did not know himself. The sword's hilt was slightly darker than the blade, but of the same metal with a small design on it. The handle was covered in black leather and tapered to bare metal followed by the pummel which bore the Brethren emblem. In fact, it was Edmond's sword which was the inspiration for the emblem. All together the sword was incomparable to any other weapon the world had ever seen, and I doubt will ever be seen again beyond the age.

"We are nearly there," Edmond stated after nearly an hour of trudging through the sickening mire.

"Good," I replied, making sure I did not slip and fall. "Let us get out of this pit."

A long pause ensued, and the gravity of what had befallen us came to me once more. The great kingdoms of the old world, the empires of the Khans had fallen, soon to be followed by Asia Minor and Europe if we were to fail. Men being slaughtered in such great numbers that the yellow river runs red. Darkness and death now reigned where once a prosperous people dwelt. I could hardly picture it. This small frail world that the Brethren fought so hard to protect, was it even worth it?

"Is this what war is?" I finally asked – not really caring about what the answer would be.

"Close enough," Edmond replied.

"How do you think Andrew is faring?" I inquired

"We only brought twenty men," he chuckled slightly. "We left hundreds with him."

"And what about us?" I asked.

"The King will know what to do," he said in a futile attempt to reassure me.

"And if not," I continued, "what do we do then?"

"We take a stand. Gather together as many loyal men as possible and pray to the LORD for His grace and strength. Then we either die fighting for our lives and the lives of our brothers, or by some miracle live to fight for Him another day."

"Why was the message given to us instead of the King himself?" I asked.

"'Tis strange. The events that have risen over the past few days, it may be..." he paused, trying in vain to place a finger on our new reality. "I do not know," he concluded.

"What do you think the King will do when we tell him?" I queried. "Do you think he will help?"

"I cannot imagine he would not," Edmond replied. "Whatever he does, we can only hope that it is the right thing."

"And if not?" I cast my gaze back down to the murky water below me.

"I do no think that is a question I need to answer for you," Edmond replied. "I doubt it will be a pleasant sight."

"Do not say that!" Feargal yelled dramatically from behind us. "Keep a good point of view!"

"Aye, but if the King will not help us, our fate is much to be pitied," Edmond stated as he stopped and looked around at the walls and ceiling. "We are here," he announced, then reached up and opened a hatch in the roof of the tunnel.

I took a look around the room once everyone was out of the tunnel. Just as Edmond had said, we emerged inside the kitchen. Darkness, black as pitch, loomed in the air. The only light in the room was bright burning coals. Accompanying the darkness was the smell of smoke and fear.

"This is not right," exclaimed Edmond as his breath quickened. He fingered his sword.

"What do you mean?" asked Feargal.

"I mean this is not right! Look around you! This place has been ransacked!" for the first time since I had met him, Edmond truly sounded fearful.

"What happened here?" I stuttered.

"You think he knows?" Feargal's voice was laced with sarcasm.

"Burned by the looks of it," stated Edmond.

"Aye, I gathered that!" Feargal replied.

"The King?" I asked out in sudden remembrance.

"Dead most likely," returned Edmond. "If they, whoever they are, were able to get this far and do this much damage. I fear his fate."

"Do you mean to tell us," said one of the men in our company, "we came all this way to find a dead King?"

"No," I jumped with surprise as a hoarse voice came from the shadows near the opening of the tunnel. "They mean to tell you nothing," the voice laughed a moment, then stopped short and hissed, "because you will be too dead to hear it!"

I gazed blindly into the darkness. "Who are you?" I idiotically shouted into the blackness.

There was a scream from the man who had spoken out. Edmond, Feargal and I immediately stared in the direction of the man. "Fools. It is not the King's fate you should dread!" The killer proclaimed in a sly, calm voice, as he threw aside the dead body of our brother. "It is yours."

"There!" I exclaimed, pointing at the movement in the shadows, but Edmond was already upon him.

Edmond threw a blow to the man's left side, but he easily parried and landed a cut on the flat of Feargal's sword who was coming around his right flank. Feargal was thrown by its force against the wall of the room. I also joined the fray but was unable to land a blow upon him. The fight continued a short while until Feargal returned and the enemy finally began to retreat back into the shadows.

I marveled at the man's strength and skill with the sword, the latter of which rivaled even Edmond. But even with his skill and strength, the three of us upon him and the remaining men at our backs pushed him to retreat.

He ran into the shadows of the hallway leading to the north wing of the Castle. "Who will you be?" he yelled as he ran. He then stopped at the edge of the darkest shadows, turned his head and looked straight at me, "When you are broken?" and he was gone.

"Bennet!" thundered Edmond pointing at Bennet once we were alone. "Go back and inform the Brethren of this new threat. Our hope may no longer lie here, and if they find the King, by England, get him away from here!"

Bennet nodded and ran away like a stag with hounds nipping at his heels.

"What now?" I asked Edmond.

"Our priority is finding the King," said Edmond. "He may still be here, however unlikely."

"And what about that-that thing!" I nearly began to stutter.

"We do not know who or even what he is. You and I both know he is far too strong for a normal man."

"I can testify to that!" Feargal broke in, holding his back in pain. "I have been in many fights and never have I been thrown like a rag doll against the wall."

"All we know," I continued. "Is that there is at least one enemy, and he is in the north wing."

"We split up, groups of two's and threes. Our priority is not with killing him, but finding the King. Remember that," Edmond thundered. "You, Richard, come with me. We have many things to set straight along the way. The rest of you find a partner, and you know what to do if you find survivors and do not hesitate to thrust your blade into that thing if you find him!"

Edmond and I went north, following the path which the "man" had taken. The rest of our men went in all the other directions, each armed and ready for what they had been trained for.

The halls of the castle were dark and narrow, so that many times we tripped over broken weapons and warped steel armour. The stench of death filled our nostrils and the cold hand of fear began creeping its way around our throats, preparing to choke out our life.

As we journeyed deeper into the fortress, a realization slowly emerged. "I do not think it is just the - whatever he was," I stated as I glanced around at the fallen fortress. "Even he could not have done this alone."

"Agreed. There must be more than one of them," Edmond replied.

A long unbearable silence ensued.

"How could we not know about this?" I blurted in anger. "This is what we are here for. To stop these things from happening."

"And we would have!" Edmond yelled, clenching his teeth, clearly feeling the same sting of failure that I felt. "We would have stopped it! We could have!" he hesitated. "What is worse is that we are too late," he stopped walking. "We were too late." he echoed.

"How could we have known?" I asked.

"Our men are stationed all over England, France, Scotland, and beyond!" Edmond protested. "Roger's district covers France and the surrounding area. He should have known."

"Roger," I said remembering his actions in Birmingham and on the Silver Star. "Do you think he was keeping something from us?"

"I do not know Richard," Edmond answered fretfully - a tone I feared hearing from him. "The King is gone; and an enemy we do not know whence he came has waged war upon us and destroyed the Khanites. The great empires of the East. I do not know."

A sudden scream echoed through the halls, followed by a horrid inhuman shriek and then another scream.

"Two cries," I said. "At least three people in the battle judging by the sound."

"We need to get to them!" Edmond said.

"Right then," I said pressing the triggers on my gauntlets to release the blades.

Edmond drew his sword. "Come on!"

We rushed to the scene, veering off our path, and heading toward the east wing of the castle, but all we found was smoldering leather armour and glowing deformed metal from their weapons.

"What is this?" Edmond asked in horror as he took in the sight. "Richard?"

"I do not know," I replied, "it is like they just burned away," I knelt down and examined the armour laying there. "More or less," I stared at it in confusion as I stood up.

"What in the name of England?" he said kneeling over close to the soot covered floor.

"What?" I inquired.

"Look at it!" he demanded.

"It looks like a footprint of some sort?" I stared at it in confusion. "Do you know what it is?"

"It is like nothing I have ever seen before," said Edmond. "How large would you say the creature is that made it?"

"By the looks of it," I paused, "bigger than a man. I would say, judging by the depth of the imprint in the soot, maybe, biscuit's blood! I cannot tell a thing about it!"

"If this is what we are up against," Edmond's voice trailed off in thought.

"I know," I stammered.

"Aye," Edmond replied. "Look!" he exclaimed a moment later, pointing to the left.

"What is it?" I inquired.

"You said three in the battle, right?" asked Edmond.

"Yes, but I could have been mistaken," I replied.

"Two would be ours, but where is the third?" he paused and pointed to the footprint. "And, what is the third?" he bit his lower lip lost in thought.

"Two cries..." I stammered, "two sets of armour," I stared at him in utter horror. My face grew cold as I turned to see where the footprints came in. I turned to see where they went out, as sweat formed on my hands. "Edmond?" I stuttered as I continued looking back and forth, hoping that what I was seeing was a coincidence.

"What is it?" he followed my gaze and froze. He saw it too. Only one set of footprints came into the hallway, but three walked out the other side.

"How?" I implored.

"I do not know. There is no way they could have survived," Edmond responded. "The screams were not of pain, nor of horror, but something else entirely."

"How do you know?" I asked

"I have been to war. Bloody, terrible war! I have heard all horror of dying men and I have seen their blood spilled across the field," he then drew his sword and thrust it into one of the pieces of burned leather armour lying at our feet. "But this," he raised the leather to my eye level, "this is no act of war!"

"Then what?" I struggled to keep my voice under control. "What could do this?"

"Nothing!" he thundered with anger and fear. "Nothing can make someone disappear! And then you add the screams. Those screams were not of fear."

"What then?" I yelled. "Were they cries of death?"

Edmond looked at me, his eyes bloodshot with fear. "I do not know," he looked back at the tracks and the remains of our comrades, "as surely as I stand here, I do not know."

We fell silent for a while and pondered what should be done.

Edmond broke the silence with the most obvious answer, "We

need to find the rest of our men."

"What is the point?" I answered in despair. "The King is gone, our men have been picked off one by one."

"No!" Edmond yelled. "We will stand and we will fight. I do not care if we do not know who they are! This war has just begun, and we have been placed within it! To fight the good fight. To bring honor to the men who fell."

I stared at him blankly.

"This is not the Richard I know, the Richard who came to Durrington ready to do anything for justice!" he thundered. "What is the point you ask? What does it matter is my answer. What matters now is that we stand strong. Even if I am the only one, and I know I am not! Nonetheless, I will fight to the last breath and die with my sword in the heart of whatever foolish rubbish heap started this!" he put his hand on my shoulder, and stared into my eyes. "And the only man that I would do that with is you."

"Then," I said, "I guess that settles it."

"Now, let us go find the rest of our men," Edmond kicked the leather off his sword and gazed at the blade as if he were reading something off of it. "And bring that 'man' to his knees."

"Yes," I replied, "let this be so."

So we went searching every hall and room of the barren fortress leaving no place unsearched.

It seemed darker than before, the sadness seemed greater, and reminded me of the time when the sickness took so many in Shrewton - all the death and gloom. A powerful sense of dread was suspended in the air as we went. I know not why, or how, nevertheless, it was as real as the castle itself.

"How?" I finally spoke, shattering the silence. "How do we fight them?"

"We do not even know what they are," retorted Edmond. "It

is all so…so wrong."

"Aye," I answered, "but what is frightening is that it all happened without anyone knowing about it."

"That frightens you? This place was attacked, and as far as we know, there are no survivors," he glared into my eyes. "Where are all the bodies?" as he outstretched his arms towards the hallways. "There should be hundreds of them. But where have they all gone?"

"Burned away?" I said as I tried in vain to explain the nightmare.

"How though?" he said. "No one would just let themselves be burned."

"Killed and then burned to conceal the evidence?" I continued. "Or possibly a fire started and the people were trapped by the flames and then burned to death?"

"No, I thought of that and it is not likely," Edmond replied. "If you look around, there is no order in which the fire spread. Just random burned areas everywhere. And moreover, there is not enough burnable material in this castle to trap that many people."

"Well then perhaps the attackers carried away all the bodies," I proposed.

"If that is the case, the question is why? Why would someone, after winning a battle, carry away the bodies?"

"Aye, for there would be no reason for removing the bodies," I replied, contradicting my own hypothesis.

"And," Edmond interrupted, "why would they move the bodies and burn the castle?"

"So, if it could not have been a fire, then what?" I stopped and looked at him. "Nothing just disappears, or burns away without any cause!"

"Aye," he suddenly stopped and listened, "or something

hiding right out in the open."

"Pardon me?"

"Do you hear that?" he exclaimed.

I listened. It sounded like another fight. "Another victim?" I asked dryly.

"That way!" he yelled as he turned and ran down a northwest passageway leading deeper into the castle. He led us down two stone staircases and through several scorched stone doorways. I struggled to keep up with Edmond as we ran.

Finally, we made it down to the bottom where we thought the fight had carried out. The dungeon was dark and musty and burned. A few torn open cells were on either side of the room. In the far corner there lay a pile of burned clothing and a broken sword, but what caught Edmond's eye was the statue standing in the center of the room.

IX

VARANUS DESCENDING

"Do we really want to be here?" I exclaimed with dread creeping into my voice. "Who knows what is down here, besides that-that thing!"

"Yes," he said walking over to the statue. "We need to find out what is going on," he pointed to the statue. "Starting with that."

"It looks reptilian," I stared at the stone statue, examining it fully. It was nearly twice the size of a man, with arms thicker than my torso. Following each arm were curved claws like an eagle's talons. But these talons were cruel looking and nearly as thick as my wrist. Following the body of the massive structure was a tail like a serpent. Its head was like that of a bear without the snout or ears. The face was badly deformed and crumbling, much due to a dagger – which was not made of stone, but of steel and leather – lodged in its head.

"Well," Edmond said pulling out the dagger, "this is new."

"Where in the dark name of war did that come from?" I exclaimed staring at the dagger.

"It could be one of our daggers," Edmond replied.

"Not the dagger Edmond!" I answered.

"I was trying to stay on the bright side," he replied. "But if you want to go there," his tone changed. "It is definitely not a statue."

"What else could it be!" I cried.

"Not even the French would make a statue that deranged," Edmond replied dryly betraying his fear. "And I doubt anyone would place it in the center of a room, and have a dagger in its head."

"Look," I said, kneeling down near the feet of the statue. "I must be mad. The foot is the exact shape and size of the footprints in the hallway."

"So?" Edmond asked.

"I believe this thing is killing our men."

Edmond knelt down beside me gazing at the feet of the statue, "How is that possible?"

"It is not," I said. "Unless this thing was alive at one point, or perhaps is still alive."

Edmond jumped up, drew his sword and slashed it deep into the head of the crumbling statue, then followed up with another powerful slash, which sent the stone head rolling onto the floor.

"It is dead," he coldly remarked.

"A new plan then," I said. "Perhaps, considering the dagger in the head, it was already dead?"

"Stone does not live."

I picked up the dagger and gave it a long stare. "Check the burned clothes in the corner for a sheath or something."

"What?" Edmond asked.

"I have an idea," I smiled.

Edmond sifted through the clothes and found a sheath to a dagger. "Will this do?" He asked holding it up. "You had better not be doing anything foolish."

"Bring it here!" I exclaimed. "And would I truly be wasting time now?"

He gave it to me and I scrambled to fit the dagger into the sheath but my effort was fruitless.

"Well that is no good," Edmond said.

"Perfect," I smiled

Edmond stared at me dryly. "It does not fit, the sheath is useless to us."

"It may be," I said standing up and holding the dagger like an offering, "but this is priceless!"

"It is a sheathless dagger we found in the head of a monster-" Edmond suddenly realized what I meant. "Oh, you are very clever. This means whoever had this dagger and killed that thing is still alive. And they know how to kill them. And also that person may know where the King is," his eyes beamed. "We may just have a chance after all. We must find this person."

"But they will most likely be dead by now," I said pointing at another creature's footprints leading out of the dungeon.

"Aye," he clenched his teeth, refusing to give in, "but at least there is still a chance," he held up the dagger again.

"What about our men? What about Andrew?" I demanded. "If we go after this person or people we could lose our chance to save them!"

"I know," he hesitated, visibly torn between his duty to save lives and the mission for which we had been sent. "We need to help these people," he said with resolve.

"What is the point?" I questioned.

"Saving it. Saving all that is left. Richard, we made a promise to protect the world and those in it," he spoke with renewed strength.

"I intend to keep that promise, no matter what the cost."

"If we waste time trying to protect them, there may be nothing left of the rest of the world to protect!" I protested.

"You do not understand," Edmond gazed into my eyes. "This person could be the key to finding the King. If we let them die, we let England die. We let hope die."

"And if they kill us before we reach these people? What then?" I stammered. "We cannot save them all Edmond."

"If we find them then there is hope that we could find the King. They could show us how to win this war."

"And is that all you care about? Winning the war?" my voice was just above a whisper. "Do you even care about the cost?"

He met my gaze unflinchingly. "Never tell me that I have not counted the cost," his jaw set and he strode out of the dungeon in the direction of the footprints. I waited a moment, glaring after him until I followed.

We walked along in silence for about half an hour until we came upon a large torn open window. The sun was coming up, but it was obscure and dull – a dead sun. At the base of the wall where the window opened was severed rope floating in the moat, and next to the rope, the remains of three of our men.

"They were trying to escape this pit," I said.

"It will be our fate too if we stop for long," stated Edmond as he took out the dagger from his belt and cut the rope.

"What is that for?" I asked

"It may come in handy," he replied as he coiled it up and lashed it and the dagger in his belt.

We kept on with each step getting harder and harder to take. Our fate seemed as if it could be around any corner. Then at last that corner came.

"What is that sound?" asked Edmond as a bone chilling shriek echoed throughout the halls. It was high pitched, like the screech of an eagle, only heavier and more deranged.

"Sounds like one of them," I replied.

"One right?" Edmond questioned.

"According to the sound, yes."

"Get ready," Edmond took up a fighting stance as the sound drew closer.

"Ready?" I exclaimed. "They burned an entire castle! Death is the only thing I foresee for us today!"

"What a ray of sunshine."

Suddenly, a hideous creature rounded the corner and stared straight at us with wide fire-like eyes, like a red sun lodged in its head with streaks of green running through it. In shape and size, it matched the statue completely, only this one was black and covered in scales instead of the grey stone. Its back was covered in boney ridges and it came in first on all fours, then rose up on its hind legs like a massive scaly bear. When it did so, its muscular arms hung like vines from its hunch-like back.

Following its hideous form was its tail, only this time it moved in a snake-like fasion. Still worse was the head with a mouth like a snake, which curved up into a horrible devious smile of serpent-like fangs and bubbling up from the jagged ends of the fangs was a black venom which ran down its jaw and dripped onto a steaming dark puddle.

It was so hideous that fear rose up within me greater than ever before and made me want to vomit.

"Get out of the way!" I yelled to Edmond as it leapt at us. Thank the mercy of God that we made it out of the way before the creature bored into the wall like a battering ram. I quickly recovered, releasing both of my blades and ran at the creature. It grinned wider as it caught me by the throat and pressed me against the wall before I could do anything to prevent it. Edmond had by this time drawn his sword and rushed at the creature, but with a swoop of its tail he was thrown more than ten feet down the hall. It then turned its focus back to me, staring and snarling in triumph. I immediately struck with both my gauntlets, and severed off the arm that held me fast. The creature screeched in agony for a moment before another arm began growing in its place.

'That is why the knife was in the head!' I thought to myself. 'No head, no regeneration.'

Quick as lightening, I ran at the confounded beast in an attempt to thrust both blades into its head. But it swooped its arm around, hooking my armour on one of its claws, and then threw me in the opposite direction it had thrown Edmond. I looked up quickly to see if Edmond had recovered yet and to my surprise, he was sitting and fiddling with the rope. 'What are you doing Edmond?' I thought as I gazed up at the snarling creature bounding towards me.

"Finish it!" I yelled as it came ever closer. The creature then brought its arm down upon me, only to be met with one of my blades. It stumbled back in surprise gazing at its new arm bleeding out. I took this chance and regained my footing.

"What is wrong?" I asked playfully, trying not to fall into despair. "No one has ever survived this long? Come on! Prove to me you are more than a sack of scales!" It looked up enraged as its severed arm began to heal and then it let out a bone chilling screech which shook the stone floor. Before I could realize that the roar was finished, it charged at me in a wave of fury. I tried to leap out of the way, but the tail of the monster curled around my leg and slammed me into the wall. I collapsed on impact and lay stunned on the floor.

"Good job," I slurred, spitting blood out onto the floor. Before I could recover, the creature grabbed me and again threw me down the hall. I could barely look up once I landed, but there it stood basking in victory. As it approached it opened its gaping jaw looking more hideous than before, and prepared to strike me down once and for all. I watched it intently as its teeth began to descend but the mighty beast was stopped nearly an inch from my face. It reeled back and nearly fell in struggle.

"I could use a little help!" yelled Edmond. I stared in surprise, then saw him on the creature's back with the rope tightened around the neck of the confused monster.

"Your sword!" I shouted to Edmond as I bounded towards him. Edmond quickly took both ends of the rope in his right hand as the muscles in his arm bulged. He then drew his sword with his left hand and tossed it in my direction. I ducked under the flailing arms of the creature, grabbed the sword as I leapt off the wall, and slashed through the neck of the beast. The beast suddenly stopped thrashing and turned instantly to stone.

I dropped the sword suddenly as a burning pain entered my hands. "Biscuit's blood!" I said stunned.

"What?" stammered Edmond.

"Just take your sword!" I said as I turned to look at the stone monster. "By the way, what were you doing?"

He held up the rope, "I told you the rope would come in handy."

"You sat there fiddling with the rope instead of helping me!" I yelled. "Edmond. You have a sword on you."

"Come," Edmond chuckled. "We must go on."

***

We followed the way in which the footprints led, but nothing came of it. We did not make it far for exhaustion overtook the two of us and night came soon after. We found a comfortable place to rest and attended to the wounds we had sustained in the battle. We lit no fire even though the night was cold, for we did not want to attract the creatures.

I leaned against the wall and closed my eyes.

I was walking along as rain poured down from the dark sky. Broken weapons were scattered about like grain on a threshing floor across a great battlefield, stretching as far as the eye could see.

Dead monsters were littered amongst the dead of mankind, and not a patch of ground was left uncovered. It looked much like the halls of the castle only it stretched for miles.

Strange metal forms also were strewn about the field, the likes of which I had never seen. The forms were in the shape of a man, only larger and made of metal. The strongest metal known to man – Valinium.

I looked into my hands at what appeared to be a sword, but blurry. I looked up again to the hill and the man standing there. I knew who he was and why he was there. We fought once again. His hate was stronger than ever. The battle lasted for hours. Finally, I prevailed and felled him into the mud. As I raised my sword to kill him again, I stopped. He looked at me. His face was indistinguishable, but I could still see hate gleaming in his eyes.

"Look at yourself," he bid me with a contemptuous smile, "look at what you have become."

"I am no more than what you are!" I defended my rage as I raised the sword preparing to strike.

"Like me?" he sneered. "I never said that you were like me."

I finished the deed and was suddenly thrust into a pitch black room with the man standing in the dark corner.

"You are a murderer," he announced.

"No," I argued, "he deserved to die!"

"What else could you be?" he smiled scornfully. "Men like you are hard to come by."

"What are you saying?" I asked in confusion.

"I need you."

"Me?" I stammered. "Why?"

"Not why. What."

"What do you want?"

He was up next to me again. "To end this war!" he erupted in fury "To end an endless fight. To end the war of hope. That is what I want."

I thundered. "I know not what war you speak of. Let alone the future of it."

"Join me, you will see what I have seen."

"And what have you seen?" *I demanded.*

"The future," *he tried to sound fearful.* "A future where nothing is left, a future you wish not to know."

I answered. "If I choose to join you, by what name shall you be addressed?"

"My name will be revealed in time."

"Aye," *I looked at him bewildered. I turned and began to walk away. Then suddenly stopped and spun around to face him.* "If you want me to come with you," *I questioned,* "why then do you threaten me?"

"Dread," *he smiled.* "It is a great power," *and he vanished.*

I awoke suddenly. The sun was just beginning to peak through the cracks in the castle wall. The air was cold and the floor like the heat of a fire. I looked around. It was still dark and the smell of soot filled the slight breeze that managed to seep through the fractured walls. Edmond was still asleep in the place where I saw him last. I sat up and pulled a bit of food out of a small bag on my belt. It was not much but it was better than nothing. I cast my gaze around the hallway trying to forget what the man had told me. 'The future,' I thought. 'What does he speak of?' I tried to put it out of my mind, but it would not go. I looked around again at the crumbling fortress. As I did, a light caught my eye from a room at the far end of the hall.

"Edmond!" I shook him awake. "Look!" I pointed down the hall.

"What is that?" he asked in a daze.

"It is a light," I replied. "I am going to see what it is."

"Nitwit," he smirked.

"Come on. We have killed one," I endeavored to sound positive. "Why not add another to the list?"

"Fine, but you are still a nitwit," he said reluctantly. " At least take the dagger."

I took the dagger and hid it in a safe place in my armour.

We went silently down the hall with our weapons poised, ready, so we thought, for anything that fate could throw at us. The light suddenly was snuffed out as we drew near.

X

MASTER OF THOSE WHO SERVE ME

"Who is there?" shouted Edmond as we came before the entrance of the room. We could still see the embers of the fire within the room, but there was little light emitting from them.

Edmond was answered by the inevitable silence.

"I will ask you again," said Edmond. "Who are you?"

More silence.

"I will ask you one last time!" Edmond yelled. "Who are you?"

"Does it matter?" a Scottish voice answered, sounding much like a young woman, but the pain laced within it made me unsure. "You think you can cause me more pain?"

"That depends on how each of us defines pain," I said as I walked over to the door and leaned against the remains of the stone frame. "Who are you?" I calmly asked.

"Why should I trust you?" her voice was filled with resignation.

"You are from Scotland?" I asked.

"Ha'," she spoke with affirmation, "Englishman," she continued, "still want to know who I am?"

"In these times we must put away our differences. I may be from England, and you from Scotland, but if we let that get in the way, there will be no England or Scotland, or any other nation, except the one that started this war," I hesitated and quieted my voice. "We are all in this fight together. So I shall ask you once again, who are you?"

"Pretty words Englishman. I did not know your type was capable of such things," she insulted.

"Who are you?" said Edmond swiftly losing his patience.

"Put the weapons down and I will tell you," she protested.

"Ah, no," stated Edmond bluntly. "We do not trust you. For all we know you could be one of them."

"I could say the same about you," she returned in her thick accent.

Edmond looked at me, "Well is she not a persistent one?"

"I am still not coming out," she said.

"Then I am coming in!" roared Edmond drawing his sword and beginning to advance upon the room.

"Wait!" I interrupted. "I will go. Here," I unlatched my gauntlets and handed them to Edmond. "Fine then," I announced, forgetting the dagger stashed in my armour, "I am unarmed and coming in."

I walked slowly into the room. It was darker than the hallway and took a while for my eyes to adjust and only then did I see, if only a little. The room was small, square, and burned.

"Hello?" I asked, only to hear more silence. "Really? I come in, unarmed and alone, and you slink into a corner?" I felt something cold touch my throat. I turned to the left and found myself gazing down the blade of a sword with a feminine form standing at the end of it. Her ginger hair looked as if it had not been brushed for a few days and her armour was blackened by flame. "You are a girl," I said trying to make conversation.

"Yes," she answered. "Can Englishmen not distinguish voices?"

"Nay, we can," I teased, "it just explains a lot."

"I do not think you are in the place to criticize," she said coldly.

"Oh no, I was merely stating a fact," I calmly remarked.

"Who are you?" she inquired. "And what are you doing here?"

"Oh! So now that I am in here you ask?" I replied.

"Who?" she demanded.

"Put down the sword and I will tell you," I smirked. She simply pressed it harder against my neck as a reply.

"Who are you?" repeated with anger seeping into her voice.

I pushed the tip of the sword away with my hand and glared into her bright blue eyes. "Now look, I cannot trust you any more than you think you can trust me, so let us save each other the trouble and just say our names. Shall we?"

"And how do I know you will not lie?" she asked.

I pointed out to Edmond. "See him? I did not let him come in here did I?"

She nodded.

"Now if I was out to hurt you, why would I come unarmed and leave my only defense outside? Why did I not call for him?" I raised my eyebrow. "Think about it."

She glared out at Edmond, then at me. "Tell me your name and I will tell you mine."

"And how do I know that I can trust you?"

"If I tell you, let that be a sign that you can trust me," she lowered her sword a bit.

"All right then. But remember," I pointed out to Edmond, "he is still out there."

She nodded and waited for me to speak.

"Richard Armistead, and just in case that is not enough," I gestured to Edmond. "That is Edmond Caddarik."

"Piper," she forced a smile. "Trust me now?"

"More so," I smiled, however it disappeared as I stared intently at a sheath tied to her belt. "The dagger sheath," I stated. "May I see it?"

"I beg your pardon?"

"Just give me the sheath," I pleaded.

She reluctantly removed the sheath from her belt and handed it to me. I took it in one hand and with the other pulled the dagger out of my armour.

"Unarmed?" she asked with her sword still in hand.

"More or less," I answered. I raised the dagger to the sheath. It slid in perfectly. "You killed it?"

"Killed what?" her breath quickened.

"The creature in the dungeon," I replied. "You killed it?"

Her eyes glistened as tears of sorrow welled up within them. "Yes," she managed to say.

"Do you know the person who was killed there?"

"One of the castle guards," she answered, "he helped me escape the attack," more tears formed. "God rest his soul."

"I am sorry," I tried to comfort her.

"Do not be," she wiped away the tears and looked at me. "Be sorry for yourselves, for you have entered into hell!"

"And you have survived it," I encouraged her. "Surely some comfort can be found in that."

"The only comfort I can find is that God still has a plan," she demurred.

"That is the spirit," I said, remembering the death of my parents. 'I wish he had the same for me.' I thought. "Do you know if the King is alive?" I asked.

She nodded slowly. "He escaped when the Varanus attacked."

"Varanus?"

"That is what the Adversary called them," she replied.

"Adversary?" I stared at her in confusion. "You lost me."

"Of course I have, Englishman," she let a hint of a smile cross her lips. "The Varanus are the creatures."

"And I suppose the Adversary is the man in black?"

She nodded.

"Well, the name suits him," I grinned.

"You done in there Richard?" Edmond called in. "Or has a Scottish maiden bested you?"

"One moment Edmond!" I returned, then addressed Piper. "Will you join us? You know much more about the Varanus than we do and know what happened. We could use that information."

"May I?" she asked looking up at me.

"Why not?" I answered trying to sound as friendly as possible.

She sheathed her sword and with her piercing blue eyes met mine.

At that moment I felt as if part of myself was torn away. But not like when my parents died. At that moment, I did not feel hate, nor anger. At that moment, I felt peace. I did not know why, all I knew was that this girl had something to do with it.

"Come on," I beckoned her toward the doorway. "Let us go,"

And so, we left the room.

"Well it is about time!" Edmond exclaimed as we came out of the room and drew near to him. He took a deep breath and turned his gaze to Piper. "So there is the little shadow dweller," he smirked, trying to lighten the moment.

"Like you are out of the shadows?" she answered.

"That is enough," I admonished them both, trying to keep the peace. "We need to get out of here."

We went down westward leading hallway. There was silence for quite a while as Edmond and I pondered what to do.

Finally, Piper spoke.

"Surely you did not come here alone," she said.

"No," I replied. "Twenty men came with us. We have seen none of them since we split up."

"Only God can save them now," she stammered. "I am sorry, but your men are dead. There is no way anyone survives who does not know how to kill those creatures."

"Why?" Edmond asked, surprised at her sudden response.

"Once you see what happens when the Varanus get a hold of them," her voice shook, "Trust me, then you will know why."

"And how do you know?" Edmond asked. "Without dying, how do you know what the Var – and what in the dying name of England are those?"

"The Varanus are the creatures," I informed Edmond.

"Fine," Edmond accepted my response and continued, "but how do you know what they can do?"

"I was there!" Piper exclaimed. "I was there when they attacked the castle! I watched innocent people become murderers! I watched people being torn apart like paper! I know what those monsters can do!" her voice broke into tears. "So many died," she sobbed. "I did not know what to do."

"You have no need to lose your temper," said Edmond flatly.

"You are one to talk!" she struggled to hide her emotions. "I lost far more than that when they came!"

"And we will lose everything if we continue like this!" said Edmond.

"As if I have not already?" she looked at him, distraught. "The Varanus are your worst nightmare! A nightmare you can never wake up from!"

"Stop!" I yelled coming to the edge of losing control of my anger. "We need to get out, not fight each other!"

"This place," stammered Edmond "It is a sickness, like death. We must pay attention to the matters at hand, and not on those which lay in the past."

"Aye," I replied in a lighter tone. "But all the same, tell us what happened. How did you survive the Varanus' attack?"

"When the King came here, I was one of his servants, brought from Scotland with my brother who later joined the guard."

"Was the guard from the dungeon your brother?" I asked.

"No. That was another guard I met," she replied, "My brother was with the King when I last saw him. Maybe for the last time too," she began to tear up again. I wanted to comfort her, but knew not how.

"Please continue," Edmond said.

She pulled herself together and resumed her story. "The first few days nothing strange or violent happened, but I do not remember those days quite so well. All the memories of what happened then were drowned out the night the King was having another one of his parties. It was going all according to plan until a man leapt on to one of the tables and declared, 'I am the Adversary! And I bring doubt! I bring dread! I bring death!'"

I felt a raging fear and a spasm of pain as she repeated those words. They resonated in my ears like an endless scream of hopeless pain! The faces of my parents and images of their death flashed vividly before my eyes. I collapsed onto the burned stone floor of the castle.

It was Edmond's sword I held in my hand. Its beauty shining brightly in the darkness of the battlefield which stretched all around me. The great stone forms of the fallen Varanus were scattered about. But outnumbering the statues, men lay as far as I could see. Thousands and tens of thousands. They were without number.

Rain again was pouring from the clouded sky like waves of the sea.

I glared at the man standing there on the hill. He looked different than the other times I had seen him. He looked tired, like he had fought for many years and his eyes bore the pain. More pain than any man should have endured. Even so, he was covered with hate.

"Who are you?" I asked.

"The enemy," he sneered.

"Who do you serve!" I yelled.

"I serve my Master," he replied.

"Who is your Master?" I demanded.

"My Master is the one thing you fear he is," he grinned.

"Who do you think I fear?" I questioned.

"You have two fears," he never broke his dark smile. "An earthly fear and one not of earth."

"Who do you serve?" I yelled. My fear was mine to know and mine to own. It was my burden, and mine to carry.

"You fear death."

"No, I fear not death!" I countered.

"Yes," he replied, "you do fear death. Your death and the death of those you care for."

"No!" I thundered, realizing that perhaps this creature knew more than I thought. "What do I fear?" I tested.

"Two things you fear, three lay within one and lead into the other."

"Enough with the riddles!" I yelled. "Tell me plainly!"

"Doubt, dread and death," he spoke smiling. "Such are your earthly fears. And for the other, you fear what comes afterward."

"Are you the Adversary?" I clenched my teeth.

"To my Master, I am a loyal servant. And to you I may be an adversary," his voice was cold and dreadful. "To my Master, it is you who goes by that name."

"Are you the Adversary?" I thundered.

"I am an enemy to those who stand against my Master," he replied.

"By what name does he go?" I asked impatiently. "Who is he?"

"He goes by many names and who he is, that is beyond what even I can say."

"What then are his names?" I demanded. "Who is he compared to?"

"My loyalty does not stand with you," he spoke coldly. "Why then should I tell you the names of my Master?"

"If you will not tell me the name of your Master," I began to lose patience with him, "will you tell me your name?"

"As I said before, I am not loyal to you," he scowled. "I am loyal to him who enlightened me."

"And who is that?" I asked again, trying to make him slip.

"My Master," he grinned. "You think me so naive?"

"Tell me his name!" I cried losing my patience all the more.

"He will tell you his own name in time," he said "It is not for me to tell you."

"I am tired of 'in time'! When will I see him? When will I know?" my sword was poised to strike.

"Soon," his voice was calm as a snake and cold as the winter wind. "Soon all will be revealed."

"And what do you call soon?" my patience was draining swiftly.

"You know Richard," he hissed. "You know when he will come."

"Do I?" I replied.

"You do know," he countered.

"How do you know?" I parried.

"I am the Adversary!" his voice was like thunder. "I know the will of my Master!"

"So you want to end this war?" I nearly burst with joy that I had gained some information from him.

"My Master's orders are my existence!" he proclaimed. "Therefore, if he commands the war be ended, that then is what I fight for. That is what I die for."

"So, your Master is the other one who comes after you?" I dug in deeper to find his Master's identity.

"You speak the truth."

"Who is the other?"

"My Master!" he drew his sword and rushed at me, swinging it around and striking mine with enormous force. I took a few steps back, and there held my ground. I fought back laying a blow to his leg, which he countered and rounded his sword, pushing mine with it, until he brought his hammering down upon me. I leapt out of the way and kicked the side of his stomach. He stepped back and smiled.

"You cannot win this war," he said.

"As long as you die!" I screamed. "It is enough!"

"And that is why you will never be victorious over me! You say you are not like me," he coiled his sword and arm around his body, "and yet you yearn for blood!" he came closer, unleashed the sword, sending it crashing around and knocked my sword out of my hand. He then stepped in closer and ran his sword through me.

"He is waiting," the Adversary grinned and cast me to the mud. "He is waiting for you."

I lay there in pain as he faded away and the other appeared.

"Have you decided whether you will join me in my cause?" he asked. "The world will be a much better place when we succeed. Trust me, this war is one you do not want to fight."

"Are you the Master of the Adversary?" I gasped.

I reached with a shaking hand and grabbed Edmond's sword and with the last of my strength pointed the keen blade toward him. "Are you his Master?" I yelled as blood covered my tattered armour.

"I take it you have not decided," he sneered.

"Are you the Master?" my voice cracked with pain. My shirt was now crimson.

"To you I am not," he looked at me with his demented gaze. I studied his face in agony. It remained calm and menacing. But an unearthly pain dwelt behind it.

"Who are you?" my voice shook.

"You know me," his deranged words were a constant stinging through my heart and mind. "Did not my servant tell you?"

"He told me you would tell me who you are!"

"Not who I am, only my name," he grinned, "that will be in time, when it is revealed."

"Are you not my dream?" I yelled in desperation. "Tell me who you are! Your name! Where you live!"

"Oh Richard," it was the first time he had addressed me by name and his voice made it sound like a curse. But not a curse toward me. "I am far more than a dream."

"What?" I said in confusion.

He gripped my throat and lifted me from the place where I lay. "I am Doubt," he whispered through anger and sorrow. "I am Dread," his voice burned. "I. Am. Death." My heart melted in my chest and the pain from my wound immediately ceased.

"Richard!" Edmond ran hastily to my side.

"What happened?" asked Piper as they both knelt on the floor next to me.

"I do not know!" Edmond replied.

"We need to keep moving," she stated. "The Varanus will find us for sure if we stay here!"

"I am alright," I stammered, inching my way to my feet.

"What happened?" asked Piper in surprise.

"What he said," I stuttered, "it reminded me – never mind, it – it does not matter."

"The doubt, dread and death?" she asked

My heart skipped a beat, "Yes," I swiftly answered. My teeth gritted together as I struggled to purge the image of my parents' death from my mind.

"Can I help you?" Edmond asked.

"No," I said trying to dispel the dread in my heart. "I need to find him!" I nearly fell again. "I must find the Adversary!"

"No, not now," Edmond replied. "Now, what we need is to get out of this pit."

"Yes," agreed Piper, "we can find him later."

"I will kill the Adversary," I gritted my teeth. "You cannot stop me."

"And let this be so when the time comes," said Edmond "But not now! Now we must get out of this place."

I stared into Edmond's eyes, "I will kill the Adversary!" I fumed.

He laid his hand on my shoulder. "The Adversary is not our goal. He is not our mission. Our mission is to find the King."

I stood up. "You have no idea, Edmond, you have no idea who he is!"

Edmond rose and faced me. "I know how much it hurts, I know how much pain you have but now is not the time."

I glared into his eyes. Rage built up within me. "The Adversary killed my parents," I gritted my teeth. This dark being. The fear that had been following me for years. The messenger of doubt, the follower in the market, the man in the shadow, the form at the ring of stone were all the same. They were all the Adversary. After all these years here he is – the monster of Shrewton. The man who killed my mother and father.

"Richard, no," Edmond saw the rage and hatred. "Not now."

"You cannot stop me Caddarik! He was always there! He has followed me my whole life! I will end this!"

"No," Edmond pleaded.

"You have no idea how much it hurts. How much pain I have endured because of him!"

"Stop!" Edmond's voice rose as he forced me against the wall. Piper stood watching in fear – but I did not care. "This is not who you are. What happened to you does not define you!"

I struggled against his iron grip. "He killed them!" I screamed into his face. "He took them from me!"

"Richard stop!" Edmond pushed harder, but the pain meant nothing. "Is this what your father would want? Is this what God wants?"

"Your God is dead!"

"My God is alive!" Edmond boomed. "He always has been and always will be. From this time, now and forever more. And only He can save you!"

"Shut up!" I clenched my teeth. "Let me go!"

"Please," Edmond's eyes filled with tears. "Please, do not do this," he clenched his teeth. "Do not make me do this."

"I do not care," I hissed.

The last thing I saw was Edmond's fist, and the world went black.

THE CHINK IN MY ARMOUR

I opened my eyes and felt my head. Two large bruises stung to the touch and I concluded that Edmond had knocked me out with more than one blow. The floor of the castle was uncomfortably hard.

I turned my head to my left and saw only the dark hallway. Ash floated in the air and coals flickered in the shadows. The sky, through the cracks of the castle wall, was grey and overcast.

I turned to my right to see Piper, but Edmond was nowhere in sight.

Piper was sitting beside me. She leaned her back against the wall, her legs were curled up to her and she wrapped her arms around them. Her head was downcast and weariness hung on her face.

"I am sorry," I said with regret lacing my voice. I could hardly remember what I had done, but I knew it was bad.

She turned slowly to me, her head still resting on her knees. "Who are you?" she asked. She was afraid and I dearly hoped it was not of me.

"I am a man who has lost. I have lost my family, my faith, and my hope," I turned and gazed at the opposite wall. "I do not want to lose anything else. I cannot lose anything else."

"Back in Scotland, when I was young, I met an English soldier," Piper followed my gaze to the broken wall. "He told me that a man he once knew said that no one lives without pain," she bit her lower lip. "I never knew what he meant until now."

"I should not have lost control," I stared blankly. "I do not want to become the monster that killed my parents. All I want is for him to know the pain I feel."

"The Adversary is a monster," she replied. "But as much as I hate him, I can see pain in his eyes. I believe he has lost others dear to him too."

"You are sympathizing with that demon?" I snorted. "All I see in him is a man doomed to die by my sword."

"Hell is the only place those words go," she turned back to me. "I do not want to see you go there."

I turned and met her gaze. "Then I will drag him with me."

"Please. Do not lose your soul in this obsession," she pleaded.

"You do not know me," I replied coldly.

"I know you are a man in pain. I know enough. I know pain can rip a person apart. And I know who can put them back together."

"Did Edmond tell you to say that?" I scowled.

She shook her head and forced a smile. "I just do not want to see a good man lose sight of what is right."

I nodded in understanding. "Where is Edmond?" I asked in an attempt to change the subject.

"He went on, saying he wanted to see what is ahead so as not to lead everyone into a trap."

"How long was I unconscious?" I queried.

"Which time?" she laughed. "He repeatedly knocked you out to keep the peace."

"How long?"

"Two hours," she replied.

I grimaced. "How long has he been gone?"

"A few minutes," she began standing up. "We should probably join him," she offered me her hand but I declined.

I felt lightheaded as I rose, and pain crept down my head onto the side of my face and jaw. Suddenly a sound caused my heart to jump - the sound of steel on steel. The screech of a Varanus and Edmond's battle cry.

"No," I clenched my teeth as I released my blades. "No!" My voice rose as I broke into a sprint down the hall to the scene of the fight. Piper followed close behind, drawing her sword as she ran.

My head pounded as I ran, but I knew that Edmond's life was in danger.

We rounded the last hallway and saw Edmond holding his ground against the Adversary, and two Varanus closing in.

Smoke rose all around them and ash flew up into the air as they fought. Sparks flew off the swords as they clashed. The Adversary's cloak billowed as he fought his way through Edmond's defenses as the Varanus closed in.

My jaw set and my nostrils flared. "For my father, demon!" I charged into the fray.

"Hello Richard, nice of you to join us," the Adversary sneered as he motioned one the Varanus toward me.

"You killed my father!" I cried at the Adversary as I attacked the Varanus.

The Adversary smirked, his gleaming eyes pierced through me. He grinned as he parried a thrust from Edmond. "And yet you have forgotten my name."

I puzzled for a moment, then flew at the Varanus like lightening, desperate to destroy it and end the life of the Adversary.

Piper charged at the second Varanus and drew it away from Edmond. That, however did not stop the onslaught of attacks the Adversary pressed against Edmond. Moment by moment the Adversary's strength overcame Edmond in his weary state. With neither enough food nor adequate rest for several days, and the undying power of the demon of Shrewton, there was little Edmond could do to stand.

I glanced in Piper's direction to find her retreating from the Varanus. More fear rose up within as I turned back to the monster in front of me. It snarled at me and whipped its tail around to kill me, but I dodged it and slit the tail in half. The creature screeched and fell back. The other one raged as it ran at me and knocked me against the wall. Piper ran to it and thrust her sword through its chest. I recovered from the blow and went to help Piper. Just as I did, the Varanus I had been fighting grabbed me and threw me against another wall. Pain shot through my back. I attempted to rise, but the Varanus gripped my chest and threw me again. This time I was able to shield myself before hitting the wall so that I still stood on my feet. The Varanus then charged at me a final time as I readied my blades for the head of the fowl creature. "One less will stand in this war!" I said under my breath as my blades met their mark.

As the creature transformed I wrenched my blades from the solidifying mass and ran to Piper who was losing ground to the other Varanus. Before we could dispatch it, another figure came running down the hall, drawing a Scottish Claymore, and slashed the head off the beast.

I turned again to see the Adversary clasping Edmond by his throat and pinning him to the wall. "The blood of your brothers will be spilled," he gritted his teeth. "Let yours flow with theirs!"

"Let him go!" I yelled as the Adversary prepared to run his sword through.

"Or what?" he answered in disdain.

"You too will die!" said the man with the Claymore. I could see him more clearly now, he looked a bit younger than me.

"You think I fear you boy?" the Adversary sneered addressing the young man. "You are nothing to me."

"No," answered the young man. "But you will fear me when I am finished."

The Adversary turned and addressed the three of us standing before him. "I will let him live," he pointed to us, "if one of you is willing to die to save him."

We stood there in silence.

"No one?" he said with a smirk. "So be it," he said amused.

"No!" I yelled running at him. As I did, Edmond grabbed the Adversary's arm and spun him around exposing his side to my blades which ran through him.

The Adversary flinched. "You are willing to die for him?" he smiled. "My Master will be pleased that you are so easily defeated," he threw Edmond aside and wrenched my blades from his body. "The ruse is proved," he smiled, then stumbled quickly down the hallway into the shadows.

I helped Edmond up and turned and heard the other man speaking.

"Thank you!" he said emphatically.

"I beg your pardon?" Edmond asked. "You are the one who came to our aid."

"You found Piper!" he answered. "And for that I thank you!"

"Yes, and who are you?" I said perhaps a bit too roughly and Edmond glanced.

"Redhill," he said in a Scottish accent, "Luke Redhill."

"Well," I said as kindly as possible, trying to ease Edmond's gaze, "seeing as you are against the Varanus, would you like to come with us?"

"It would be my pleasure," he replied.

"What happened to you?" asked Piper with tears welling up in her eyes.

"When the Varanus attacked, I attempted to protect the King," he said. "Though many of our efforts failed, I was able to ensure his escape. After that, I began searching for you, but you were nowhere to be found. I searched the castle until I came upon two men who said they were looking for the King. I told them he had escaped and was heading back to England. As we gave leave of each other, I saw the Varanus attack and sink their teeth into the men. That is when I saw the transformation – the death of a man and the birth of a Varanus."

Piper's face bespoke the terror and Luke continued. "All I can say is that is the worst sight any man can behold! Seeing the black scales appear and cover the poor soul's body," Luke's voice quaked and I marveled at how much fear the Varanus could invoke within men.

"The new born Varanus turned and saw me and gave chase. I could not outrun them, but I was able to escape through a grate in the floor where they could not follow. As I emerged, I found myself in the King's armory where I availed myself of a better sword and resumed my search for you. I thought for sure they had killed you," his voice cracked as he fixed his eyes on Piper.

Luke continued. "I wanted revenge. I wanted them dead and especially the one we saw earlier in the Great Hall declaring his name. That man who called himself the bearer of death and dread – this so called Adversary. So, I followed one of those disgusting creatures which led me to him."

"The Adversary?" I questioned.

"Aye, that is the name he calls himself."

"His name certainly describes him," scowled Edmond.

"You found the Adversary though?" I asked.

"Aye, all too true. When I found him, I asked him what he had done. 'Changed the world,' he answered. I asked him why and if it was truly the best way, I then pointed to a vile Varanus snarling at me. 'Humanity though unwilling, must die!' he stared at me with burning eyes. 'You search for someone? Give it up, there is no purpose in searching.' 'No' I answered 'The Lord hath made all things for a purpose, even the wicked for the day of trouble! As yours is now so ready yourself doubty boy.' I then rushed at him, but he disappeared quickly down the hallway with two of those lizard creatures guarding his back.

"I followed at a distance waiting for them to let their guard down but they never did. After a while, the Adversary disappeared into the shadows. I waited and watched to see what would come of it. Then I saw you!" he hugged Piper. Tears streaming from his kind green eyes.

"At last I have found you!" they stood there embracing each other for a while.

Seeing Piper and Luke so relieved and in their embrace, I felt a twinge of jealousy, but thought that it is not my place.

"And who are these Piper? Not quite gentlemen I see." Luke finally said smirking at Edmond's blood stained face and my tangled mop of hair.

"This," she said pointing at me and Edmond "is Richard Armistead and Edmond Caddarik. They saved my life."

"I would not say saved," I laughed. "More like gave her company. Her actions in the dungeon showed Edmond and me how to kill the Varanus."

"Thank you anyway," said Luke.

"It is merely our duty," Edmond answered.

"Let us get out of this pit," I said, "it is high time we did."

"Aye," said Edmond. "Who knows what else is in the depths of these halls!"

"You," said Luke pointing at me. "Richard is it? Where did you get that gauntlet?"

"I made it."

"Does anyone else have one?"

"Yes, the men we brought with us," I answered. "Why do you

ask?"

"I may know where one of your men resides! In fact, two!" he said excitedly. "Follow me!"

We walked quickly through the dark halls. Hoping and praying that the worst was over. Alas, though, no war is truly ended in a day.

Soon we came to a balcony with a staircase which led down into a large room in the shape of a rectangle with great walls of stone. A large burned door stood at the far end. Thus the great hall in all its broken glory lay before us as a great tree felled in a storm.

"This is where it happened?" I asked, staring at the devastated majesty of Château de Dourdan. "This is where they attacked?"

"Yes," said Luke gazing down at where it all began. "This is where it started."

We stood there in silence for a while. No words could describe what we saw. Dread loomed like a thick shadow.

"Look!" Edmond shattered the silence, pointing towards the door. "It is one of our men!" a man in tattered leather armour came running out of the far corridor. It looked as if he were limping, and calling for something in the hallway to chase him.

"No," I whispered to myself as a Varanus emerged from the hallway and charged at the man. "There behind him! A Varanus!" I yelled to the rest as I released my blades and prepared to run to his aid.

"No!" Luke grabbed my arm.

"Let go of me!" I turned on him in perplexed anger.

"There is nothing you can do," his voice filled with pain, "he is gone."

I looked back at the man. Luke was right. The Varanus was upon him and had been bitten his shoulder. He screamed in pain as blood stained his armour. The Varanus casually threw his body aside and ran back toward the gates of the castle. Piper looked away not wanting to see the sight.

I looked on in horror as the man lay for a minute, then twitched and looked up. His eyes seemed to be on fire and that fire spread completely through him. All of the armour he was wearing tore off like paper. The flames engulfed him for at least a minute and the room heated like an oven. The flames licked at everything in search of something to destroy. When the flames finally cleared, they revealed an imposing black scale covered creature, a Varanus. I could not believe my eyes. There was no sign that the man had been there!

Suddenly, just as quickly as it began, it was over as the creature reeled back with an arrow in its head. I looked at Edmond.

"It is not mine," he said.

I looked back at the fallen enemy. Our fallen brother. At the door, a man stood with a bow in his hand. He was tall and had dark brown hair that fell to his shoulder. He leaned against the door frame, and the morning light shone upon his face. It was Feargal.

"That is him!" yelled Luke. "That is the man!"

"It is Feargal!" Edmond exclaimed.

Seeing us at the balcony, Feargal yelled. "It takes more than lizard monsters to kill me! Then again, that was the last of my arrows," and he began to make his way toward us.

"Stay there!" I yelled back. "We will come to you!"

"If that be so," Feargal gasped. "I could use a rest," he leaned weakly back up against the wall again.

The room was covered in soot and ash. Nothing remained except the melted weapons of the garrison. As we got closer, I realized that Feargal's condition was not good. Edmond too saw Feargal's poor state as we both approached. The Adversary had held nothing back with him. Feargal's eyes were no longer bright, but filled with dread.

"What happened?" inquired Edmond.

"I met the Varanus!" Feargal answered. "What does it look like?"

"Come on, we have your friend," said Piper. "Let us go."

"To where?" asked Feargal suddenly getting serious.

"Out of here!" exclaimed Luke. "I do not know about you, but I personally dislike giant black beasts that are out to kill me."

"I would have to agree on consideration of them trying to kill us," Feargal replied, "but we would be better off in here."

"Why?" asked Piper, speaking for all of us.

"Do you not understand!" he exclaimed.

I shook my head.

"The Varanus are leaving! All of them! That one that ran through here, it was the last!"

"Leaving?" questioned Edmond. "Where? Why?"

"To their master," my face flushed as I lost feeling in my fingers and toes. "The Varanus have gone to their master. Now that they are out, nothing can stop them."

"Are you all right Richard?" asked Feargal.

"I will be fine," I took a deep breath trying to calm myself.

"All right then," Feargal laughed, "but you look worse than me!"

"Well then, we had best chase those scaly flames of grime to our own turf. Surely they will see the futility of their attack and run," Luke grinned. "Or we could die here alone."

"I for one would rather not die alone, as Luke left me to do," Feargal stated.

"I had other priorities, besides dealing with the grumpy, frightened captain of the Big Dipper!" Luke exclaimed.

"Silver Star is her name! Silver Star!" Feargal yelled.

"Silver Star, big dipper, what does it matter! We need to get out of here!" I yelled impatiently.

Feargal and Luke gave each other a scowl and the five of us

walked out of the great hall into the passageways toward the great iron gates of the main enterance. I tried to piece all of it together as we walked, trying to see the Master's plan. Nothing fit, not one scenario. In a short time, we came to the gates and found them melted together.

"Now what?" asked Luke in despair.

"We open it," Edmond replied cooly as he was prone to do.

"Or we could go back through the tunnels," I suggested.

"Do we have time?" asked Edmond.

"Do we have time to tear through a plate of iron?" Feargal asked. "I say we go back through the tunnels."

"Hold on," interrupted Luke, "what tunnels?"

"We came in through tunnels under the castle," Edmond replied.

"Why in secret?" asked Piper.

"Our mission called for it," Edmond said. "We could not risk anyone knowing we were here as our message was for the King and him alone."

"Well I am no expert on the matter," said Luke, "but I would say you failed in not letting anyone know you are here. Would you not say?"

"What mission?" Piper ignored Luke's comment.

"The mission that came with this letter," I said, putting my hand inside of my leather armour trying to find the letter Andrew had given me. I fished out the paper and handed it to Luke, still grinning. He opened it, went fully pale, and his grin disappeared.

"You?" his eyes searched mine like mouse eyeing a cat. "How could you?" he threw down the paper and drew his sword. "Run Piper!" he screamed. "Get out of here! Find the King!"

He charged toward me and brought his sword crashing down on my blades, which I thankfully had released only moments before. Piper surprised and bewildered, turned and began to run back down the hallway. Luke brought his sword up again and let fly a more powerful blow. This one I almost dodged, but it hit my armour and got lodged in it. I shook myself loose and went on the offensive trying to loosen his grip on the sword. He gripped my right arm and bent it behind my back.

"You scum! Why?" he continued to push and twist my arm. "How could you?" he yelled and gave my arm one more push and dislocated my shoulder. I let out a scream of pain. Edmond then realized that Luke was indeed intent on killing me. He did not even draw his sword, but ran at Luke and landed a massive blow to his jaw. Luke was instantly off of me and on the floor holding his jaw in pain. He looked up at Edmond.

"Why?" he said with tears of anger dripping down his face.

"Why what?" Edmond asked.

Luke gave a pained scowl as he sheathed his sword and ran down the hall behind Piper.

I lay there for a while as Edmond began to put my shoulder back in place. Pain shot up and down my arm as if someone had turned my bones into a thousand red hot needles. But even though the pain was great, I hardly noticed it, for Piper and Luke occupied my thoughts and worries.

"What had they seen?" I thought aloud, then let out a sudden scream as Edmond pushed my shoulder back into place.

"Something bad I would say," Edmond gave my shoulder a pat and stood up.

"What?" I asked through clenched teeth as I tried to clear my head. "Why would Luke do this?"

"I do not know," answered Edmond. "Maybe," he paused briefly. "I do not know."

"Was it something in the letter?" Feargal asked as he leaned up against the wall.

I reached for the letter laying on the floor where Luke had left it,

I pulled it towards me and picked it up. My heart fell like a stone in the sea and what seemed like a cold wind chilled my soul. There on the paper, in large splotchy letters, as if they had been written in blood, were the words which would drive men mad. The words which broke mankind and burned the halls of Château de Dourdan. The Words which broke the might of the Khans and destroys hope itself:
I bring Doubt, I bring Dread, I bring Death.

    I stared at it dumfounded as my heart raced. "He," I faltered. "He thought we were..." I looked at Edmond, "in league with the Adversary and the Varanus!"

    "No," Edmond declared. "It cannot be!" he snatched the paper from my hands and gazed at it in frustration.

    "How did this happen?" I entreated as I stood up from the floor.

    "I do not know," Edmond answered. "It does not make any sense!"

    "However it happened," Feargal broke in, "we need to find those two and make sure they know we are not working with the enemy."

    "Aye," answered Edmond in a thunder-like voice. "We are going to find them. Then get out of this God-forsaken pit."

    We were about to take off running when Feargal interrupted:

    "Do I look like I can run?"

    I looked at Feargal, then at Edmond and we realized with Feargal in such a bad condition, there would be no running. Edmond and I walked over and helped him up, and allowed him to lean on each of our shoulders.

    Our progress was slow and mind numbing. I could not stop wondering how the letter had changed. Could the Adversary have planted it when he realized how to strike me? 'No' I thought 'He found that out and then left right after his attack. There is no way he could have; even he could not do it that quickly!' I came up with countless more scenarios, but none were logical or reasonable.

THE BRETHREN RISE

Darkness engulfed the day in shadows as the three of us made our way through the castle again, calling out for Piper and Luke. I walked slowly with my companions, staring through the darkness, hoping, praying that Luke and Piper would return. I realized that day that I did not want to be alone. A seed of longing began to grow, but it was quickly suppressed by duty to my country, and duty to the Brethren. I could not let my mind wander into thoughts of love and a life of peace. And how could I ever be at peace? A man whose mind was bent on revenge. My mind was distressed, but my mission was clear, 'We must leave Château de Dourdan, with or without Piper and Luke.'

XII

THE BATTLE OF CHÂTEAU DE DOURDAN

Through the windows of the desolate fortress, the only sight to be seen was a great grey cloud looming around the castle. So thick was it that I could neither see the ground nor the surrounding trees.

We walked through the castle on our way to the tunnel, searching for Piper and Luke in every room we passed, but to no avail.

Time passed slower. I began to recognize the castle and forgot about the King. All I was focused on was getting out, but I still felt the longing to be with Piper again.

Everything was dead and burned. All color had faded. There was little talk from anyone that afternoon.

Finally, Edmond spoke. "I think we all know what we need to do," Edmond said. Beads of sweat dripped from his brow as the day warmed.

"And what is that?" I asked.

"We need to get out now, without any more distractions," Edmond replied. "We cannot waste any more time looking for Piper and Luke."

"We stay in here," Feargal blurted.

"What do you mean?" asked Edmond.

I stood to the side watching them talk.

"The Varanus are gone," Feargal looked straight into Edmond's unflinching face.

"Exactly," Edmond countered. "We must follow them before it is too late."

"Do you know what that means?" yelled Feargal. "Can you not hear me?"

"I think I am beginning to hear you," Edmond declared.

"The Varanus are out there!" Feargal's face was red as blood. "They are finished here! If we stay, we might have a chance to survive! But if we go out there we may as well be asking for death!"

"What is the point of surviving if all others die?" Edmond questioned. "You know that is what the Varanus will do."

"Maybe it will not be! Maybe Europe will win!" Feargal protested.

"Then why stay if we could survive out there?" Edmond pushed harder into Feargal's heart.

Feargal walked to the nearest window and pointed out into the black mass of smoke. "I cannot see another man die because of them!"

"You are a ship's captain," said Edmond, "surely you have seen death like this?"

I began to see that Feargal was hiding something.

"Edmond, there is nothing in the world that is comparable to this! You know that! You are no fool!" Feargal's voice trembled.

Edmond grabbed Feargal, fiercely gripping his armour and pushing him to the wall, prying harder. "Be a man Feargal! Look at yourself! Our home dies and you stand here in fear?" It was clear that Edmond was pushing now as well to find what Feargal was hiding, pushing him to the breaking point.

"I have a reason to fear!" Feargal yelled in distress as he pushed Edmond off. "I have reason to stay back in hiding!"

"And what is it that you fear?" thundered Edmond. "Death?

The Varanus? Pray, do enlighten me Feargal Elmsbirch. Come on captain!" Edmond's eyes blazed.

"I fear," Feargal stammered, "him."

I glared at Feargal in greater interest. "Him?" I asked.

"The one behind all this!" answered Feargal in dread. "The one behind all of it."

"Who?" I questioned. "Who is he?"

Feargal looked at me with broken eyes. "I do not know."

"Have you seen him?" Edmond pressed further.

Feargal trembled. "No."

"Why then do you fear him? You have not seen him and you do not know who he is," I questioned and stared at him harder than I thought humanly possible, but Feargal still remained silent.

"Why then do you fear him?" I yelled.

"The Adversary!" he cried out in terror.

"What about him?" Edmond responded.

"His master-" Feargal stopped and turned away. His hands shook and his teeth chattered. His face was colorless and it looked as if all life had abandoned him.

"Spit it out, Captain!" Edmond yelled. "Who is this master?"

"Edmond wait," I said under my breath, but Edmond did not hear.

"He told me," Feargal stopped again and collapsed to his knees. "He said he would kill me if I told you," his voice quaked with utter terror.

Edmond lay his hand on Feargal's shoulder. "We cannot make you talk, but we need to know."

"Edmond stop talking!" I yelled.

Feargal remained silent and Edmond continued. "Is your life so important to you? That you would let them win?"

"Edmond," I shivered as I thought of the Master. The being of pure darkness which plagued me with dread.

Edmond ignored me. "They will destroy everything Captain. You must tell us what you know or else it is all over," the last straw was torn away.

"Apollo!" Feargal's voice reverberated like an earthquake. "His name is Apollo!"

The hall grew darker as Feargal spoke his name and my heart sunk as I felt myself go pale. Utter dread encompassed the name of death, the name of horror.

"Did I not warn you, Elmsbirch? Perhaps I was not clear?" The Adversary's voice thundered from the darkness behind us.

All three faced him, but only Edmond was ready for a fight for Feargal cowered and I was far from ready to face my parents' killer.

"This is the last time, demon!" Edmond yelled.

"Oh no Edmond," the Adversary's voice was calm as a summer breeze and yet menacing as thunder. "Perhaps for you, but as for me, my life will remain."

Edmond scowled at the monster and struck his left side. The Adversary met it with the flat of his own blade and pushed Edmond's sword away. In the same movement, he lay a blow into Feargal's right leg and Feargal collapsed under the force of it.

Edmond regained his footing and kicked the Adversary in the chest sending him stumbling back on the impact. Then, reorienting himself into a more opposing position, the Adversary swung his sword around and smashed it with immense force into Edmond's blade. Edmond was thrown back several feet from the sheer power of the blow.

I then felt the rage of revenge enter my blood and advanced onto the Adversary's left flank which he left unguarded. I had almost met my mark when he gripped my right arm and twisted. The pain returned to my shoulder, far greater than before. I grabbed the Adversary's arm and hit a pressure point near the elbow with my left blade. The Adversary let go of my arm as the Valinium pierced his forearm. He glared up at me with a grin and readied his sword with both hands for another engagement. The dark being swung his sword around towards me, however, I ducked underneath the demonic blade as it crashed into the crumbling stone wall. Edmond then engaged again with all his strength, laying a blow with his heel to the Adversary's hands. The Adversary let out a slight grunt of pain as he released his sword and it slipped through the crack in the wall, plummeting into the moat. Seeing a chance to strike, I gripped the Adversary by the back of the neck and brought his face slamming into my knee. He stumbled back desperately trying to regain his footing. As he fell, Edmond delivered another powerful blow to his shoulder which sent him sprawling to the stone floor. Edmond leapt upon him the moment he was felled and lay his sword on the Adversary's throat.

"Who stands behind this!" thundered Edmond. "Who is Apollo?"

The Adversary smiled, "I believe Richard can answer that question for you."

"Enough!" Edmond yelled as he pressed the blade further against the Adversary's neck. "Tell me who Apollo is!"

The Adversary nodded to me, "Ask him."

"What are you talking about?" asked Edmond. "Who is Apollo? Tell me or your life ends here!"

"I told you," the Adversary answered calmly. "Richard knows."

Edmond and Feargal looked at me, "Richard?" stammered Edmond. Both of them with an expression of disbelief and the intensity of battle.

"I-I do not know," I stuttered.

"Yes," his words were smooth as a serpent, "you do," the

Adversary smiled. "Remember Richard. Remember."

"Richard what is he talking about?" Edmond's voice seemed to shake.

"I do not know!" I tried to remember all that I could.

"Remember," yelled the Adversary. "To end the future of this war! Have you forgotten?"

My heart sank like an anchor.

"Future?" Feargal exclaimed.

"That is it!" howled the Adversary as he grabbed the blade of Edmond's sword and struck his fist into Edmond's jaw. He then kicked Edmond in the chest, throwing him back against the wall.

I flew at the Adversary attempting to bury my blades into his body. As I lunged at him in fury, he leapt over to the right and gripped my back, and slammed my chest into his knee. I collapsed to the floor under the blow. It felt like my heart had been crushed as I laid there in agony.

I did not lay there long before he grabbed my leather armour and slammed me into the wall. My head was clouded. The castle seemed to be spinning all around me. I struggled to a standing position somehow, only to get punched in the gut and thrown more than twenty feet down the hall.

"It is over Richard!" he hissed in utter cruelty. "You have been beaten once more!"

I laid there on the dark stone floor, fighting the defeat.

He smiled as he walked over to me and knelt down, wrapping his fingers around my throat. "Do you really think you can win?" he began tightening his grip.

"Not alone, not now," Edmond's voice boomed from behind the Adversary.

The Adversary released my throat and rose to face Edmond. "Do you ever get tired of being beaten?"

"Not when my friend is about to die," Edmond said.

I turned slowly where I laid and saw Edmond standing there and Feargal cowering in the corner. Edmond's gleaming blade laying on the stone floor as the masters of combat advanced toward each other.

"Always the hero," the Adversary's step quickened. "But I have news for you," the two ran at each other and met in the middle of the hallway. The Adversary threw the first blow to Edmond's side.

"Heroes die," he hissed as he kicked Edmond's leg out from under him.

Edmond glared up at the Adversary. "Heroes sacrifice," he leapt to his feet and dodged the fist of his foe. "Heroes give their all!" he spun and kicked the Adversary's chest.

The Adversary sneered as he flew upon Edmond with a volley of blows, but Edmond dodged and blocked them all. Even though he was as weary as a soldier on the front lines, he still fought. He still gave his all.

The Adversary threw another punch, but Edmond swept it aside and struck the Adversary in the throat. The dark menace stumbled back for a moment grasping his neck. "How?" he gnashed his teeth. "How?" he plowed himself into Edmond in fury.

Edmond was thrown back by the force and was just getting to his knees when the Adversary began choking him.

I watched in horror as Edmond struggled to breathe.

"You are a fool," he dropped Edmond's beaten and bloody form unto the stone floor. "Do you really think you can escape from the shadows? Escape from me?" He kicked Edmond and turned to Feargal. "Escape from Apollo," he grinned at the terrified captain.

"Please," Feargal cowered before the imposing darkness. "What do you want?" he quaked.

The Adversary pulled Feargal up by his hair. "You know his name," he spat. "You all know his name," he punched Feargal in the gut. "Never forget," he punched again. "Never in all your days will you forget," he loosed a blow to Feargal's face which felled him.

"That I bring death!" he kicked Feargal again and left him just as unconscious as Edmond.

The harbinger of death turned his gaze to me. "This is what happens when you play with darkness," he turned and lifted Edmond's sword from the ash. "A shame," his voice echoed with victory, "that you should all die like this," he gave a kick to Feargal. He rose up the sword above Feargal and glanced at me with a sadistic grin. "Broken," both hands clasped the sword as he stared, preparing to strike the captain once and for all.

I closed my eyes to block out the sight and clenched my teeth. A sudden scream of agony shattered the silence of the halls, but it was not Feargal's scream. I opened my eyes to see Edmond's sword falling to the floor, and the Adversary howling in pain as flames engulfed his hands and crept up his arms.

He flailed around for a few minutes until the flames were finally extinguished. Gazing upon his hands, burned nearly to the bone, he clenched his teeth and glared first at the sword, then at me, then Edmond. He let out one last cry, then turned and threw himself through the castle wall into the small moat. From there he rose and ran northward.

'There is a way out,' I thought desperately, staring into the dim light coming from the hole. I glanced at Edmond and saw the rope, still tied to his belt. I sighed in realization that the nightmare of Dourdan was finally over. But the horror of what I saw outside snuffed out all relief.

XIII

VOICE OF THE PAST

I struggled up onto the shore of the moat and gritted my teeth as I gazed upon the land surrounding the castle. All around the smoke was rising from the charred earth, and the smoke entering with each breath came the unmistakable odor of burned flesh. Chills ran down my spine as I gazed across the smoldering remains of the province. Nothing but ash remained of the countryside – nothing but desolation.

Edmond was the last to lower himself from the rope and rose up from the water next to me and Feargal.

"I told you the Varanus left the castle," Feargal sat up and gazed around us. "I told you there would be nothing left."

I shook my head. "We cannot give up," I pushed myself up onto my knees. "We must find out who is behind all of this. Only then can we stop him."

Edmond sat up as well. "How?" he asked. "There is so little we know and understand."

I stood up and began walking north toward England. "I do not know," I said as I turned back to them. "But somehow, we have to stop him."

Edmond and Feargal joined me a moment later and we walked together in silence.

The smoke obscured most of our vision. Glowing embers from the surrounding trees were scattered like rubies as far as the eye could see, and interwoven were the dastardly tracks of the Varanus in every direction. Holocaust was the only word that described the destruction.

'Who are you?' I thought as we walked. 'Who is Apollo?' I gritted my teeth as I thought back to anyone who knew the Brethren. To anyone who hated us or longed to control the world.

'But then there is the Alignment,' I thought, 'Edmond mentioned that it was odd that the Alignment was happening as the war unfolded. Could it be that this Apollo knows of it? That he knew of its power?' my breath quickened. There is only one way he would know. If he was part of the Brethren, but not just any member. He had to be a leader.

I bit my lower lip as all the leaders of the Brethren flashed through my mind. Then I came to Roger Wilson. 'He knew about the Alignment,' I thought. 'He knew how to tear us apart. He was in league with the Adversary, for that was the dark being who attacked me when I was sent to Birmingham!'

All the pieces fell into place.

'He is in charge of the Brethren in France and let the Varanus in,' anger rose within me. I did not want to believe it, but it was all there. He had to be Apollo. 'Roger wants the King dead,' I stopped walking. Edmond and Feargal glanced at me in confusion.

"Are you all right?" Edmond asked.

'His family had position to the throne and if the King was out of the way, what would stop him from assuming it? And the slave trade that is how the Khans were overthrown. Roger sent them to the Khanites so that they could rampage through the countryside!'

'Roger is a man of power, and he lusts for it. He will not stop until he gets it.' Henry's words echoed in my mind.

"Richard?" Edmond asked again.

I turned to him. "Roger is Apollo," I stammered.

Edmond's brow furrowed. "What?"

"Roger Wilson is behind all of this," I remembered what he said on the ship. 'You have no need to protect me from the secrets of this world, I know how it burns.' "He testified to it. Back on the Silver Star he said that he knows how the world burns," I gestured to the abyss all around us. "This is what he did to the Khans and he told us, but we were too blind to see!"

"Do you hear what you are saying Richard," Edmond glared into my eyes. "He is our brother."

"I was not the only one who thought he was acting strange," I protested. "So did Andrew. We told you to be on guard and you agreed!"

"To be on guard, yes, but this is madness," Edmond said coldly.

"But what if he is?" Feargal asked Edmond. "What if Roger is..." he stopped, dreading to say the name. "It would be our fault if we did nothing."

"We need to find Andrew," Edmond fumed through his iron set jaw. "That is all we can do now."

I knelt down and lay my hand upon the stone foundation of a smoldering house. The heat of the stone warmed my chilled fingers, but nothing could warm my thoughts.

'You have no need to protect me from the secrets of this world, I know how it burns.' Roger's words came to me as I stared at the coals in rage. "He knew this would come," I stammered as I looked up at Edmond "He wanted this." I looked back down at my own hands. "Do you think I want to believe it?"

"Richard," Edmond replied. "He fought with us. He dedicated his life."

I leapt up and faced Edmond. "He used us!"

"No," Edmond clenched his teeth.

"Who would you choose to be King when the entire royal family is dead? A peasant? Or the last leader of the Brethren? A man who brought peace to England. A man who knows policies and politics. And who could stand against him?"

Edmond was silent.

"Roger has betrayed us Edmond," I bit my lower lip and sighed. "I am sorry."

We walked in deep silence until nightfall. When we found a cave to rest, Feargal went right to sleep. I however stayed awake with Edmond for a while.

"I am sorry," Edmond said after a long silence. "I do not want to believe it."

"Neither do I," I replied.

Edmond gazed slowly at the land surrounding the cave. "Do you remember when we were young?" the corners of his mouth rose.

"We worked on the farm, trying to get all the work done so we could be taught by Andrew. Be it sword or science, we were always happy to be with him."

I nodded. "Days of peace," I sighed. "Days when we did not have to worry about war and peace."

"I remember the harvest. You always came to help us," he smiled.

"Because I knew how it felt, not having a father there for you," I answered.

"How is it that we came to this?" his smile disappeared. "How did the world come to this?" his jaw set. "I remember the days of peace. I remember the joy."

"We became the Brethren to help people, and that is all we have done!" I turned to face him. "We have fought and died for hope, it is not our fault."

"Roger is our brother," Edmond stared deep into my eyes. "He is our fault. It is just like that castle – we were too late to stop the destruction."

I shook my head. "We have to stop him. We cannot let him do any more harm."

"I am willing to do what is necessary, but I will never forgive myself if he is innocent," Edmond gritted his teeth. "I will never forgive myself if I strike down a blameless brother."

"I know," I put my hand on his shoulder. "I wish we were still in Durrington."

"No," Edmond replied. "We were put here for a reason. We are here to make a change, and if I have to, I will go to any length to achieve it."

I nodded.

"Get some rest," he forced a smile and I obliged.

At the far end of the cave, I laid down as exhaustion swept over me.

The world was dark and rain poured from the sky. But it was different, there was no Adversary upon the hill. In his place, a great scepter stood. It was made of a black, cloudy metallic substance. It was around 5 feet high and was covered in foreign writing that was carved in gleaming red along the handle. At the top of the handle, there was a carved crimson dragon so detailed that it made my best work look trivial. Each of the dragon's scales were perfectly aligned and sized. The eye of the dragon gleamed like a glowing emerald which cut to the soul. Above the dragon were three blades which seemed to pierce through reality itself. Suspended in between the blades was an orb – a dark globe of impending doom. The sight of the scepter melted any courage I had left.

"Look around you," a dark, menacing voice pierced the silence.

A dark figure rose up upon the hill, grasping the scepter, and directing it toward me. "This is where your path leads."

The battlefield stretched further than I could see. Millions of dead were everywhere and I could not help but feel that I was responsible.

"Roger," I gritted my teeth. "Apollo. All this time it was you!"

The being's face was indistinguishable, but his eyes were filled with pain.

"Come out of the shadows!" I yelled. "I am coming for you!"

He shook his head. "You will find me," he said as he raised his scepter, "when shadows mark the line and five stars rise,"

As he said these words, a wave of darkness flew from the scepter's orb and enveloped me. And as the searing pain bit into me, I heard one more whisper.

"Words are over."

XIV

ONE WAR

I sat up and glanced around the cave. 'Roger is Apollo,' I thought in grief. 'A man who fought alongside us, a man we trusted,' part of me wanted to hate him, but I could not. All my hate hung upon the Adversary.

I rose up as I contemplated the two men who seemed to have overcome the world. As I stood, I remembered the words of the Adversary. Piper and I were fighting the Varanus, before Luke came and when I accused him of killing my father, he said, 'And yet you have forgotten my name.' The words haunted me like a great burden.

I came to the entrance of the cave and sat down beside Edmond.

"What is wrong?" he asked as I came.

"It is all wrong," I took a deep breath. "Edmond, I remembered something."

He raised an eyebrow as he turned to me.

"I think I knew the Adversary," I clenched my teeth. "A long time ago,"

"We also know Roger, what else is new?" he dryly turned back to face the desolation.

"The Adversary killed my father," I said.

Edmond slowly turned back to me. "He what?"

"He killed my mother and my father," I bit my lip. "He killed them."

"I am sorry Richard," Edmond replied with sympathy lacing his voice. "But we cannot think about that, it will only bring more death,"

"No matter what we do there will be death," I countered. "I have been having visions Edmond, visions of where we are going. We are going to ruin and chaos."

"There is no way of knowing that for sure," he sighed. "Chaos and ruin are always the consequences of war."

"Not like this," I objected. "What Roger plans to do is far more than war," I suddenly remembered the poem. 'When shadows mark the line and five stars rise,' the words repeated themselves over and over in my head. "When shadows mark the line and five stars rise. Where Have I heard that before?"

"When shadows mark the line and five stars rise, when truth fails and mercy dies, now the light shines in the skies," Edmond said.

"Part of an old poem, Bennet was singing it on the ship."

"The light," I exclaimed, "it means the Alignment. Roger means to use the Alignment."

"How do you know?" Edmond asked.

"Why would he not?" I asked. "Roger has always wanted power."

"But how does that help us stop him? Knowing that he desires the power to destroy the human race does not help us find him and stop him. Even if it is him."

"There are four possible places Roger may be: Durrington, our base of operations, Birmingham, his home, the ring of stone and Shrewton," I shuddered at the name. 'My old home,' I thought.

"Why Shrewton?" Edmond asked.

"The Adversary killed my parents in Shrewton when the plague swept through," I replied. "He was in the city when it was quarantined therefore he must have lived there. No one would have let him in for several weeks after we were sure the plague was over."

"So you are saying he must have lived there? But that was thirteen years ago," Edmond retorted. "Surely he would not still live there, with all that has been happening."

I continued. "Shrewton is closer to the ring of stone and the Alignment. If the Adversary lived there, it would be a likely place for them to regroup."

Feargal sat up and looked over at us groggily. "What are you all jabbering about?"

"And why would he be at Birmingham then?" Edmond asked.

"If Shrewton is closer to where he wants to be, then that is where we will go. But first to Durrington," said Edmond, "we must resupply."

I nodded in agreement.

"What is going on?" Feargal stumbled over to the entrance of the cave.

"We are going to Durrington," Edmond announced as he stood up. "Roger is likely at Shrewton, but we must resupply first."

Feargal nodded. "If resupply means food, then I like that plan."

The three of us threw on our armour, and coming back to the entrance of the cave, looked out over the desolate landscape.

I turned to look at Edmond. "Whatever happens," I said, the memory of Apollo's words rose within my mind, 'This is where your path leads,' I shuddered. "You are my brother."

He turned to me. "So was Roger."

We both turned again and gazed over the landscape. Smoke rose from every direction and rubble was strewn everywhere. This is what England would come too. This is what the world would come to if we fail. "If we cannot do this. If we lose this war, we lose the world."

"That is why we lose it," a voice came from beyond the cave. A voice of peace. The voice of Piper. I whipped my head around and laid my eyes upon her and Luke. Tears entered my eyes as I hurried toward her and laid my hand on her shoulder.

"You came back?" I stammered.

"I saw who you were," she said. She seemed to begin to tear up as well. "My brother was wrong to judge you so quickly. And I was wrong in following him. I am sorry."

"Brother?" I could almost feel Edmond's gaze. "He is your brother?"

"Who did you think I was?" Luke stated bluntly. "I am not her husband. Were you worried Richard?" Luke asked with a smirk.

"Anything I thought before no longer matters," I answered trying to hold back the tears. "He judged me rightly. Though I may not be on Apollo's side, I am still unworthy of your kindness. There is no need to be sorry."

"What made you change your mind?" Edmond asked.

"I was blinded by fear," Luke explained. "When Piper and I fled from you, I did not know where the tunnels were. So we followed you for quite a while, and in that time we overheard some of your conversations. We now realize that you were fighting the Varanus and the Adversary as much as we were."

I walked over to Luke and embraced him. "All the same," I said, "it is good to have you both back."

"Aye," stated Edmond, "but I am afraid that the worst is still waiting for us."

"The Varanus will not be too difficult to defeat with England by our side," Luke said. "The majority of those burning stench buckets are already dead."

"Dead?" I asked. "What do you mean?"

"I mean dead, is there any other definition?" Luke retorted. "Dead, not alive, deceased, without breath nor stench. Clear?"

"How?" asked Feargal.

"We do not know," replied Piper. "They are everywhere though, the statues."

"Do you know how many are still living?" I asked.

"Not many on this side of the channel," Luke said. "I cannot figure out though why they all died."

"In any case," Piper spoke out, "even if the Varanus made it to England, they would not make it far. The Irish, English and Scots have the upper hand and a defensive position, seeing that the Varanus would come from the sea."

"Perhaps," Feargal spoke, "however, there are few who know to be alert and none who know how to kill them."

"True," I replied. "And we do not know if he is still alive," I said, referring to Andrew.

"Well, where would he be if he were alive?" Asked Luke, "and who is this 'he' you are talking about? Not another Adversary person is it?"

"No, thankfully. Durrington most likely," replied Edmond. "His name is Andrew, Luke. He is the backbone of the Brethren. He is a light in great darkness, standing out even among our brothers. It is because of him that we are here."

"Well then we go to Durrington," Piper answered. "There is no use staying here as the Adversary goes on the attack."

"No, not Durrington. Andrew would be at the ring," I continued. "It is not the Adversary we should worry about," I hesitated. "It is Apollo. However, I believe I know where he is."

"Apollo?" asked Luke. "What kind of name is that? And do all of them start with an A?"

"His name does not change who he is. He is the one behind all of this, behind everything that has happened here in France and in Khan Kipchak," I said. "And we believe he is in England."

"Where in England?" asked Piper.

"We do not know yet;" said Edmond, "however the most likely location is in Shrewton. Richard?" Edmond inquired.

"He will be in Shrewton, waiting for us to gather for the Alignment," I replied.

"Alignment?" asked Piper.

"Aye," I explained. "The Alignment is a phenomenon which happens only once in every one thousand years."

"And it just so happens that it is occurring in the next few days?" asked Piper.

"Yes," I replied, "but what it does is more amazing. You see, the sun and moon align on either side of the earth, and the sun releases energy which passes through the earth and reflects off the moon and back up through the ring of stone."

"So what you are saying," Luke remarked, "is that the sun and moon are aligning and sending a beam of death or life through the earth, which this Apollo character wants to control so that he can become all powerful. And you want to be there when it happens, eh?"

"Precisely," remarked Feargal, then began a befuddled look on his face as though he disbelieved his own words.

"Well, that is one I have never heard before!" Luke announced. "But count me in! Might as well see the 'Alignment' if there will not be another for the next thousand years."

"We are all in this," I said. "There are no more sides to it – it is just him and the rest of mankind."

"What are we waiting for?" Piper asked.

"There are no more options," Edmond spoke out, "it is either die here or die there. That is all there is to it."

"Way to put a good view on it, Edmond," Luke slapped Edmond's shoulder. "I choose to go," Luke continued. "I do not care who this Apollo is. He has done this much, and I will not see him do any more. Even if I perish in the end, I choose to face this threat head on – no matter the cost!"

"Then it is on to the ring of stone," Edmond said. "To Andrew and to death."

"More wonderful views Edmond," Luke clapped. "More encouragement!"

And so the five of us left the cave.

France, though it was dead now, had brought us together, and together we made our way to the coast. Nothing more remained in France except the thousands of dead statues littering the countryside. Even the rivers seemed dead, like they had somehow been burned.

Although the road was rough, nothing mattered more to us than getting back to England and unifying the Brethren once again. Within three days we made it to the coast at Cherbourg, where we had left Andrew. The town was burned to the foundations like every other town we had seen since leaving Château de Dourdan.

We walked out onto the gloomy beach. Ash mixed with the sand and painted the water a dull grey color. There were no more ships in the harbor, neither was there a harbor. The Varanus had come and destroyed it all.

I ran my fingers through my filthy hair, hoping to find a solution. There was nothing to build a boat with, nor was there any chance we could swim so far to England. But my mind soon drifted to the Adversary. Every second we delayed, he and Roger got closer to their goal. I collapsed into the sand and lay there. Exhausted and beaten by a strip of water. 'Surely we have not come this far to fail,' I told myself. 'We must find a way.'

"Richard," Piper quietly spoke my name after a moment of

silence.

I looked up and around, and everyone was watching one thing, looking to the water.

I glanced to whatever it was that caught their attention. Edmond's broad form stood out of the water twenty feet away from the shore. He waded slowly deeper into the sea, with the waves breaking against him. He seemed neither cold nor tired.

"Edmond!" I yelled as I stood up. "Edmond!" I cried again. He stopped walking, but he did not turn around.

"There is a ship!" exclaimed Piper. "There!" she pointed far in front of Edmond.

The ship caught my eye, but it was hopeless, there was no way we could get there. It was at least two miles away. "Edmond!" I yelled. "It is impossible! No man alive can swim that far!"

He turned his head to face us, "None of those men had a reason," his expression was resolute as if the cold of the water and distance to the ship was of no account. "It is time," he continued, "To do whatever is necessary," his voice was the strongest I had ever heard it, but a tinge of fear was still in it. "No more will I hide!" his voice rose to a shout above the sound of the waves crashing against the beach. "No more will I let darkness reign!" he turned back and faced the sea. "The time has come to unify mankind!" he unbuckled his armour and let it fall into the water. "To let the Brethren rise!" he unstrapped his gauntlet and threw it into the sea. He looked back at us for a moment and his eyes locked with mine. He was ready to do what had to be done and it was clear that I was to follow. Then he disappeared into the water.

I ran to the shore throwing my gauntlets and armour into the dark sand. Feargal caught me just as I was about to leap in after Edmond, who was now over forty feet away.

"Let me go!" I shook Feargal off of me.

"You will never make it! It is too far!" he yelled at me. "No man alive would make it! You said so yourself!"

"He is my friend!" I protested. "I am not letting him go alone!"

"Richard there is no way!" Feargal thundered.

"Then we will be food for the sharks," said Luke as he leapt into the sea. Piper was close behind him. "Or the fish," he swam forward "Or the rays," he gulped up a bit of water by accident "Oh you get the point!" he coughed out water and continued swimming.

"It is time Feargal, as Edmond said," I began to tremble, for I still doubted what would come from our endeavors and what would become of us. "Are you with us Feargal? Are you willing to do whatever is necessary?"

His eyes filled with fear as he stared at me. "Are you?" he stammered.

I let my head fall and locked my gaze upon the ground for a moment, then faced Feargal once more. "If it means the Adversary's death," I turned and began walking again into the water, "I am willing!"

"I am but a ship's captain," Feargal protested. "I do not think that is what the Brethren needs. You need warriors, soldiers, and I am neither. I am not enough. None of us are!"

"If we are not enough, nothing is! We are all this world has got left. Peace is over, it is time for war," I gritted my teeth and looked back at Feargal who still stood where I left him. "I would rather die bringing justice to that murderer, than die in his trap!" With that, I leapt into the water and began swimming toward the distant ship. Feargal hesitantly followed. But as I swam I could not forget Feargal's words, 'I am not enough,' I thought, 'none of us are.'

The waves rose and fell higher than I had ever seen before. It seemed as if we would be swept away at any moment. The cold of the water bit through me like a thousand needles. As soon as we began, a strong west wind began blowing us off course. It was unbearable with the biting cold and the water stinging our eyes like bitter tears. Still, Edmond swam boldly forward, uncomplaining and showing no pain. Piper and Luke continued behind him at a close distance. Feargal was close behind me, swimming slowly, yet keeping a powerful steady pace. I knew not how they could continue.

After about half an hour the pain in my shoulder returned. It felt like a fire, steadily increasing with every stroke. I smiled through the pain though, remembering that Luke caused me this pain, but now he and Piper were once again with us.

Within the hour, I found myself using only one arm, trying to keep my pace, but steadily slowing down. Finally, I stopped, my arm felt as if it would fall off. I floated and looked out – the ship seemed just as far off as when we had begun. I looked up at the cloud-covered sun, and it, like us, striving to break through its bonds and reach across the world. Feargal came up next to me within another minute.

"Well it seems that all the world has got is about to die," Feargal stopped next to me and began treading water. "There is no way we can make it to that ship. We have been led to our death!" he scowled.

"I told you we should have stayed in Château de Dourdan!"

"Perhaps," I gasped and pushed onward. "But I have a meeting in Shrewton that cannot be missed!"

After a short while, I caught up with Piper, who was slowly falling behind Edmond and Luke's strong pace.

"Come on," I told her as I approached. "We must keep going!"

"I am fine," she gasped, catching her breath. "Go on ahead."

I smiled as I tread water next to her. "I can wait."

Slowly the ship came within shouting distance as it sailed in our direction and we came up to the side of the ship with the waves now higher than ever, and the wind steadily getting stronger. The pain in my arm was nearly unbearable.

"Well then," said Luke looking up the side of the ship, "if they are pirates, I will strangle you, Edmond. Three times, just to make sure."

"We have seen monsters rise and kingdoms fall," Edmond replied coolly. "I doubt anyone, even pirates would be reluctant to help us after all that has happened."

XV

THE MAN OUT OF TIME

"Ahoy!" a voice from the ship rang out from the deck and we all looked up.

"Captain," the man shouted, "lads overboard off the port bow!"

The captain came to the side of the ship, "By England," the captain gasped, "I do believe you are right!"

"Well if you do not mind," shouted Luke, "these 'lads' would like to come aboard!"

"Quite right," the captain said to himself. "Hoist them up!" he yelled.

Several ropes were thrown over the side of the ship. "Loop the ropes around yourselves," the captain ordered.

We did so, and the ropes began to tighten. Slowly we were hoisted onto the ship. Piper was the first aboard, Luke second, Edmond third, then Feargal and me last. I untied myself and looked around the ship. It was spotless. It was by far the cleanest ship I ever saw.

The crew stared maliciously at us. They were well dressed, but their smiles were forced and their eyes bore malice. At first glance, I saw nothing, but as the sound of swords scraped out of their sheaths, I realized that there was something sinister afoot.

"Luke," I leaned over to him, "I do believe you were right

about the pirates."

"Why do I have to be right," he sighed, his head downcast. "Why could not Edmond have thought it was pirates? He is the soldier!"

"What is it?" Piper asked as she drew near to hear what Luke was saying.

"Pirates," Edmond stated just as cool headed as he was in the channel.

"Wait," Luke exclaimed, "You knew? Make it four times then! Five, maybe six! After I hang you!"

Edmond drew his sword and readied himself for a fight "I did not know, but I do believe we will arrive in England a bit behind schedule."

"My sincere apologies," said the captain smoothing back his shimmering black hair, "especially for the fair maiden," he grinned mischievously at Piper, flashing his deep amber eyes. "However," he looked at Edmond, "a man has got to make a living, no matter how much inconvenience to his inferiors," he motioned his hand, and all the crew was upon us. Edmond had his sword and Piper her dagger, but the rest of us faced the crew with no more than our fists. The first crew member was quickly dispatched by Edmond and thrown aside, followed by several more as Edmond's mastery of swordplay and hand-to-hand combat was quickly revealed.

"Oh, I have missed enemies who do not regrow limbs!" Luke yelled above the rage of battle.

Edmond wrenched his sword from the body of a crew member, "Who are you?" he demanded. "And what is the meaning of this?"

"This is the Crimson Sea," smirked the Captain, "and I am her captain, Victor Blackheart – Victor over the Varanus; the deliverer of France, and the dream of hope for humanity!"

"You and I both know that is not true!" hollered Luke,

slamming his fist into a crew member's jaw, knocking him off the ship. "You have no concept of dreams!"

"Perhaps," replied Victor straightening his black coat. "But that threat is gone now. Left dead on the coast."

I stopped instantly. "What?"

"The Varanus," a crack of thunder interrupted Victor's voice. "They cannot cross the water!" he laughed. "So mighty are they? Yet beaten by the English Channel. So, now there are hundreds of ships coming from the mainland on their way to England for safety, and they are all just waiting for me."

"You monster!" I shouted as I ran over to him. "You have no idea what you are doing!"

"Oh no," said Victor just as I reached him. "This," he pulled a vial of black liquid from his coat, "this is the monster."

"What is that?"

"This, young fool, was taken from the mouth of a Varanus as he attacked me at the harbor. This is what transforms them."

I stared at him, "No," I stammered, "you would not do that. That would kill every man on this ship!" The rain began to pour.

"And how do we know you are telling the truth?" Piper yelled.

Luke threw his hands up. "That is a chance I am not going to take. Where is the brig?"

"One of us gets this in our blood and we all go down in smoke," Victor smiled.

I clenched my teeth and felt for my absent gauntlet. "You would not do that!" my rage boiled.

"Do not doubt what I am capable of. I found out the Varanus' weakness; do you think I would not find yours?"

I fell silent.

"So," he smiled triumphantly, rain streaking down his pompous face. "I suggest that you surrender." He held up the vial, pulled out a dagger and laid it on his arm. "I will not let you go alive."

"Done!" Luke held his hands higher. "Where is the brig?"

We stood back in silence.

"Fine then." He put a gash in his arm and opened the vial. "Think of their lives," he gestured to the crew. "Think of your friends. Must more blood be spilled?" he asked. "You will surrender, or everyone here will die."

I looked back at our company, Piper handed her dagger to a crew member, and she, Luke and Feargal were led down below the deck. Edmond walked up to Victor, and, staring straight into his eyes, stabbed his sword into the floor planks.

Edmond let go of the sword and left it lodged in the floor. "Keep it safe, I will be needing it later," he threw down the sheath and walked confidently below deck.

Victor sealed the vial and put it in his coat. He then grabbed Edmond's sword for a moment, but let go in searing pain. "It is cursed!" he yelled in pain. "The sword is cursed!"

The crew stared hatefully at us then at Victor.

I turned and followed Edmond below deck toward our uncertain fate.

A large wave hit the ship and caused me to slip and tumble down the soaked steps. The moment I was down I was harassed by two of the pirates to one of the three prison cells and pushed inside.

"You will regret this!" I yelled at the guard as he locked the cell and walked away. Another large wave hit and threw me against the bars. "Mark my words," I clenched my teeth through the pain shooting through my jaw, "you will regret it!"

"Unless you find a way out Richard," a man spoke from behind me, "he won't regret anything."

I turned in surprise to see a familiar face with me in the cell.

"Bennet?"

Bennet stood up and with a weak salute said, "It's me," he smiled and then collapsed back onto the waterlogged bench in the back of the cramped cell. "Andrew is back in England now."

"Bennet Burnell survived all this time? The man who runs?" I exclaimed elated to see my old friend.

"Chief messenger of the Brethren," he said, "you think I would go down that easily?" he chuckled.

"You said Andrew was safe?"

"As safe as he can be for the time being," continued Bennet. "As you probably know, the Varanus cannot cross water. So, they died in France from their own poison."

"Their own poison?" I asked.

"My theory is that when they run out of people to infect, the venom builds up eventually killing them."

"Clever," I commended. "What did you say about the water though?"

"They cannot cross it."

"Yes, that is what the captain said, but they must have crossed rivers and such on their way to the coast," I pointed out. "And they must have experienced rain?"

"How?" asked Bennet, questioning his own knowledge. "None of them got in the water! They chased me to the coast. I saw that they would not follow me once I had gotten to the ship."

"They chased you?" I stared at him "How? You should have been long gone by the time the Varanus left Château de Dourdan."

"I would have been, however, I came back to tell you of Andrew's escape and also that the King was with him."

"Edward?" I asked.

"Aye," he replied.

"That makes one good report," I replied. "But what stopped them? What stopped the Varanus from coming after you?" I thought through it over and over.

"Salt," Piper shouted from the cell she and Luke shared. "It must be the salt in the channel!"

"Salt," echoed Bennet thoughtfully, "that must be it!"

"So," I said, breaking up Bennet's thoughts, "they cannot stand the salt in the water. It is like a fish in a lake that cannot stand the ocean."

"Precisely!" Piper exclaimed.

I nodded and began thinking it through. But what good was it to know the Varanus' weakness, when we were bound up here by a pirate's folly.

***

The ship rose and fell. Feargal and Luke had long since fallen asleep. Edmond however, who had not said a word throughout the conversation, sat thoughtfully on the bench running his hands through his hair. "I am sorry," he spoke.

"For what?" I asked.

"I got us into this. I thought we could get to England."

"Edmond it is not your fault," Piper said. "You got us here, and you would have taken the entire ship to get us back. There is nothing to be ashamed of."

Edmond looked up at me and then Piper. "We will get out of here," he said. "No matter what the cost." We all fell silent and slowly drifted off to sleep.

A few hours later, a pirate came down and threw food to us, then left without saying a word.

One hour later another pirate came down and opened my cell.

"Get up," he snarled.

I stood up slowly and stumbled out of the cell.

"Keep your head," Bennet nodded to me. I raised an eyebrow. "You will know when you see it," he said as the cell door clinked back into place.

I was led past the stairs which lead up to the main deck, and then through a hallway adjacent to the brig and stopped in front of another door.

The pirate grabbed my shoulders and stared into my eyes with his one. "As your friend said, keep your wits about you!"

I bowed my head and entered the small, damp, putrid room. A man sat on the other side of the room at a desk with his back toward me, but I knew who he was by the length and shine of his back hair and the manner in which he postured himself.

The pirate strapped me down in a chair, opposite the one Victor sat in and with one last sorrowful glance, he left. And that is when I why Bennent had warned me to keep my head.

I stared all around. Lining every wall, shelf and desk were jars, dozens of them with hundreds of eyeballs inside them. And one in Victor's hand.

"My apologies sir," Victor spun around and faced me as he placed the eye into a jar, "I did not get your name."

I stared at him in horror and strained against the leather straps which held me down.

"Fine then," he grinned and stood up, setting the jar onto his desk with a loud thud, "you have two options," he plucked up a knife from the desk and stopped smiling. "Option one is what I like to call the hard way, in which I pluck out both your eyes and leave you in the brig forever if you do not cooperate."

"What is option two?" I asked, still trying to take in horror.

"I lied, there is no option two," he scowled, "most men start screaming once I mention option one."

"I am not like most men," I scowled back.

"Well then I will have to come up with an option two," he leaned forward to me and laid the knife onto my face. "But in the meantime. Let us have a little fun shall we?" I spat in his face and he reeled back, wiping his sleeve across his face, momentarily hiding his deep amber gaze. "Option two!" his eyes gleamed wide with hatred and pure spite. "I go get the pretty Scottish girl, and I take her beautiful blue eyes, rather than your green blobs of kelp!" he scowled.

"I choose option one," I replied.

"And you will answer all my questions to my satisfaction or else I will use option two. Am I understood?"

"Aye," I clenched my teeth. "What do you want?"

"Who are you?" Blackheart asked cooly.

"My name is Richard Armistead," I replied.

"Who do you work for?" he asked.

"I work for no one," I answered.

"What do you call yourselves?"

I shook my head, but was reminded of option two. "The Brethren," I said reluctantly.

"And who are you?" he inquired as the ship began to rock. "What does the Brethren do? Besides get themselves captured?"

I struggled against my restraints and clenched my teeth harder. "We are no one you need worry about," I grimaced.

"What do you know of the Varanus?" he changed the direction of his assault.

"I know they are dead. And where they came from," I replied.

"And where is that?" Victor grinned. "Where do they come from?"

"Same place you came from," I replied.

"Oh? And where did I come from?"

"From hell," I scowled.

He punched me in the face, throwing me and my chair back from the impact. He then knelt down and grabbed my throat. "And I will make you go there if you ever speak to me like that again!" The ship rocked once more and Victor was thrown off balance. He straightened up and glared at me. "Today is your lucky day," he glowered. "For when I take your eyes, I want it to be clean. Like this one!" he pulled one out of a jar and stared at it, stroking it. "I do not like messes. Back to the brig!" he hollered and I was dragged back and thrown into my cell.

I lay on the floor of the cell, dwelling on the horror of Blackheart. I could not bring myself to believe his brutality.

I looked up and saw that Edmond and the rest were staring at me as if to say, 'I am sorry,' I supposed Bennet told them of the eyes. I turned and faced Bennet who was staring off into the distance, rather, at the pirate as he walked away.

"You had better rest," Bennet said.

"How do you know the poem?" I asked, trying to divert my mind from the eyes.

"The poem?" Bennet asked, with equal exhaustion. "What poem?"

"When shadows mark the line, and five stars," my voice trailed off as I realized how tired I truly was.

"It is the Song of the Dream," Bennet replied.

"Where did you?" my voice trailed off again.

"Learn it?" Bennet replied. "It is one of the few things I remember from my father."

"Who was your father?" I asked.

"A poet and a warrior," Bennet sighed. "We had better rest,

we must..."

I heard no more as I entered my sorrowful sleep.

"Richard," a voice entered my head. "Richard!"

I looked up and saw the Adversary. "What do you want now?" we stood near the bow of the Crimson Sea as it sailed on a sea of darkness.

"Beware," he said. "The ship you are on holds great danger."

"You want me dead, so why would you care?" I grimaced.

"I do not," he replied. "My master wants you. Not your corpse lying dead on this ship."

"Why does he care? Roger betrayed us!" I yelled.

"Your fear is misplaced. Do not fear Roger," the Adversary countered.

"I hate him. I do not fear him; what I fear is not getting off this ship!"

A large bang shook the ship.

"Richard, do not fear surviving the ship, fear her captain," the Adversary's voice carried into my soul as I felt that he was truly warning me.

"Who is he?" I questioned.

"It is what he will become that you must fear," the Adversary replied. A crack of thunder followed his words.

"Why do you care?" I asked in confusion.

He gripped my throat. "I do not," he stared into my eyes, then threw me to the deck. "And the rest is not for me to say," another bang hit the ship and threw me from the vision.

My eyes opened swiftly and I stared anxiously around the cell. I could hear a storm outside and the crew running about the deck. Another bang snapped me back to my senses. I looked around the brig and saw Edmond and Feargal battering their door with the wooden bench from their cell.

"What are you doing?" I asked dully.

"I am getting us out," Edmond replied as he and Feargal readied themselves for another ram.

Another bang rang out. "There has got to be a better way to get out!" I yelled.

Piper, Luke and Bennet awoke to the sound of another bang.

"Do you have any other ideas?" Edmond asked.

"I just do not believe it is a good idea to go up there."

"And why not?" Edmond demanded.

"I am not sure," I spoke in confusion and fear.

Another bang.

"Edmond," I said, "I had another vision! He warned me about what would happen if we went up there!"

Suddenly, the sound of footsteps could be heard coming down into the brig. A pirate, one of the two who pushed me to my cell, returned and angrily came up to Edmond's cell with his nostrils flaring and hair tangled like a wet mop on his head. No more courtesy to hide his wretched nature.

"One more noise out of you!" he yelled sticking his arm through the bars and pulling Edmond to the door. "And it is into the sea! There is a storm out there and you do not want to be swimming in an angry ocean!"

"You mean to say that all the crew is occupied?" Edmond grinned.

"By the way," interrupted Piper reaching through the bars and taking the keys to the cell off the man's belt "Would you be wanting these?" she held them up.

The pirate let go of Edmond, drew his sword and lay it on Piper's throat. "Give them here!"

"Yes but," Piper paused and watched Edmond and Feargal

preparing to batter the door again. "Would that be considered an order or can I say no?" she asked politely.

"It is an order wench!" the pirate screamed. Another bang rang throughout the brig. "That is it!" the pirate brought his sword from Piper's neck and grasping the bars of Edmond's cell. "That was your last chance fool!" he yelled, while Piper silently unlocked her cell and Luke's; then began to work on mine.

The pirate looked over at them. "No!" he exclaimed in horror and fury.

"Nothing to see here, be about your business," answered Luke as Piper opened the door to my cell and let me and Bennet out.

"No!" the pirate thundered and raised his sword. Edmond meanwhile, reached through the bars, grabbed the man and slammed him against the cell knocking him out. The pirate slumped to the floor.

"Well that is done," said Luke taking the keys from Piper and unlocking Edmond's cell. "Next comes the dirty work."

"Were you all planning that all along?" I asked staring at them.

"Aye," replied Edmond. "Well, I was, Piper and Luke just played along. And if you do not mind," he ran to the bottom of the steps which lead up to the main deck, "I have a sword to retrieve and a crew of pirates to take care of!"

He turned and ran out under the wailing sky.

"What are we waiting for?" I exclaimed as I ran up onto the deck, fully forgetting the Adversary's warning. I was instantly followed by Luke, Piper, and Feargal who was carrying the fallen pirate's sword.

Edmond ran over to his sword, still standing in its place. He pulled it out with ease. "No one could pick it up?" he announced to the frantic crew as they ran to and fro trying to secure the ship. "Come on then, are you not men?"

Torrents of rain poured from the sky such that the ship was slowly foundering and the crew, seeing Edmond retrieve his sword, and hearing his taunts, scrambled over to the challenge.

"Alas!" cried Edmond, as he poised his blade to meet the oncoming horde. "I am ready for you now!" he slashed with the flat of his blade and hit the first man's legs sending him crashing to the deck. I then ran up, took the fallen man's sword and fell upon the rest of the rabble.

And so, the battle for the Crimson Sea, turned crimson indeed.

"What in the name of England is going on out here?" Victor burst out of his cabin and stared at the battle unfolding before his eyes.

"By the blood of armies," he stammered, "how can they stand so long?"

"Blackheart!" Edmond yelled out stretching his arms. "Come on then, enough of your schemes, show me the power of your steel and we shall see your pride then!"

Victor straightened his black coat and drew his sword, "My pride, as you presume, is not misplaced," he smiled. "Your attempt to escape shall cost you," I remembered my vision as Victor brought his sword crashing around and hit Edmond's sword with a loud clang that deafened the rest of the battle. The clang was followed by the chilling screech of Victor's blade scraping down Edmond's sword and slamming into the hilt.

'What have we done?' I thought to myself as I froze upon the deck and watched Edmond and Victor face off. Two master swordsmen. Both equally passionate for their cause, both ready to pay the price.

The Adversary's words echoed in my mind. 'It is what he will become that you must fear,' his words were so loud it seemed as if they were being spoken at that moment. 'What will he become?' I thought.

My attention returned to the battle as Feargal slapped me on the back and gestured me to the back of the ship to access the rudder.

I leapt up the stairs to the stern and darted at the man controlling the rudder. He jumped up, drew his sword and rushed at me and Feargal. The helmsman swung his sword around, nearly hitting Feargal, who narrowly escaped by sliding on the wet wood under the blade. I then brought my sword crashing down scathing his left arm. He let out a scream of pain, though hardly noticeable during the rage of the storm and swung his sword slamming into mine causing me to nearly slip down the stairs. I gripped the railing, pulled myself back up and with my new momentum ran my sword through the marauder's chest. He staggered back, fell to his knees, and collapsed onto the wet planks of the forecastle.

    I looked down at the man at my feet. Blood was covering his shirt, and his face was beginning to morph in my mind, twisting and getting darker. The Adversary's grinning face soon captured me. 'It is what he will become that you must fear,' his words rang aloud in my thoughts, but my hatred of the monster was stronger. I raised my sword and struck him with all my strength.

    "Richard!" Feargal stared at me in astonishment. "He is dead!" he yelled.

    I looked down at the dead man, his face was splattered with blood and no sign of the Adversary. I nearly dropped my sword at the sight of my brutality and my hatred.

    "What have I done?" I stepped back in horror. "What have I done?"

    I felt someone punch me in the gut and looked up into Bennet's face. "What are you doing?" I gasped.

    "Get back in the battle!" he yelled. "What you've done is wrong, but," he grabbed my hand which held my sword and lay the blade on my chest, "the Lord forgives our sins, even as the battle rages." I looked down at the dead man and ignored Bennet. He shook me. "Richard," his tone was calmer. I stared back into his unflinching eyes. "War will always show us who we really are. It'll make the light brighter and the dark darker. Don't give in to the darkness!"

I gripped my sword tighter and pushed Bennet aside as I looked out onto the deck. Piper and Luke were on the port side of the main deck and were holding off many pirates. Edmond faced off with Victor and three other pirates, and was steadily falling back to the starboard bow. Each time one pirate fell under Edmond's blade another would take his place, but each one became more hesitant than the last.

Bennet leapt off the forecastle and began thrashing his sword upon the crew. I clenched my teeth and my fingers curled into fists around my sword as I stepped down the stairs to the bloodstained deck. Rain was thrown into my face with the blinding force of the wind. The cold also tried in vain to hinder me, but I would not heed it. Two crew members began running at me. I raised my sword and struck down the first and caught the second by the throat and cast him onto the deck.

I continued my advance with Victor always in sight. Yet another marauder swung his sword which I blocked and delivered a thrust into his shoulder. He stumbled back clutching his shoulder in pain as blood trickled through his fingers. The other man I had thrown down attacked me again, but this time with more care. I remembered all of Edmond's training and quickly put a gash in the man's left leg that sent him to his knee. Just before I was about to finish him off, the other, the sailor with the wounded shoulder assaulted me from the right. I parried his attack at the expense of my footing and hit the deck, rolling out of the way as the pirate's sword crashed down. I kicked the pirate in his wounded shoulder, which sent him screaming in pain as his sword clattered to the deck. I then grabbed his fallen weapon and dispatched him with it.

The second pirate was up again and ran at me with vengeance. Within a moment, he too lay next to his fallen comrade.

I turned back to Victor who was now backing away from his duel with Edmond. 'Coward,' I said to myself as I advanced toward him.

As I drew closer, a shred of doubt and shame entered my heart, but the hatred was too much to let go.

"It is over!" I yelled as I thrust my sword into the captain's back. He stopped as cold as the steel which pierced through his chest and slowly slumped down onto the wooden planks.

"What have you done?" Victor stammered as he lay on the deck in front of me.

I pulled out my sword. "Ended this pointless battle," I said.

All the pirates stopped fighting and stared at their fallen captain. "Surrender!" I yelled.

"Never." Victor stammered pulling himself to his feet as everyone stared in awe. "I…will not die…like this!" he pulled the Varanus venom from his bloodstained coat and smashed the glass vial into his wound. Screaming through the pain, he stumbled about the deck, coughing up blood as the venom of the Varanus seeped into his veins. "On the contrary," he slumped over the deck ten feet away from me. He coughed again and turned his head to face me. His eyes burned with hate and a new fire which I knew all too well. "I will not die at all," Black scales began to form on his face. "As this creature burns me," he yelled. "It will do the same to you!" he grabbed my throat, burning me with his touch "You are the one who will die!" Fire began to consume him and burn me. At that moment, I felt the weight of shame. I knew that death was coming for me and was coming quickly. I fought it at first, then in resignation, closed my eyes.

"No!" Bennet ran up tackling the monster and pushing him to the rails. I collapsed upon the deck and turned to Bennet. "Tell me, Victor, how does a Varanus feel about the sea?" Bennet yelled as he pushed Victor over the railing. But as Victor's burning form fell he caught hold of Bennet's neck pulling him over the side with him.

Bennet grabbed the rail with one hand and with the other tried desperately to loosen Victor's scaled burning hand fastened around his throat.

"Bennet!" I cried as I leapt up to grasp his hand. "Do not let go!" I cried. "Do not let go!" I struggled to keep my grip, but he was slowly slipping away from me. "Why?" I asked. My rage turned to sadness and regret. "Why?" I screamed in confusion as Bennet seemed resigned to release.

He looked up at me with bright green eyes that I will never forget. "The Dream of hope will come," I reached down in a vain attempt to pull him up, but my hand only caught his emblem. I stared in horror as blood trickled from the corner of his mouth and Victor's other hand fastened around his head. "I will meet Jesus today," he smiled and let go.

XVI

"REMEMBER"

I stepped back from the rail as tears mixed with rain streaked my wretched face. The shame and loathing of living while others died returned. It pulled at me, stealing away my will to fight. I clenched my teeth together to resist the urge to scream. I stared at Bennet's medallion with his blood upon it. My heart felt as if it would break within my chest.

"It should have been me," I groaned. The medallion in my hand no longer looked like a sign of hope, but of my failure and my shame. "It should have been me!" I threw it onto the now crimson deck, and hung my head as I steadied myself against the rail. My will was broken and my strength gone.

Edmond walked up to the medallion and picked it up off the deck. "He saved us."

I clenched my teeth as Edmond spoke.

"One man," he held up the medallion. "This symbol is meant to bring hope and peace, this emblem is what he saved. He saved our will to fight and our hope. He saved, not only us, but he saved you too. And your captain was willing to kill all of you because of his pride."

My sadness gave way to rage as Edmond spoke.

"As the world falls apart, as thousands die, see what one man can do. One man changed the course of this battle, as one man was willing to die to save you. It is not too late for each of you to turn and fight with us, to ride with us to war, to put an end to this darkness. To let Bennet's legacy live on. To remember that he died for hope!" he held the emblem out to the men. "And for the hopeless."

The crew was silent for a long time, and no one moved. Finally, one man plucked up his courage and stepped toward us. "I had a wife," he stammered. "I had a family, and I saw them all killed by the Varanus," he paused. "I was helpless to do anything about it," he drew his sword and held it high above his head. "I do not care if it costs me my life, I will shed the blood of those wretched monsters and avenge my family!"

"Anyone else?" Edmond asked.

Another man stepped up. "My brother was murdered by those creatures. I did not even get to say goodbye," he drew his sword. "My blood for his blood. I will not rest until those beasts are dead."

"I guarded that man, Bennet," another pirate spoke out. "I brought food down to him. He was a good man. He showed us mercy and love even though we did not deserve it. I would be a fool not to remember his sacrifice!" After him, the other pirates looked at each other, trying to figure out what to do, then they all agreed and raised their swords in allegiance.

"Very well then," Edmond spoke. "Feargal! Turn us to England."

"Aye!" he replied, taking the helm.

The ship swayed to the right and slowly began to move northward as the sails fell and caught the wind.

"Finally," Piper walked up and leaned against the rail next to me, "we are on our way to England," she sighed. "Thank you for not leaving me back there," she smiled as I glanced over.

I forced a smile in return and searched for something to say that would not make me sound like a fool. "It was nothing."

"If that is the way you see it," she looked back out into the water. "Nothing?" she repeated and my head dropped at her words. "Really, it was not nothing?"

"I know," I forced a smile again. "I have a problem with watching people die," my smile disappeared as I remembered my parents.

"Will you be all right?" she asked.

"Why would I not be?" I replied as I tried to regain my composure.

"You are a strange man Richard," she said. "You say you can have a 'problem' with watching people die, but you want to kill the Adversary more than anything. Why is there such a war within you?"

"You are asking questions that I cannot answer."

"Cannot or will not?" she asked.

"Questions I prefer not to answer," I replied.

"The captain's cabin is empty," she said, "there should be a place to sit in there. No one else has to hear."

"Why do you want to know so badly?"

"Because I find it hard to trust a man who keeps so much anger held up inside," she smiled.

"What if I do not want to hear it?"

"You cannot keep the rage in forever. You will push away all those closest to you and you will lose your life."

I nodded and we walked across the deck to Blackheart's cabin. The rain stopped, but it was still dark and cloudy. A chilled wind blew the ship on its way. We entered the cabin and sat at the table with one side against the wall. Along another wall stood a chest and a large bed. Besides a few portraits of Blackheart and others who presumably were within his family line, the rest of the walls were covered with mirrors.

Piper seated herself at the table across from me.

"Rather vain was he not?" I commented on the décor.

"Who are you Richard Armistead?" she cut through my futile attempt to change the subject.

I looked straight into her eyes and met a piercing yet compassionate gaze. I took a deep breath and resolved to tell the story.

"It happened thirteen years ago. I was eleven at the time," I hesitated as horrid memories flooded my mind: the darkness over Shrewton, the plague that took so many, the cries of mother and father screaming for me to run, the horrid thundering voice of the Adversary.

"Are you sure we cannot talk about something else? Perhaps about what we are to do once we are in England? Would not that be more profitable?"

"That profit is not what I am after. I want to know who you are, more than just the man trying to fight a war," her warm smile swayed my heart. "I want to understand why you hate him so much."

"A man of war is all I am," I replied. "With the Adversary, with the Varanus, with Roger, with myself, with the Brethren. My life is war! And with war comes hatred, I cannot change that."

"You do not have to hate the other person in a war, you are just standing against them."

I sighed and decided to carry on, realizing that I had never shared this much of my history with anyone except Andrew and Edmond. "I lived in Shrewton, England. My family and I moved there from London. I and my family were close friends with the Baron of the town, and all things were going well. We had a friend there as well, a good friend. It was lovely." It felt as if a stone had risen into my throat; I fought to swallow it, but it would not go away. It loomed there, threatening to break me again.

"It was lovely," I repeated. My breath quivered. "But then plague broke out in the town. The Baron Aundray's wife passed by its hand. My father was with her at the time of death, and he said Angus changed that day," I lost myself in thought.

"Continue," Piper broke the silence.

"Well," I said, "later, another plague broke out causing the death of many more. My father talked to Baron Aundray and got his permission to help contain and hopefully stop the plague. The two worked together and succeeded by quarantining the sick. Right after they finished, my father returned home, with a bloody wound and was with my mother," I paused to control the tears, "murdered by the Adversary on that very night."

"But why?" Piper asked.

"I have spent thirteen years trying to figure that out, and still the reason for their murder is hidden to me."

"So that is why you want to find him, the Adversary, to get revenge?" she continued as she tried to understand. "I know how much you hate him, but would it not be better to forgive him instead of continuing the bloodshed?"

"I cannot!" I exclaimed. "I cannot forget what he did or let him do it to anyone else. Is it not better to kill one man than let him murder more?"

"Is this what your father would have wanted?" she returned.

"He is dead now!" I yelled. "He cannot want anything anymore because of what the Adversary did! Even if he did want me to follow him in his ways, he would be sentencing me to death!"

"You could be dead too! That night you were spared. At Château de Dourdan, it is a miracle you survived the Varanus. And today Bennet laid down his life so that you might be saved. God has something planned for you, no doubt about it! Otherwise, you would be dead, and there would be no more for you to do here."

"But how?" I asked. "How can I forget?"

"You need not forget, no one can forget something like that. I will never!" she said, "What matters is that you forgive."

"You," I paused, "will never?"

"I did not ask to become King Edward's servant, nor Luke one of his guards," Piper stated. "We never had a home. We were left on a doorstep of a church when we were young. We grew up there until nine years ago when they took us away and forced us to serve the King."

"I am sorry." I stammered. "I did not know."

"We have all lost something Richard," she smiled as Andrew's words echoed in my mind. "And I know what I have been through is not the same, but I do understand. If only a little," she laid her hand on mine. "I do understand."

"And that is what defines us, is it not?" I said, "The things we have been through. It is what makes us who we are. But what I cannot see is how you cared about the King, through all that pain."

"I would not have if I did not know the truth. And no," Piper declared, "it is not what we have been through, or the pain of it, it is how we stand when the trials come. And the trials do come and will always come. It is who we stand for that matters."

"I wish I could just fix it! All of it!" I clenched my teeth. "All the problems. All the pain. All the hatred," I stared down at the table.

"Christ did," she interrupted calmly. "He made a way. What He has already done is enough for not only us, but for all people, all nations, now and for all time! You need only to accept what He has done."

I looked at her. Tears filled her eyes. "I," my mind clouded. I remembered that night. I remembered the defeat and the anger. "I cannot," my head hung as I stared at the table. "I can never feel that kind of pain again. That kind of abandonment and loneliness."

"You are not alone Richard!" Piper exclaimed. "Bennet just

died for you, how can you feel abandoned?"

"My parents were murdered!"

"And mine left me and my brother," she was no longer smiling. "Richard, loss is painful, but you cannot dwell on it forever. It will rip you apart."

"I am already broken," I tried to scowl, but all that came was tears. "I broke that night!" I sobbed.

I continued to weep and cursed myself as the ship rocked onward. I could not find any way to stop. The only comfort was Piper, who sat across from me as the hours dragged on. Her hand never left mine.

I finally looked up and found Piper's head resting on the table. Her eyes were closed and she breathed softly. I stood up slowly and stumbled as quietly as I could to the door. I laid my hand upon the handle and looked back at Piper. Piper, the girl who could forgive her parents for leaving her and her brother.

I turned back to the door and stared down at my hand resting on the handle. My hand slipped off the knob and I crossed back to the table and sunk into the chair in front of her. I brushed the loose strands of hair from her face and leaned back.

"Why do you even care?" I sighed and watched her and listened to the crew outside.

An hour passed. Piper's hand clenched around where mine once was, as she lifted her head and looked at me. I smiled.

"Was I asleep?" she asked.

I smiled again.

"And you sat there and stared at me the entire time?" she laughed.

"I felt bad about leaving," I replied.

The door opened suddenly and Edmond entered.

"We have spotted land on the horizon!" he exclaimed.

Piper and I stood up slowly and walked out onto the deck. On our left, the sun cracked through the wall of clouds suspended in the sky.

The once crimson deck now faded into brown and gave off a putrid smell. A strong cold northern wind blew and slowed our progress. The sights and smells sent chills up my back, yet the dread of what was coming loomed stronger.

"We cannot bring her ashore," Feargal yelled from his seat at the forecastle. "And there is no boat or anything that we can use to row to the beach."

"How close can we get?" Edmond asked.

"If I push her any farther," Feargal sighed, "we will run her aground for sure. And there is no telling how long I can hold this course as the wind is picking up again!"

"Bring her closer Feargal!" Edmond ordered.

"We will wreck the ship!" Feargal protested.

"Biscuit's blood! I do not care a wit about the ship!" Edmond yelled. "Bring her as close as possible!"

"So it is another swim?" Luke asked.

"Are you up for it?" I asked Piper.

"I will manage," she replied with a grin.

We sailed on for another few hours. Feargal was able to find a route which brought us closer to the coast, but it was still a good way off. We talked back and forth about our plan and steadied the crew as they grew restless. Then a sudden jolt nearly threw me over the bulwark. The sound of splintering wood filled the air as the ship scraped against the bottom of the channel.

"Edmond!" Feargal shouted above the crashing noise.

"Keep her steady!" Edmond replied. Another deafening crash filled the air.

The ship thrust forward and hit the bottom again and turned the port side to shore. The current then rushed against the starboard and began turning the ship over toward the shore. Wood floated everywhere as the mast cracked and tore off into the sea.

Feargal ran up next to us as the ship fractured.

"This is madness!" Feargal yelled.

"Aye, it is!" Luke rested his hand on Feargal's shoulder. "Who is steering?" Luke shouted above the mighty roar. Feargal shook his head and simply pointed into the water as the rudder floated by.

"On my mark!" Edmond prepared to leap into the water as the ship tore apart and the deck began descending into the sea. "Ready?"

"No!" Luke replied.

"Now!" Edmond leapt into the water.

I followed into the water. Luke, Piper and Feargal came a second later, and then the rest of the crew.

We crashed into the water, plummeting below the surface. I swam forward through the icy water and burst up gasping for breath.

I pulled myself onto a very large plank and turned around, desperately searching for my friends.

Within a few moments, all five of us were together on the plank. I turned around and found that most of the crew also made it up, however, a few were lost. We then turned our sights to shore, and began the long swim back. The water was unbearably cold and the wind made it even worse.

I finally threw myself upon the shore and stared up at the sun, which was just barely breaking through the clouds.

"Where is the crew?" Piper asked as she stared back into the waves. I turned and followed her gaze, the crew was nowhere to be seen. In their place, scarlet patches of water filled the waves. I watched for a moment and then collapsed onto the beach. My eyes closed and for the first time in weeks I slept in peace.

I was awakened by Luke's screaming and running off the beach. I jumped up, ready for a fight, when I saw what had startled him. Half a dozen bodies lay in the sand around us. Each fatally wounded and missing their eyes. I stared in horror as I realized who these men were – they were the crew.

XVII

COLD REUNION

N o one spoke. There was nothing to be said. Edmond turned away from the bodies and began walking north, away from the beach.

"Where are you going?" I asked, not taking my eyes off the body of the crew member who lost his family to the Varanus.

"There is nothing we can do for them," Edmond shouted back. "All we can do now is hope that we have not lost our chance to stop Apollo."

I stood up and stared down at the man. I then turned in frustration to follow Edmond. I glanced back to find that Luke and Piper were following, however Feargal was still staring at the bodies.

"Are you coming Feargal?" I called out.

He nodded and began walking after us to find the rest of the Brethren. All of us knew, no matter how much we wanted to deny it, that there was more coming; that Apollo was going to do all in his power to destroy us, and if we did not stand together, he would succeed all too easily. And not only would Roger defeat the Brethren, but he would also defeat what we stood for, he would destroy the hope that the Brethren tried to give and peace that we had sown.

The road stretched out like a parched desert path. Our clothes, now dry from our swim, were covered in dust from the road. The only thing which was still unsoiled was Edmond's sword hanging from his side.

The sword was very bright as the sun shone off of it and it brought a glimmer of hope; however, its beauty was obscured by the painful blisters forming mercilessly on our feet and the hunger biting into our strength.

Finally, on the morning of the next day a few houses emerged as the town of Durrington lay before us, but our joy was short lived.

The town was completely empty. There were no bodies or sign of a struggle, therefore we concluded that the inhabitants had fled and were most likely hidden in the forests and mountains. 'Little do they know' I thought, 'that even there they will be found. No matter where they go, Roger's cunning will hunt them down like a wolf on its prey!'

I found my house and entered in. It was just as I had left it. The weapons were still hanging on the wall with the table standing and chairs all around.

"Come in," I told them, "help yourselves to anything still here." I walked inside and over to the wall where all the weapons hung.

"Not many of these will be useful, not nearly enough for an army," I sighed, "Most of the more effective weapons were given to our men who went to Château de Dourdan. Like the gauntlets, or the bow or-" I hesitated, "well," I said as I pulled a sword off the wall. "this might do."

"Look's like a normal sword," stated Luke from the table where he sat eating a molded loaf of bread.

"That is the idea," I said laying the sword on the table, "However, I forged it in such a way that it alters the structure of carbon steel so that it absorbs the shock of any blow. Then Andrew added in the remnant of a stone he had found years ago," I glanced at Luke. "I call it Valinium."

Luke smiled at me. "I have no idea what that means."

"It should not break," I paused, "easily," I pointed to several more swords on the wall. "Same with those there."

"Oh, well could you not just have said that?" Luke took another bite of the bread and cringed at the taste.

"Fascinating," stated Feargal as he pulled a sword off the wall.

"What is this?" asked Piper gesturing to a leather chest piece lying in the corner.

"That," I explained, "is one of the primary reasons I survived the Varanus. It is made of leather, with several thin layers of Valinium in it," I pointed to the sword. "I have several other pieces of armour over in the shop. I wish I still had that bow though!"

"Amazing," Piper said smiling. It felt as though my heart skipped a beat hearing her praise.

"And that is all I have that is worth using," I said after we chose our weapons.

"Are you sure you do not want another sword Edmond?" I asked. "I have one more and you are more than welcome to use it."

"No," he replied, "mine will do just fine."

"Are you sure?"

He pulled out his sword, allowing me to take in its magnificence and quite frankly putting my work to shame.

"Your point is taken," I replied.

I walked out of the house into my blacksmith's shop, and came back with several other chest pieces. I admired my work as I lay them on the table. I remembered how Andrew had helped me create the Valinium. All those seemingly endless hours of testing and creating. The blood, sweat and tears which created this marvelous metal. Here it was, Valinium, the most durable metal in the world.

I jolted myself out of the memories and spoke. "I would have made more pieces of armour for the rest of the body," I paused. "I just never got the chance."

"A helmet maybe?" Edmond asked in jest.

"We both know I do not like helmets," I paused. "Or hats, or caps-I do not like things clinging to my skull or obscuring my vision."

"Neither do I!" exclaimed Luke as he put on the armour.

Edmond leaned up against the door frame. "It is time we reunited the Brethren," his face was strong and would make any man fear for his life and the judgment. "The time of us defending ourselves has ended. Now we are on our turf, our land! And we will bring the war to them."

Evening was near as we drew close to the ring of stone. I could already tell that the night would be cold. Dark clouds loomed in the sky, and a shadow loomed in our hearts – increasing with each passing step. Surrounding the ring was a great horde. Countless men swarming all around ring. I could hardly believe my eyes as the scene unfolded. Thousands of men all armed and ready for war, thousands of men from other kingdoms all encamped together, and on the southern end of the camp, the majestic banner of Edward III flew gallantly in the wind.

"No," I said. "There are too many here. The Varanus," I hesitated. Memories of Château de Dourdan returned to my mind, all infected with dread. "We need to get them out of here!" I exclaimed. "He will kill them all!"

"What are you talking about?" Edmond stared at me strangely. "What do you mean get them out of here? We have an Army! At least now there is a chance."

"This is exactly what he wants!" I exclaimed as I saw what Apollo was trying to do. "He wants all of us here, so he can destroy us all in one blow. That is the only reason these people are still alive."

"Roger is not capable of that," Edmond's face hardened. "No matter what he has done, he would not murder thousands without a reason! Make no mistake, Roger is still our brother!"

"He broke that bond when he murdered the millions in Kipchak

Khan," I said. "At Château de Dourdan, and beyond! Think of them! Were they not murdered as well? Roger is a murderer and must, at all costs, be brought to an end!"

"Do not forget Richard, you too have taken lives. You too have had murderous desires and longed to avenge yourself."

I stared into Edmond's eyes. "When have I violated your trust? When have I betrayed you?"

"What I am saying, Richard, is that Roger does not have to die!" Edmond yelled. "If not for his sake, do it for the Brethren. Do it for yourself. Save your own soul from that torment."

"Torment is my life!" I yelled, and would have continued, but Piper exclaimed.

"This will not help us defeat the Varanus or the Adversary!"

"She is right," Luke grinned, "as always. A point which deserves some thought, do you not agree? Never argue with a woman." He raised an eyebrow as he looked in my direction.

"Fine then," Edmond spoke, "I will go alone and warn Andrew of Apollo's whereabouts and our plan."

"No," I objected, "I will go. I know Roger, our former brother, I dare say better than you do. And I know Andrew like a father."

"Fine," Edmond relented, "Go. And God be with you."

"Thank you," I said turning toward the camp. "If He is still there, may He be with you as well."

I bid farewell to our small company and entered the encampment. I could hardly make out anything through the mass of men. So many were there that the tents stretched over a mile in every direction. 'Seems as if Andrew got our message and took it to heart.' I laughed to myself.

I made my way slowly toward the center of the camp, where stood the stones making up the ring. I stopped in front of it. All my dreams came upon me like a tempest. I gazed around the massive stones, and the night of the murder came suddenly back. I could almost feel myself running through torrents of rain, the one difference was that it was not on a hill as the ring in my dreams had been.

I walked slowly to the middle of the ring and gazed up at the large stones, towering up around me in all directions. I felt secure in the shadow they cast upon me. But a deep dread still loomed inside. I closed my eyes and inhaled deeply and tried to remain calm as I felt the crest of the war approaching. The air chilled my nostrils and my spine. 'There is no security,' I thought. 'Only war. Only fear.' I examined the grass at my feet and sighed. 'Who am I trying to fool? Other than myself,' I looked up. A bird perched on top of one of the stones. It opened its black beak and outstretched its dark wings, but no sound came, nor did it fly. It simply huddled down into a cleft of the rock and hid as a chilled breeze blew from the west and sent another shiver down my spine.

"Richard?" Andrew's voice resounded from behind me and drove the chills away.

"Andrew!" I exclaimed as I spun about and ran to where he stood. Tears streaked my face by the time I threw my arms around him.

"Richard!" he gripped my shoulders and held me at arm's length. "They said you were dead!" he looked brighter than ever – and younger.

"Very near dead, I might say," I smiled. "Have you heard anything about the King? Is he safe?"

"Biscuit's blood! Forget the King! You are alive!" Andrew beamed.

"Aye, it would seem so, but not for much longer if I forget the King," I replied in jest.

Andrew laughed. "He is here, along with the Kings of France, Spain, Scotland, Sweden, and even the Holy Roman Emperor himself! They are all here! All the remaining armies of Europe are here as well as countless refugees from the Khanates and beyond! There are nearly a million of them! Maybe more! I would not be surprised!"

"Well at least now we have a chance," I sighed.

"A chance? Richard, what I found when you were away could save us all," his eyes beamed with excitement. "Come this way," he raced to the center of the ring. The black bird was still huddled in the corner. In the center of the ring stood a three-sided stone. It was smoother than glass and shimmered whiter than snow. Andrew lay his hand on it. "The Alignment."

"What about it?" I asked in annoyance, wishing more to be like the bird.

Andrew took a glass shape from his pouch which matched the stone in dimension and quality, and held it in direct sunlight. The light beamed through it and split into several different colors. "It is the same with the Alignment. It will split the light into four parts! I was always trying to figure out how to harness the power when really it harnesses itself," he pointed to the stone. "Look inside of it. Trust me, Richard, it will amaze you."

I knelt down and gazed into the three-sided stone, "It looks like a ball of dim light," I finally said.

"I believe that is the fifth, or first, whatever you wish to call it. I believe it gathers all the light of the Alignment, then illuminates the four others," he pointed to the spheres inside the other stones surrounding us. Each shining with the same dim light. "And it has been getting brighter each day since I have been here!" his excitement surpassed even his own expectations. "The Egyptian lights," he smiled.

"Aye," I replied trying to wrap my head around what he was trying to predict.

"They exploded when I brought them near the center stone!" he exclaimed. "Nothing left of them!"

"Amazing?" I laid my hand on the stone, still unsure of what he was saying.

He pointed to the four surrounding stones forming the ring. "Each of them will be hit by a beam coming off the center stone. And each of them has a sphere."

We walked over to one of the other stones in the ring. Andrew pointed into the stone which now, like the center one, was clear as glass. "As the alignment draws near, the stones lose their disguise and become clear revealing the other spheres."

I gazed at the orb in the stone, and noted that it could have easily been taken out. However, no one would know it was there unless they watched the Alignment as Andrew had. "And what about the center one?" I asked. "What will become of it?"

"That," he beamed, "will be the best and brightest of them all!"

"Andrew?"

"Aye," he answered.

"What has happened?" I asked. "You look somehow younger and more impassioned than ever."

"The light from the Alignment feeds the body and renews us. I am no younger than when you saw me last, but I am being renewed, with God's mercies each morning," he said and then paused. "All my life I have waited for the Alignment, trying to learn about it, learn what it could do and what I could do with it," he turned to me. "I have shown you this, now let me show you why."

"What?"

"Come with me," Andrew turned and led me through the masses of tents until he stopped before one and threw open the canvas flaps.

A mattress lay at the far end and a stood table at the near. Andrew and I sat at the table and faced each other on opposite sides.

"I know you are going to think I am mad but just listen," he began. "Everything that has happened has led up to the Alignment, but that is not the point of it. I knew that I was not the only man searching for it, but one question always loomed in my mind. Why?"

"Why?" I asked at a total loss.

"Why would God make this happen?" Andrew replied.

"Oh, no more of this Andrew!" I yelled. "I have heard enough of your madness!" I slammed my hands down onto the table. "We are in the middle of a war!"

"Listen. I know you do not understand, and for reasons of fear and vengeance you suppress the truth, but just listen," Andrew pleaded. "When we formed the Brethren I knew that we were creating a loose allegiance that would either fall within the year, or an ideal which would span the ages. I prayed dearly for the latter. I wanted to use the power of the Alignment to strengthen the Brethren, to sow peace in the world. So as time went by and I watched our fellowship grow, I also watched the Alignment. I saw the pain of mankind, the hatred and corruption and I assured myself that the Brethren would not be corrupted by that power. But from what I have now seen, I was wrong."

"What are you talking about?"

"Richard, your hatred, your sorrow – it has made your eyes blind and your heart dark. My hope for you was to lead the Brethren in that power, to carry on my vision. But my vision of an all powerful Brethren was wrong. My vision for peace was wrong. My vision for you was wrong."

"What?" I asked in exasperation.

"There are five orbs that will be released. Each will possess a different power. But one cannot be changed. There is evil in this world and there is darkness, but in the darkness, there is a great light. The light of Jesus Christ is the greatest power and the only power that cannot be corrupted! Richard that power, that light surrounds you! That greatness! The king of the universe died on the tree for you. That sacrifice, that power is so much greater than anything the Alignment can give, and it will never change – never be corrupted – never be diminished no matter how much is taken from you! No matter how much you have been corrupted. He will always save. The Alignment is not what I want for you. I want you to see that endless majesty and goodness of Christ. I want you to turn from your sins, believe and be saved. Richard, I want you to live."

"Andrew it is very thoughtful that you are trying to help me, but we must not talk of fairy tales and holy men when before any good may be wrought, we will be dead!"

"Richard, you are missing what I am trying to tell you. It is not about the war, it is not about the Alignment! It is what you -"

"Shut up! You are wasting time! He is coming for us," I yelled. "And biscuits blood he is going to kill us all! And all this talk is doing nothing to stop him. Andrew, I do not care about your faith or your God!"

"Richard please, He is calling you!"

"Then tell Him that He should have kept me when He had the chance! Tell Him that it is His fault! Tell Him I want nothing to do with Him!" I gritted my teeth. "I do not care about Him! What I do care about is the man who is coming to kill us. Andrew, he will slaughter us all! Every man, woman and child here!"

Andrew leaned back in his chair, wiped one of his eyes and crossed his arms. I almost felt sorry for a moment, then scowled and blamed him for bringing it up.

"Why does he want to kill us? And who is he?" Andrew sighed.

"Have you not heard of the Varanus?" I asked, still angry.

"Varanus," he hesitated thoughtfully, "no."

"What about monsters attacking and killing everyone?"

"Yes, from King Edward and many of the soldiers."

"Well, they are one and the same with the Varanus."

"And who is 'he'?" Andrew inquired. "You said he was going to kill us, but who is he?"

"He," I clenched my teeth as I thought of our brother – our enemy, "is behind it, all of it! Behind the Varanus, behind the death and devastation over Europe and Asia, behind this entire war."

"Who is he?"

"It is Roger!" I exclaimed with tears and choking breath.

Andrew stood up and with a look of disbelief and confusion said plainly, "No, it is not him. It is not possible."

"It must be him. Everything points to Roger. You just do not understand what we have seen and heard."

"I do not know what you saw nor what you heard, but I know Roger," he replied, "I know that he wants to do the right thing. I have faith. Roger would never betray us."

"My father's faith got him killed! Are you as blind as he?" I screamed. "Roger is coming to kill us all."

"Your father's faith was what made him strong enough to face death. To heal the sick. To seek justice. To stand strong and alone if needed!" Andrew's powerful voice filled the air around me and made me shudder. "Do not ever forget who your father was."

"You never knew my father!"

"I know you. I have heard the stories from your very lips. Your father was a great man, and he would be ashamed at how you interpret his faith. How you have become the very thing you hope to destroy!"

"No! It is a lie!" I yelled. "I am not like the Adversary! I am nothing like that murderer! He killed my parents Andrew, he is the last person I wish to be like!"

"Alas, though, you are, no matter how much you deny it," Andrew's words pierced my heart and unleashed my hatred. "But it is not too late - for either of you. So long as you live there is always freedom and redemption. There is always the way to Him."

"He is going to kill us all!" I yelled. A few of the soldiers wandering about began to listen to what we were saying.

"Let him come. Whoever he is!" Andrew's voice grew again in resolve. "And let me die if need be. For death is not to be feared. Death is the end of all woes, for after death comes life everlasting for those who believe! And by England, I cannot wait until Christ calls me home. I do not care when it is. Be it now, or in a thousand years!"

"How?" I stared at him. "How can you not see that there is no hope? The Alignment cannot save us and neither can anything else in this world!"

"Then it is a good thing that He is not of this world."

"Then what are we supposed to do?" I asked reluctantly. "Trust in a God who could not save one town?"

"We must get Edmond," he ordered.

"Edmond is not here, he is outside the camp," I replied.

"Why is he not with us?" asked Andrew.

"If we are all here together then Roger will surely attack and destroy us in one final blow."

"First of all, it is not Roger! And second, we should stay, await the coming attack and keep our enemy at bay. Once the Alignment comes, then we should strike."

"You do not understand!" I yelled with my rage rekindling once more. "Of course you would not! You are an ignorant old man! If we do not attack now there will be no other time! The Varanus will swarm and destroy us all!"

"Fine," Andrew replied coldly.

"What?" I said exasperated.

"Fine," he repeated. "We will attack this enemy – wherever he is."

"Shrewton most likely," I added.

Andrew interrupted me and continued. "But know this! The blood of the men who die due to your impetuousness is not on my head. It will not be on the Brethren. And it will not be on this villain!"

"Then let it be on me," I replied.

"Those are words that must never be said in war," Andrew rebuked.

"I do not care what cost I must pay as long as we win. Now, where is the King?" I demanded.

Andrew nodded slowly and looked back at me with his bright, lively blue eyes. 'repent Richard,' they screamed louder than I could shout. 'Please!' I looked away and walked out into the chilled night air. Andrew followed and then led me on through the camp for nearly an hour and stopped. "There," he said, pointing to a large tent with many banners around it. "That is the meeting tent where the kings gather each night to make ready for war."

"When?"

"They will gather soon," Andrew replied.

"How soon?" I asked.

"Now," Andrew pointed at the Royal English Guard coming toward the tent from the south, and then to the Maison du Roi of Philip VI of France from the east. Others in varying degree of dress and strength descended upon the main tent.

"How soon may I enter?" I asked.

"Give them twenty minutes," Andrew replied as he turned and began walking back to his tent.

"Andrew!" I yelled to him. He stopped. "How can you be so sure that it is not Roger?"

"The way I always know," he replied as he turned back to face me. "I have faith."

"Have you seen him of late?" I asked.

"He left a few days ago," Andrew answered.

I stared at him. "Where?"

"I am not sure; however he said he would be back tomorrow," Andrew replied.

"Andrew where did he go? Please even a direction!" I demanded.

Andrew paused realizing the direction of Roger's departure, "Toward Shrewton."

"What about Henry?"

"He went with Roger." Andrew looked at me. Once more his eyes screamed at me. 'No! No Richard! Do not go!'

"Andrew, post guards around the camp to make sure Roger does not make it back through an alternate route. I will rally the army and get them to Shrewton but I also need you to get Edmond."

"And why is that?" Andrew asked.

"Because he has the will it takes to rally an army!" I ran down to the king's tent leaving Andrew to find Edmond and post the guards.

The tent was one of the largest I had ever seen. It had eight sides with a large wooden post in each corner. In the center, a taller post gave the tent a pointed tip with a large open grommet for ventilation. I trudged through the muddy ground to the entrance, flung open the flap and entered.

On the central post, mounted fifteen feet high all around, were torches lighting the tent. At six separate corners there stood a large chair and surrounding each was a guard of soldiers wearing their country's coat of arms. In each chair sat the king or ruler with his

kingdom's flag behind the right side.
    Everyone turned to me the moment I entered.

XVIII

COMMANDER OF KINGS

I gazed around the room not realizing that I had entered through the back of the tent onto the main platform. To my dismay, all the rulers and their men stared back at me with expressions of anger and despair.

"Hello," I could not say anything else as I entered the presence of the kings, nor did I want to.

"Who do you think you are?" The Castilian King sneered, pointing at me. His fair skin turning red with rage and his finger quivering with the fear of war. "And what are you doing here?"

"I-uh." I smiled in an attempt to smooth over my rough entrance.

"Quit stumbling over your words boy and explain your intrusion upon these proceedings," King Edward of England demanded.

I bowed and regained my composure. "I, your majesties, am Richard Armistead of Durrington, third head of the Brethren and your humble servant."

"We already have English here. We need no more!" King Alfonso of Castille blustered. "Be gone!"

"I submit highness," I raised my voice, "that you are in England, and therefore a guest and shall be in need of every English man!" I took a deep breath. "You have no idea what we are facing – what this war is bringing to us."

"Watch your tongue lad!" Edward rose from his gilded chair. "I watched good men die in the most brutal ways imaginable. So have each of these men here," he pointed at the other kings around the tent. "You do not understand these matters. This is much more than just a war."

"With all due respect your majesty," I pulled out my medallion, and his face flashed with recognition. "I lost good men trying to save your life in France. You know me and I know more than you can imagine," I strode over to Edward. "They will come and this land will burn!" I yelled. "I know who is behind this war!"

"Who, pray tell, is it that started this holocaust?" taunted Alfonso. "Fool of an Englishman – I am tired of your impudence."

"Let him speak. I know this man as a leader of the Brethren, as he has already said and has now proven. They have kept peace in England throughout my reign. He is an ally to me and to all of us."

I stood there, silent and still wondering what to say. What if Roger was not behind any of it? What if Andrew was right? I would never forgive myself if I maligned his name and caused his death in error. But if I let this devastation continue then thousands more will die – perhaps millions.

"Speak up Armistead," Edward beckoned me. "Who is it?"

I turned to face the other kings, "He was once like a brother to me," My anger and hatred for Roger wavered. "He was also a friend. A good man." I swallowed the lump in my throat. I had made my decision, there was no turning back now.

"You speak foolishness!" Philip of France shouted as he rose from his throne. "Silence this man for his words are empty and shall discourage my army!"

"His name is Roger Wilson! He is a traitor to the Brethren and a disgrace to our name!" I yelled in my prosecution. "And if your men waver so easily, you have no army. This is a herd of sheep waiting to be slaughtered," I unleashed my rage. "And mark my words, if you do not listen to me, all of them will be slaughtered!"

"Where is this man that we may end this war?" Louis IV, King of the Romans, King of Italy, and Holy Roman Emperor stood up.

"He is here, in England. He is less than three miles from this very spot."

"So then it is England behind this destruction?" Alfonso spoke out again, glaring from me to Edward.

"I knew nothing of this plot," Edward thundered. "I would have never have allowed this to happen if I knew – you Castilian warmonger."

"What is that supposed to mean English fool?" Alfonso hollered. "Are you insulting the King of Castile and disgracing the Regent of León?"

Philip of France shouted. "You are the disgrace for your own people. You have done that for yourself."

"There are no fools here. You speak far too highly Philip!" laughed the Emperor. "You all are merely children playing kings and regents!"

The guards readied themselves to defend their leaders as the tension escalated.

'They are going to destroy themselves!' I thought to myself as my fingers curled into fists. I gazed around the room as the anger grew hotter. 'At least the men are loyal.' I thought as some of the guards drew their swords.

"Children?" thundered Edward. "You, Roman, are permitted to leave whenever you please. I will not force you to stay with us upon my regency. But know this, I will not have my people or my honor disgraced."

"Disgraced?" Magnus IV of Sweden spoke out for the first time.

"You insult the King of Castile and cannot receive your own reproof? You speak so much of wars and great conquests. Is this name calling more disgraceful than all the blood you have spilled?"

"What is disgraceful is your judgment," Edward recoiled and half hissed as his kingly composure peeled away. "You yourself have swindled kingdoms from their rightful rulers. How is war worse than conniving?"

"I am sorry to interrupt Edward," the King of Scotland, David II spoke, "but you sir have done that as well. All of you have!"

"I will not tolerate your speech here Scottish child," Edward pointed at David and addressed Louis, "This is who you shall address as 'children' in England, Emperor."

"Enough!" I yelled. "You must quit your bickering and deal with the matter at hand!"

"And what pray tell is that?" Edward turned on me.

"Sire if we do not attack Shrewton now we will lose the war," I pleaded. "There is simply no other way."

"And who is leading this attack?" asked Philip of France.

"Aye," King Edward interrupted. "I am not following any of these who have already lost their kingdoms. The honor of England stands alone!"

"And neither shall we follow you," retorted the Emperor. "For the honor of England is nothing to anyone but yourself!"

"Stop this debate!" I demanded incredulously.

"I will not follow a Frenchman to battle!" hollered Alfonso. "Was it not the French who fell first? What reasons do we have to put our trust in a fallen king?"

"Neither will the French follow you, Alfonso!" Phillip snapped back, with rage and pain in his eyes.

"Why can I not lead you?" David asked. "Was it not David who slew the giant in the Holy Scriptures?"

"Correction, boy," Louis announced. "It was David's faith in God that slew the giant."

"I see no reason why God will not do the same for me!" David's voice cracked in pubescent alacrity.

"And pray tell what makes you like David other than your name?" asked Magnus. "Have you ever tended sheep? Killed a lion or a bear? Become king of a blessed nation?"

David was silent, but I could see anger in his eyes at the affront.

"Exactly. You are a boy and no more. David was trained in leadership from birth by God. Such is not the case with you!" Magnus insulted him once more. "I will lead Europe to victory."

"And what?" responded Edward. "Take two-thirds of England in return for your schemes? You certainly will not! This is my land. My people. And I alone will lead the attack on this enemy!"

"Quite strange is it not?" Louis laughed. "The King of England attacking his own countrymen? Surely there is some other way. I almost think France should lead as routine."

"I would be glad to lead it," Philip answered. "The French shall go first in the charge!"

"I said almost, subject." Louis objected.

"And I will not follow a Frenchman," Alfonso said again. "Let the Castilian cavalry ride first! Followed by whosoever wishes to bury the bodies!"

"Never!" thundered Edward. "Never shall I follow a Castilian upon my lands."

"Why not?" demanded Alfonso. "Why can Castile not have the honor?" Alfonso stood up and marched over to Edward, standing tall in front of his throne. "Give me one. Reason. Why!"

Edward leaned forward in his chair and with a smirk upon his face said, "Because when you say charge in your Castilian babble it sounds like 'cobra.'" he leaned back as in a victorious repose. "Then everyone who hears you loses their wits and starts scrambling for snakes! Little do they know that the only snake is you and your foolish language – leading them to death! Castile will not lead unless Castile is alone!"

"Cargar! Es la carga! Serpiente!" Alfonso muttered disgustedly under his breath as he walked away.

"The language does not matter, for the only snake I see is you, Edward," Philip sneered as he stood up from his throne. "Twisting it all into your favor, in favor of England," he turned to the rest of the men and gestured to the English king. "Can you all not see? Edward wants England to win the war, then he will say we owe him for saving our people. He will make us give him our land and enslave us all. But I say 'no more!'" Edward sat silently on his throne with a scowl on his face and hatred in his eyes as Philip ranted. "No more shall England stand alone on their little island trying to pretend they rule the world! Trying to rule us from their pedestal!" the French guards cheered for their king. "No more shall they stand alone, for today, the might of France and her people will ride forth and then you will see how wars are fought! Then you shall see who truly is willing to die! For harken to my words, O kings of Europe, if you let England lead you this day, you let them lead every day hereafter!"

"Fine then," I said loud enough for everyone in the tent to hear. "Let it be known that Philip of France leads us."

"Nay!" Magnus yelled back. "You have no place among kings! You have no right to order us!

"Sweden shall lead the battle and that is the final decision!" Magnus continued. "Though France is right about England, they fail to see that they too will follow the same path. Sweden however, will not. The Swedes, though achieving the victory, shall return to former borders in peace. Let us avenge our brothers who lost their lives protecting those borders, and keep them intact," Magnus stood up and drew his sword followed by his guards, "And whosoever wishes to object faces the armies of Sweden and the remnant of the Khans who have sworn allegiance to me!" All the other kings stared in disgust and horror at Magnus. Until now, the Khans had been open ground for them to snatch, but now that Magnus had them on his side, it would take both Spain and England to oppose him.

Suddenly a voice from the entrance of the tent thundered forth, shattering the silence and turning the expressions of resentment fully to surprise. The voice was more powerful than any they had ever heard. Save one.

"Look at yourselves!" Edmond's voice shook the tent as thunder shakes the Earth. He had been waiting for the opportune time to speak and one could see, he had heard enough. "Look at where your pride is leading you. All of you are ready to murder one another. And for what? To lead a battle in which you should be united? I am ashamed to call myself English, and so should all of you to your own nations and kingdoms!" he strode out to the middle of the tent and his sword swayed at his side. He stood proud representing all that remained good in the broken world. "Is this how you want to be remembered? Is this your legacy?"

Louis stood up in fury, "I am the Holy Roman Emperor! Fool! You shall pay for your-"

"Pay for what?" Edmond interrupted without flinching at the Emperor's threat. "Yelling at a King who says he is holy? You are a man, born of a man and nothing holy comes through man except by faith in God! And from all I can see you have given that up!"

Edmond turned to King Philip of France "And you! You and I

both know France is in no place to lead a war. Much less this one. Why then do you pretend? I remind you that the war entered Europe through France. The French people are scattered and broken. Now be their King and protect them better than you did in France. Be the man they need you to be," shame flooded over Philip's face as Edmond spoke.

He turned to Edward, his eyes burning with anger at his own King. "You," he gritted his teeth, "I said it before and I will say it a thousand times over - I. Am. Ashamed. I am ashamed to be called English and I am ashamed to have risked my life and the lives of the Brethren to a man that is parrying names instead of marshaling swords! How can this be?"

"Silence!" Edward stood up. "I will not be insulte-"

"No, you have talked enough! See - your men see it as well. Now it is my turn for words." Edmond's fiery eyes made the torches look dim. "You are not my King. You are no one's King, not even your own, for you have let darkness be your king and shadows the ruler of your people!" In his voice was pain and sorrow, but still his strength flashed. "I wish I had never tried to save you if this is the man that you are.

"And you are all the same," he stormed turning to Magnus, "And you all know it. The moment the battle is over, you will all turn again and start another war. You know it is true. Your ambition and hatred rule your heart rather than the King of Kings!" The kings all looked at each other in unified anger and fear toward Edmond. "For this alone, you should be dethroned. For your pride and selfishness! That in this time of great tribulation you stand divided, and not only that, but ready to shed each others' blood! I am surprised you have not killed each other yet!" Edmond walked around the room, gazing at each king with blazing eyes. He saw their hatred and the fear which brought it up, and he despised it. "But as you stand divided, our enemy prepares to destroy us in one stroke. One blow and we are gone.

But!" he outstretched his arms toward the kings now all sitting on their thrones. "He may not have to lift a finger!"

"You had your chance and only stirred our wrath peasant!" Alfonso hissed. "Be gone from us!"

"I am not finished!" Edmond's voice made Alfonso's seem like a wisp before a hurricane. "And you Alfonso, son of a dowager Queen, curse your pride and your brutality!" he gestured to all the kings, "You are ripping yourselves apart!"

Edward leaned over to his captain of the guard. "Kill him," he turned back to Edmond. "Do you know the punishment for treason?"

Three guards drew their swords and advanced upon Edmond. He stood motionless as they approached. "You think you matter to our enemy?" Edmond set his face like flint. One of the guards grabbed Edmond's arm. Like lightening, Edmond drew his sword and sliced the guard's forearm. He screamed and stepped back.

The two other guards advanced and Edmond quickly sent them stumbling back with bloody wounds.

"You think you are more important than these men you send to kill me?" Edmond turned toward the King as he gestured to the guards laying on the ground. "Think of who they are. I want you to remember every person you have ever killed, or sent to die. Remember them. And how does that make you feel?" Edmond marched up to Edward whose face betrayed fear and shame. Not one of the guards stirred when he approached. "Hear me, Edward, remember them and multiply the shame ten fold. A thousand fold! That is what you are sentencing your kingdom to if you suppress the unity needed to defeat our enemy," Edmond laid his hand on the king's shoulder and said,

"Repent and believe. The LORD forgives, but our enemy does not, he is coming to kill us all," Edward's face was downcast as Edmond spoke. "He is faithful to forgive," Edmond then straightened himself to full height and gripped the English flag with his left hand. Then, with his sword in his right, sliced a strip off of it.

"What are you doing?" Edward's captain of the guard screamed. "My king, do not listen to him! He has committed treason against your Majesty!"

Edward was silent.

Edmond took the torn piece of the flag and tied it around his arm, "I am not committing treason – for I am a man with only one King," he walked across the tent to the French king and was unhindered as he reached beyond Philip and sliced another strip and tied it next to England's colors. "My King is the only King," then on to the Castilian flag. "My King, is the King of Kings," and then Scotland, Sweden and finally to the flag of the Holy Roman Emperor saying to Louis as he cut through his flag. "He is your King."

He walked calmly to the center pole and turned to face them all. He stabbed his sword into the ground and spoke:

"A time comes where all men will stand, not only for themselves, but each will see the need for unity and strive toward it," his eyes blazed with passion and his voice bore the strength that comes through trials. "The time. Has. Come! England shall not lead, neither France, nor Castile, neither Scotland nor Sweden, nor the Khans, not even the Empire! But as surely as I stand this day, because of the Brethren this war began, and because of the Brethren, it shall end! We stand not for England, or any nation. We stand for all that is right and good! We stand in the name of Jesus the Son of God! And if any of you wish not to come with us, so be it! But nothing, not even an army of monsters can stop me from dying for my King!"

The tent rose up in the cheers of all the men present, then slowly fell silent. And the silence remained for a full minute. The kings looked back and forth at each other, waiting for one to speak first. The guards whipped their heads left and right and then back toward

Edmond. One look at them told me that they understood.

And then he rose up from his throne, smaller than any of the other Kings, but a boy in the eyes of all the men present. "Scotland shall stand with you!" David, King of Scotland drew his sword and held it high.

Magnus looked around at the other kings then stood. "I cannot argue with that - Sweden stands. And with us the remnant of the Khans."

Louis stood up. "There is nothing more to be done nor said," he sighed, "The Empire will fight with you."

Philip stood. "I have nothing more to lose. I will renew my honor, and the honor of my people!"

Alphonso and Edward looked at each other. Neither wanted to stand up and hatred for each other blazed in their eyes. Alphonso broke away from Edward's stare and stood up. "Castile fights with you, to the last man."

Edmond fixed his gaze upon Edward. The tension in the room built for a moment, and a moment only. He sighed and breathed. "England stands."

Edmond pulled his sword from the ground and sheathed it, "Either we die alone, or stand together for the one true King," he turned his back to the kings and marched out of the tent. I followed close behind leaving everyone staring in awe after their new commander - the commander of kings.

XIX

WHEN HEROES FALL

I spoke once we were safely away from the king's tent, "I knew you could get them to follow you to Shrewton, but that was quite the speech!"

"I told you the time was coming," he replied soberly, "the time is now here," he sighed.

***

I stood outside Shrewton, the town before me, an army behind, and friends on either side. Wind blew in my face and sent chills through me, but nothing compared to the cold fear. I knew that what we were about to face would cost, but I could never have fathomed how much.

Andrew broke the power of the silence, "We shall enter alone first and talk to whoever is in there. If it is Roger, we will seek peace before war."

"There is no other way," I exclaimed. "The Roger we once knew is dead. That creature must die before we rest tonight!"

"Vengeance is mine, says the LORD," Andrew replied. "If Roger is who you say, then God will give justice in His own time. It is not your place to cast judgment, lest you be judged by the same standard."

His words stung. "Very well," I growled. "We will talk first."

"Thank you, Richard. You, Edmond and I shall go in," Andrew said to me then turned to Piper, Luke and Feargal. "You three stay here. If battle breaks out before we return, hold your ground for thirty minutes. If either I, Edmond or Richard do not return before that time is up, then fall back to Durrington and ready yourselves for the defense of the town."

"As you wish," Luke replied.

Andrew nodded. "And Richard, you will talk to him."

"Me?" I asked.

"You believe that Roger is against us," he sighed. "That is something I cannot believe."

"Fine," I answered, turning toward the town.

Andrew placed his hand on my shoulder. "If it is Roger, do not go to war. Remember who he is. He is our brother."

I nodded and faced Shrewton once more and began walking toward it with Andrew and Edmond.

"I demand an audience with Apollo!" I shouted to whosoever was waiting for us.

One man emerged from behind a house and walked out of the town. He was dressed in a black surcoat and cloak which billowed in the wind and his hands were covered with black leather gloves. At his left side, he bore a sword so black that it seemed to reflect death itself. With each step of his advance, I could sense the dread of our army and feel their withdrawal of several paces.

"You wish to speak with my master?" the Adversary's voice plunged deep into our conscience, provoking an unearthly fear in its wake.

"I demand an audience with Apollo," I repeated.

"He is the master to me. And to you, he is your judge," he grinned sadistically.

"He is Apollo to me and all these men here with me," I said as calmly as I could, "and I demand an audience with him, on threat of war and overtures of peace. Terms of which will be the safety of me and my companions. Are we understood?"

"An audience you shall have," the Adversary replied. "Follow. He has been expecting you. Your terms are met. Harm will not come to you."

"Very well," I replied.

The Adversary slowly turned himself around, quizzically staring at Andrew as he went. "Follow," he said with something like pain in his voice, then shook himself and scowled. We followed him into Shrewton. So much had changed that I hardly recognized my old home except for the one thing which remained unchanged. I looked at the house and tears came to my eyes. I stopped and stared at it for the first time in thirteen years. The most painful memory came back to me as if it had just happened. Our home where I once lived, the home where everything I loved was lost. 'Of course, he would keep it the same!' I thought in hatred of the monster. 'Curse him!'

"Move on," the Adversary nearly stammered, pressing the flat of his sword into my armour. "He will not wait forever!"

So onward we walked along the deserted roads of the desolate town. Past the silent alleys and through the streets where my fear and hatred was born.

"Where are the people?" asked Andrew as he searched every crossroad we passed. "Where are they?"

"They are here," replied the Adversary.

"Where?" Andrew repeated.

"You will see," the Adversary smirked then turned again to confusion as he looked at Andrew.

Soon we came to the center of town where the Aundray manor stood, but not exactly as I remembered it. This time the manor was much darker and it looked as if it had not been occupied in many years.

Surrounding the manor was a gruesome sight – hundreds of statues, perhaps even thousands, led in a trail to the western end of town.

"What did you do?" asked Andrew as he stared at the army of stone. "Are these the citizens of Shrewton?"

"Are they dead?" I asked.

"The ones closest to the manor are delivered," the Adversary smirked again. "The rest are alive – more or less."

"You are a monster," Edmond scowled.

The Adversary drew his sword and met Edmond's already drawn blade. "I promised safety from harm," he glared at Edmond in fury. "I never said I would not retaliate!"

"And I promised nothing," Edmond fumed.

"If you face me, you will die," the Adversary threatened.

"Face me without your black magic," Edmond challenged, "and see who remains alive, villain."

The Adversary lowered his sword. "Your time has not yet come and it is unwise to keep my master waiting."

"Where are we going?" I asked.

"To the comfort of home," the Adversary jeered.

We navigated through the statues and continued our course westward toward the end of Shrewton.

Finally, we came upon an old, run down house. The shutters were torn off, one window and the stench of death emanated from it.

The door swung open to reveal the form of the man I dreaded to see.

"Come in! Come in!" Roger beckoned us like a mad man. I began walking toward the house. Andrew stared in disbelief at Roger. Pain filled his eyes as he realized that I was right. I turned away from him and facing Roger, entered the house with Andrew and Edmond reluctantly following.

"So here we are, old friends now leading opposite sides of a war," he laughed hideously. "Leave us," he scolded the Adversary.

The Adversary left us alone. I almost wished he had stayed, for the man before us was even more dreadful.

"No more lies, no more riddles," I demanded. "I want to know what you want."

"Oh Richard," his demeanor remained terrifyingly calm, "are you such a fool?"

"If I am a fool, I will be remembered as the one who stood against you."

He smiled again, more demented than before. "Oh but you will not be remembered by anyone because they will all be dead!" he chuckled. "But all the more excited I am!" he outstretched his arms. "For your army surrounding the town will be such a glorious ending to my conquest of the world!" he seated himself at the table and beckoned me to sit as well. I sat down while Andrew and Edmond stood on either side of my chair.

"Tell me what you want and all of this can end," I said as I sat down in the chair. "No one else has to die."

"I do not want to kill them! If you thought that, you are a bigger fool than that man Solomon always talked about! Or was that David? The fool that fought the giant. Much like you, only, this time the giant will gain the victory. Your faith is weak and your hatred is strong. The Brethren shall fall. But all of these people - I do not care whether they live or die."

"Have you seen this town?" I said. "You say you do not want to kill them! Meanwhile, you have a graveyard right outside and the rest of the world burning in ruin!"

Roger smiled again distantly.

"And it was you who took their lives!" I yelled. "You are no giant! You are a monster!"

"I am no monster! Not all of them are dead. They are merely waiting," he laughed. "In fact, I am giving them eternal life! I have given them what all men dream of!"

"That is not life," I pointed outside. "That is torment!"

"If that is what you call it," he sighed, "then you lack vision," he sneered. "Why can you not see that I want the same thing as you?"

"Your madness even surpasses your servant!" I returned.

"Look at yourself! Your hope is foolishness!" his voice rose. "Your hope is nothing but conflict! Distress! Thus, you come to me to either destroy or confirm it! Oh, Richard, why can you not see? We are the same. We want the same thing, we both want the end of conflict."

"We are not the same!" I slammed my hands on the table.

"Yes," he laughed. "Yes, we are."

"I will never be like you!"

"Both members of the Brethren. Both lost what is dear to them. Both on a path that few have trodden. Both willing to die for it. No matter what it does to our conscience and soul!" he paused. "Only on your path you doubt your life, fear me and die for nothing!"

"I do not fear you!" I drew my sword and slashed it into the table.

"Richard!" Edmond placed his hand on my shoulder. "That is enough," he glared at Roger. "That is quite enough! Surrender now Roger or die in your cause."

"So, 'Fearless Edmond'," Roger sneered, "let us test that claim shall we? Say, a horde of Varanus?"

"Surrender or die!" I echoed Edmond's words as I felt Andrew's hand upon my shoulder. I shook him off.

"And if I say no?" Roger grinned. "I know you all too well. You would never kill me. After all I have done for you."

"Roger," I stared into his eyes. Both anger and sorrow welled up. "If you bring more death to this world, you leave us no choice but to end your life."

"My answer is no."

"Then you choose death," I warned.

"No," he smiled and motioned his hand to where the Adversary had just returned. I turned to the door where the Adversary stood with Henry's beaten form in his clutches. "One step closer." Roger pulled the vial of the Varanus' venom from his cloak. "And Henry, 'our brother,' will die."

I could no longer think clearly through my anger and hatred. How could he? How could Roger do this?

"Finish it!" Henry screamed in pain as the Adversary put a gash in his chest. "Help me. Before it is too late."

I yanked my sword from the table and Andrew grabbed my shoulder saying, "The moment you give in to hate, you become as they are."

"I am not like him!" I shook Andrew off. "He betrayed the Brethren! He betrayed his people! He betrayed mankind! Death is what he deserves!" I tightened my grip on the sword in my hand.

"Your beliefs mean nothing to me," Roger hissed as he threw the vial. I watched the glass fly quickly past yet it seemed as though time had stopped. The vial shattered on impact upon the open wound in Henry's chest, and the venom mixed with his blood as it seeped into his body.

"The Brethren lives!" Henry screamed. "The Brethren rise!" he threw his head back and screamed. Smoke began to rise from his clothes and black scales pierced through his skin.

I snapped to my senses at Henry's dying cries. "What have you done!" I yelled. Edmond and I readied our swords.

"This negotiation is over," Roger replied. "I always planned to turn him into a Varanus, all I did was delay it until I saw fit," he grinned. "Until it would hurt the most," he looked thoughtfully around the house. "Do you remember the last person to die here, Richard? So long ago was it not?"

"You cannot play God!" Andrew yelled. "That is a man you are burning! Roger, mark my words; if you live by the sword, you will die by the sword."

"Dying is not part of my plan Andrew. And playing God?" he sneered. "Why would I be playing?"

"Who died here?" I asked with Henry's cries filling my ears.

"I believe my friend here can tell you that," Roger replied. He laid his hand on the Adversary's shoulder as they both walked out of the house.

The Adversary let go of Henry, now a Varanus, who flew instantly upon us. Edmond maneuvered his sword and tried to sever its head, however, its serpent-like tail wrapped around Edmond's torso and threw him into the wall. The impact splintered the rotting wood and sent Edmond crashing out into the cold.

The Varanus turned to me, grinning with black venom streaming down its devilish smile. I readied my sword – but not my heart.

"Come on!" I cried in rage, yet quivered in fear and anguish. "Come on!" I paused. "Henry," I clenched my teeth, knowing he was dead.

It let out a horrifying screech, gripped my armour and lifted me from my place, venom ever dripping down its jaw. It screeched again revealing rows of teeth ready to sink into my body.

"Henry!" Andrew's voice startled the creature into dropping me. "Henry, fight it!" he yelled. "Fight the monster!" Andrew laid down his sword, and walked up to the creature. "I know you are still there!" he thundered. The Varanus scrambled over to the door.

"Henry is dead," A voice came from the door. The Adversary towered in the splintered frame.

"Not as dead as you," Andrew glared at him.

"Oh, but Andrew," he lifted off his hood, "I have never felt so alive!"

"Who are you?" I stared into his eyes. I had never seen his face in such light. I could tell I knew him, but I could not place where.

He snapped his fingers and left with the words, "Soon blind man, soon."

The Varanus turned and stared at me. It snarled and leapt across the room opening its gaping mouth with its venom pouring like steaming rain onto the floor.

I looked into the Varanus' eyes awaiting the end. It matched my gaze and nearly my hatred as it made the final lunge. But it was cut short quickly by Andrew's sword piercing its shoulder and capturing its attention.

"Oh, Henry," Andrew poised his sword. "Even if you are no longer there, know this - I will never give up my oath to protect mankind! I will never give into the hatred and I will always fight for the glory of God and Christ my Savior! And there is nothing you can do to change that!" The Varanus screeched. "You want to kill me? Come on then," Andrew nodded. "But let him live."

The Varanus leapt at Andrew who jumped out of the way and thrust his sword into the side of the beast.

I readied my sword and joined Andrew in his assault. I aimed for the head, however the beast ducked and sunk its claws deep into my armour, but did not fully penetrate. Andrew slashed off its arm that gripped me and then lay a blow to its leg. The Varanus hobbled back as its arm regrew and crouched down again, ready to pounce.

I dislodged the claws from my armour and advanced upon the Varanus on its left flank. My blade sunk into its back and it screeched.

I wrenched my blade out as it writhed in pain for a moment then I watched as it healed again. I began to lose heart in the fight. But in that split second of doubt, the creature cast me into one of the remaining walls. The impact weakened the wall just enough so that the roof collapsed upon the fight, but far from ended it.

I struggled to free myself from the rubble as the Varanus burst forth in fury. It fixed its fiery gaze upon me and leapt in my direction. I searched frantically for help but Edmond was nowhere to be seen.

I almost closed my eyes and later wished I had, for suddenly Andrew came up behind the Varanus and leapt onto its back with his sword imbedded in the creature. The Varanus spun around trying to get Andrew off. Finally, it threw itself backward onto the ground. Andrew tried to get off in time but his leg was caught under the crushing force of the beast. I tried with all my strength and rage to free myself but all my efforts were in vain. I watched in horror as the Varanus pounced upon Andrew. "For Christ, I live, and for Him I die!" the Varanus sunk its venomous bite into Andrew's shoulder and teeth into his flesh. It looked toward me, and then toward the east and ran off in that direction.

With new strength, I broke myself free and ran to Andrew's side.

"Andrew!" I cried in horror and anger as I collapsed next to him, "What have you done!" I stared at a black bloody wound on his side. "What have I done? It was coming for me!" my voice fell to little more than a whisper. "It was coming for me."

"It is all as it should be," he coughed. Blood spilled from his mouth. "Do not worry about me," scales began to form on the sides of his face, he clenched his teeth, sweat began to form on his brow. He put his hand on my shoulder. "Do not let him go," he stammered as he gazed up at the sky and weakly pointed to my heart. "Save him."

"Andrew, you are the one who must not let go!" I cried as the tears broke their bonds and streaked down my dirt covered face. "You can fight it, Andrew! You can beat the monster!"

"No," Andrew pointed weakly up again, "He is waiting for you to accept Him!" he gasped and winced from the pain.

I clenched my teeth, even in the shadow of death he could not leave me in darkness.

"Andrew hold on! Do not let go!" he slowly began to go pale and weaken in my arms. "Do not let go!" the image of Bennet's hand slipping away entered my mind. Henry's screams and my parents' blood. "Please! Andrew please..."

"The door is opening for me Richard," his clothes began smoldering. "I will see Him today, I will tell Him about you! And I want you to see Him too when your race is done," he arched back letting out a scream of pain. He lay his scaling hand on my shoulder. "Finish it!"

"No!" I stammered.

He looked up at me with loving eyes – they looked exactly the same as Bennet's. Joy in the pain. Hope in suffering. Triumph in death.

"It is okay," he grabbed my hand and lay it on my sword. "It is all well."

I raised my sword. "Do not make me do this!"

He smiled and nodded. "He is waiting."

"Andrew no!"

He laid his hand on mine, "He is waiting for you," he whispered, "run to Him!" as he pulled my sword into his chest. And let go.

LEGACY OF OUR BROTHERS

I felt a hand on my shoulder. "Edmond go away!" I cried in anguish as Andrew's final words reverberated like cymbals in my mind; echoed like the beating of dying drums.

"Richard." A powerful voice spoke, so powerful that even Edmond could not have been its source. "I told you we would meet again."

I did not look up to see who it was but somehow I knew the white rider had returned.

"He is with me now," He said.

"Why did he have to die?" I cried.

"My son, such things are not for you to know," I could feel His warmth and compassion. "But this you must know, he is with the angels glorifying God. His faith was great and his hope the same. He loved me with all his heart, and he was willing to give up what was most precious to him on this earth to see me."

"He gave his life and he gave up the Alignment," I stammered. "Because of me! He will never see the Alignment because of me!"

I paused and closed my eyes tightly. "He will never see his son again," tears welled up in my eyes, "because of me."

"No, my son," He said, "his life was not precious to him. The Alignment was only a passion for truth, to fill his life and give him hope, but now he is consumed in truth, eternal life and his hope is fulfilled. And he is at peace knowing that you will restore his son to him."

"Then what did he give up? What was possibly more precious to him than finding his own son? Or his life? What was it?"

"It was you," His words pierced my heart. "You were the most precious thing to him. The most precious one to release to me. In the end, he did release you. To me. And I will never let you go." Indescribable shame engulfed me; my hatred and anger had accomplished nothing except tearing Andrew away from me.

"Who are you?" I wept.

He proclaimed, "I am the Son of God, who loves you. I am, and I always will be! I am here as I was then, and I will be forevermore. I am the King of Kings and Lord of Lords. I am One with my Father as I will be with you, even until the end of the age. And forevermore. I am Jesus, whom you have pushed away so many times."

"I am ready," I stammered. "My heart is open. Please. I cannot do it on my own anymore. I never could."

"I know," He knelt down next to me. "I know," I felt His smile. "Go now my son, the Brethren awaits, for five stars will rise, for the war is fought on both battleground, and in the heart of mankind," and before another word was spoken, He was gone.

I sat there alone for a few minutes in silence. I had no words to say nor any thoughts, all I had was hope. And that was enough.

"Richard!" Edmond returned to the rubble of the house. "It is madness out there! The Varanus have attacked the army!" he looked around the pile of rubble and saw Andrew's body.

"What happened?" he asked. His jaw was clenched so hard that I could see it shaking. A tear splashed into the rubble.

I stared back at him. "Pull back the army. There has been far too much blood for one day."

He put his hand on my shoulder. "Do not do anything you will regret. Honor Andrew's legacy." he drew in a deep quivering breath, "Will you do it?"

"There are things that must be done," I set my face like flint. "The war is not over yet."

Edmond and I left the ruins of the house and ran stride for stride until a Varanus met us in the street. A battle ensued, but Edmond ordered me to press onward. I refused to leave him, but he would not have it another way. And so, after running through the streets of Shrewton, I found the traitor – the puppeteer. I stared up at Roger as he stood upon the roof of one of the houses, gazing out at the chaos he had created.

"Roger!" I shouted to him. "The Brethren live! It is not over - even as man dies and legions fall. As surely as I stand before you this day, the Brethren live!"

Roger leapt from the roof onto the street. "Truth fails and mercy dies," He drew his sword. "Now the light will die!"

I drew my sword and met his as he sneered. "You are not my final prize Richard. You have no idea what you are doing!"

"It is not too late Roger," I said as our swords scraped down and locked on the hilt. "You do not have to do this."

"Too late for what?" he smiled. "Death?" he kicked my chest and sent me stumbling backward. "For you, it is right on time!"

"Can you not see what you have become? Roger please, I do not want you to be as I was."

"I have always been as you are Richard," he swung his sword slamming into mine, "a hateful wretch!" he let loose a wave of attacks which I thwarted to the best of my ability.

"You speak right about the past, but I am no longer as you are," I slashed and almost hit his left side. He leapt out of the way and swung his sword around. I dropped down as the sword slashed the air above me. "For I have seen Him! I have seen the Son of God! And if He forgives me, He can forgive you!"

"He let your parents die!" he blocked another hit from me and countered with a slice to my leg. I blocked and positioned my defenses for another attack.

"No," I stood strong for the first time. "He gave them a new life, I do not know how, but I see the truth now."

"No!" he came in and gripped my throat. "They died because of their weakness! They died because you were not able to save them! You ran in your dread and cost your father his life! And now Andrew is dead because of your weakness!"

I was silent with the fear and weight of my former shame.

I looked around and caught a glimpse of the Adversary, then gazed back straight into Roger's eyes. I kicked Roger in the gut and ran my sword through his right shoulder. He reeled back in pain, gripping his wound. "Do you really think you can kill me?" he spoke through gritted teeth.

Out of the corner of my eye, I saw the Adversary walking toward me.

"Roger," I said lowering my sword, "end this now."

"I cannot," he gasped.

"End it!" I commanded.

"I cannot, fool!"

"What-" my words were cut off as the Adversary tore my sword from my hand and wrapped his other hand around my throat. The

Adversary's iron grip tightened even stronger than Roger's. I knelt before him quickly losing air.

"Think of the cold and the pain," the Adversary grinned. "Think of the hunger and death that you were unable to stop. Think of how the Brethren failed in their attempts to save these people!" he lifted me from where I knelt. "Think of me when you slump over and darkness settles upon you!" his eyes blazed.

"Who?" I gagged.

He threw me down and kicked me in the chest. "Who died in that house?" he said. "Can you not remember?"

"What?" I stammered.

"Who died in that house?" he screamed. "The first death you ever saw! Tell me, Richard! Who was it?"

I thought as hard as I could. Running my mind through every person I had seen die in Shrewton. The Adversary drew his sword and prepared to strike. Despair came over me and clouded my thoughts. I thought about my mother and father. I thought about Bennet and Andrew. Then it came to me. The first death. The death which thrust me into years of torment.

I stared up at him, blood trickled from my mouth "Norwood?" I stammered.

His sword missed and dug into the ground next to me. Tears fell from his eyes as he bent over his sword. His eyes were bright for a moment. "I thought I could save her by joining him. I thought I could do good. But he killed her! He killed them all!" he shook himself and stood up while his eyes blazed with hatred once more. "Just as you will be killed!" he raised his sword again, but immediately a blade came through his chest and stopped him.

"He is mine," Roger hissed as the Adversary fell to one knee. "And so are you, as you have always been!"

The Adversary looked up at Roger. "You know you cannot kill

me," he said. "Not even with that!" he gestured to the sword which had laid waste to the people of Shrewton.

Roger gazed at the sword, then at the Adversary. "Hundreds turned to stone because of the blade I have been given. Why are you different than them?"

"Because," the Adversary stood up. "I am part of the reign," he brought his sword around and slashed Roger's tunic. "The question is, are you?"

Roger leapt backward and ducked under another blow. He then sent a thrust to the Adversary's chest but missed and was caught off balance. The Adversary instantly used this chance and laid waste to Roger's shoulder.

"Roger! It is not too late! I know now!" I shouted above the clanging of their swords.

The Adversary lifted Roger by the throat. I ran to his aid, but was thrown back by the Adversary's blade.

"You underestimate me," stammered Roger.

"Perhaps," The Adversary readied his sword. "Let us see your fate," After a brief moment of silence the Adversary turned to me and said, "Behold Richard, you have brought about the destruction of your brother!"

'No!' I thought, but could not say.

"I bring Doubt!" the Adversary grinned as he grabbed Roger's hand and forced his sword toward him.

"No! Please have mercy!" screamed Roger. "This was not supposed to happen! It was not to end this way!"

"I bring Dread!" the sword inched closer.

"You cannot kill me! I am immortal as you are! I know you!"

"Not anymore!" the Adversary replied.

I stared in horror.

"Would you kill your friend?" Roger stammered. "The one man who knows who you really are?"

"I bring Death!" the Adversary thundered.

"Kill me, and you will never be at peace. Kill me and you will always be searching. You will be in torment for eternity!"

I turned and ran from the town just as I had so long ago. I wished not to see another death in that town. Screaming in pain was the last I heard of Roger Wilson that day.

I ran out of the town, to the east. The Varanus tracks lead in the same direction. 'They have taken the ring,' I thought as I made my way skirting their location and moved past - onward to Durrington and the Brethren.

XXI

"WE STAND AS ONE!"

It began to rain as night fell. I tried to accept that my nightmare had ended, but I was reminded of all the times I had failed. 'Henry is now dead, and no one even knows his name,' I thought in shame. 'Roger, lost in pride and anger, destroyed by his own servant,' I strained to forget. 'Norwood is alive, but has been bewitched by darkness,' I fell to my knees. 'And Andrew – now gone forever. Like a father to me – he never gave up,' tears entered my eyes and I collapsed. 'Like my father before, he was strong through death!' I stood up and stretched my arms to the sky. "It is all in Your hands LORD God!" I cried. "Your will be done!" I put my head in my hands, trying to dispel the doubt and dread. "I will stand for You!" I clenched my teeth and fought the darkness. "I will fight for You!" My voice rose to the greatest height and strength. "Onward, oh my soul!" I commanded myself. "To end the lying tongues! To the end of this war! Forever I will fight and stand for You! By Your hand, I will be made new. Wipe my shame away, wipe away the darkness and hate oh God!" I turned back to the east and continued running to Durrington all the while repeating over and over: "When shadows mark the line and five stars rise. When truth fails and mercy dies now the light shines in the skies. There is something about the Alignment. The Stars, the Orbs. Truth fails and mercy dies," I ran harder as rain stung my face as it had that night, thirteen years before. But now a new man ran, with faith not dying, but becoming stronger with every stride. "Where are the shadows?" I yelled. "It is time to shine the light!" I pushed onward to Durrington to rally the Brethren once more.

I soon slowed to a walk from exhaustion and came to Durrington in the early morning, later than I had hoped. The sun slowly rose on the horizon, but it was covered as though shrouded in darkness and cast only a dim light upon Durrington. The rain had subsided but still the clouds ever darkened. It felt like night had fallen upon the world. A night that no dawn could end.

"Richard!" Piper ran out to meet me and we embraced. "We thought you were dead."

"I did," I said. "I died in Shrewton."

"What?" Piper queried.

"The man I was," I gazed into her eyes, "he is dead," I smiled with a laugh. "And I am alive!"

"What do you mean?" she asked, but her eyes said that she knew. Richard Armistead was a new man.

I nearly fell to the ground, "May I sit somewhere?"

"Of course, Edmond is at your house waiting for you. Do you wish to go there?" she replied.

"Yes, please. Thank you," I said as I took in her radiance with new eyes.

We journeyed slowly through the town passing thousands of soldiers, French, Castilian, English, Bavarian, Swedes and the strangest men, the remnant of the Khanates, with rounded sabers and bows that looked like snakes. All of them were beaten and broken.

"What happened?" I asked.

"The battle of Salisbury Plain happened," Piper explained. "A Varanus came out from your direction and attacked. It infected first two men of the army, and then ten succumbed, and chaos ensued. The Scotsmen were not prepared for the attack because of the absence of leadership and their inexperience with the Varanus. The French field commander rallied his troops and the remainder of the Scots and formed a barricade against the Varanus, allowing the remaining men to retreat."

"God help us all," I breathed as I stared at the battered troops.

Piper only nodded and continued with me through the ranks of beaten soldiers.

"I am so sorry," I said many times as we walked. I thought of their families. I wondered how many were married or had children. It took all my strength not to collapse in grief, and throw my head into my hands, for all who fell on Salisbury Plain were on me and their blood was my responsibility.

Finally, we arrived at my home and Edmond ran out to help me inside. He led me to a comfortable chair where Feargal and Luke were waiting.

"What happened?" Edmond asked.

"He came to me," I paused staring at Edmond. "Your King. My King," tears began to well up as I recalled our meeting, and all that ensued. "All my life I have lived for myself. I helped create the Brethren to protect myself," I paused. "I have sinned so much. I sinned against you when we formed the Brethren. I wanted you for your strength, not for your faith. I did not trust you when I should have. I murdered a man and slashed his body apart in my rage and vengeance. I did not uphold what I vowed," I clenched my teeth. "But back there," I stammered, "back there in Shrewton I felt something new," the tears broke through their bonds. "I felt a fire – a fire that has ignited a blaze in my heart," I looked at Edmond. "A fire I have not felt since my father was murdered. I felt faith and freedom! I felt that no matter what happened, it would all be all right, even if we died, even if we failed. It is as Andrew said, 'this world is only a place to display our faith.' And for the first time in thirteen years I truly have it. I have faith!" I stood up and looked at Edmond directly, "Can you forgive me?"

He gripped my shoulders and looked at me with tears in his eyes, "And I have waited all these years to hear you say these words!" his voice carried the most emotion I had ever heard come from Edmond. "I forgive you Richard!" he embraced me. "And a thousand times more I forgive you!"

"Thank you," I groaned, "thank you." I leaned back in my chair and looked around.

Luke stood motionless next to Piper. "Did I miss something?" he asked.

"No, nothing is amiss," answered Piper. "If anything, something has been found."

"What now?" Feargal asked. "We are finished. There is nothing more we can do. We have no advantage, an army that stands against us and another army in ruin."

"Andrew selected you," I said, "but he is dead now, so you are free to go. Find your family, or anyone you hold dear to you and run. Run as far from here as you can. And to you Piper and Luke, perhaps the Varanus will not make it to Scotland. You too may go if you desire."

"No," Piper spoke, "we cannot leave now. After all this, there is no way to leave. No world to go back to."

"Please," I urged her. "I cannot see you die, not today. Not ever."

"I have no family, my parents are gone, my brothers are too," said Feargal. "Where will I go that they will not find me? I am with you, even if it means death! I want to be part of the Brethren."

"As do I!" Piper exclaimed.

"If it is not always this fun," remarked Luke. "I stand with you and against those wretched bags of stench. And, and. Oh biscuit's blood! Onward to the end of them or us."

I looked at Edmond. "Well then - I guess a pledge is in order?"

"Aye," Edmond said.

"Right then," I said, "repeat after me," I turned to Edmond briefly. "I have never done this without Andrew," turning back to Feargal, Piper and Luke.

"On my honor, in union with the Brethren, I hereby pledge to do Christ's will and all in my power, to Heal all Offenses, to help all those in need, and to Protect the Earth and those in it from whatever perils should come."

They repeated the words with more passion than anyone I had ever heard; even Roger whose passion surpassed all of us when he spoke the pledge, paled in comparison to the hope that resonated and was resurrected by their conviction.

"Andrew was right," I said. "We should have waited for the Alignment."

"When is it?" asked Piper.

"It is today." I said remembering Andrew's words from our voyage on the Silver Star. "When the sun rises over the ring of stone."

"The Varanus and the Adversary will be there," Feargal stated, "there is no way we can get through them all."

"We have an army," I said.

"They will not help us anymore – not after what happened at Salisbury Plain," Feargal countered.

"They either die with us or die later," I said. "And we need their help."

"Pardon me Richard," Luke said, "I believe that is too close to Edmond's line."

"You will have to try to convince them," Feargal appealed. "It will not be easy."

"Is anything?" I turned and left the house followed by Edmond. We walked down the streets of Durrington, each one lined with countless soldiers. We found Edward and the rest of the kings in the town hall with our welcome exhausted.

"You!" hollered Alfonso as he pointed his finger at Edmond when we entered the room. "You led us into a death trap. How dare you face us?"

"I am sorry for your losses," Edmond spoke. "But what we did saved so many more. For it was not you who risked his life. You did not go into the fires. No! The Brethren walked through hell to give you a chance! It is true you lost men, but the army still stands. The Brethren lost their leader; the Brethren risked everything and lost just as much. And you are there on your throne – safe away from danger! Always remember what the Brethren did for you and do not cast your reproach on us!"

Alfonso was silent.

"But even so," Edmond's tone changed. "I hereby resign as Commander of the Alliance."

Surprise spread over each king's face as Edmond spoke. "My leader is dead. It is no longer my place to lead. That position belongs to another," he laid his hand on my shoulder.

"That man is no commander! That man is nothing!" Alfonso spoke out again. "He will lead us to ruin!"

Edmond retorted, "The Varanus are now at the ring awaiting midday for the Alignment. If they succeed, there will be no war to fight – it will be a slaughter for all mankind! But this man before you knows more about the Alignment than any man! The man he was yesterday is dead. This man is new. This man is alive with hope! This man will lead us out of the Varanus' flame and into battle like no other!

A battle that will decide the fate of the world. This man stands for our King, for our Savior!"

"And what if I say no?" Alfonso snarled.

"Then I will gather whoever has strength to stand and fight without you," I thundered.

"Then prepare to go alone! I am finished dealing with peasant boys and fantasies!" Alfonso crossed his arms and leaned back in his chair with a scowl.

"You saw the Varanus. They are no fantasy!" I responded with equal force pointing my finger at Alfonso.

"No, your hope is the fantasy!" Alphonso hissed.

"Wait," King Edward spoke. He walked over to me, "I heard the accounts of Salisbury Plain. I heard the stories of the men who laid down their lives for their homeland," he turned back to face the other kings. "Is that not worth fighting for? For their memory? To make sure that they are never forgotten!" he drew his sword. "I stand with the Brethren! And with God for whom they serve! If we perish, it is God's will! But let it be known!" he laid his sword upon the table. "England stands today!"

"France is no more," Philip spoke. "We have nothing to lose. We have nothing to go back to," he stood up. "The people of France will avenge themselves this day." he drew his sword and laid it next to Edward's.

"This is madness," Alfonso gasped. "You really believe this fool?"

"The Holy Roman Empire stands at your disposal," said Louis as he too drew his sword and laid it upon the table with its tip nearly touching the other two. "I trust you will do God's will."

David was silent.

"Why not?" said Magnus. "One more fight. Our final stand!

Our legacy shall be remembered with our fallen brothers! Sweden will stand!" and he laid his sword next to the others.

"And you Alfonso?" I said. "What will the Castilians die for? What will they stand for?"

Alfonso gazed at me. His bitterness was depleted. The fire in his eyes was dying and he knew it. He opened his mouth and spoke. "Castile rides one more time with you. Their lives will be remembered," he said as he too placed his sword upon the table.

David's head was downcast. I walked over and laid my hand on the boy's shoulder. "I failed my people," he wept. "I failed Scotland!"

"No David," I said. "Scotland fought the giant. Scotland stood at the front lines. They gave up everything. Scotland saved the world."

"We have only a remnant – only three hundred."

"Then show the enemy Scotland's faith and stand as Gideon against the foe and by Christ, we will see God's hand deliver us!"

Tears welled up in his eyes as his faith was rekindled. "The giant falls today. We are with you, till the final day!" he declared and his face turned as flint as he walked to the center table and placed his sword down with the five.

Edmond drew his sword and walked over to the table. "Forever the Brethren shall stand!" he thundered as he sunk his sword into the center of the table just grazing the tips of each king's sword. We all watched dumbfounded as a light began to shine from Edmond's sword and carried down onto the other six blades. A moment later, smoke rose from the table as the swords blazed and then flashed.

Edmond drew his sword from the rest as the kings stared in awe. "No matter what the price may be."

"No matter the pain," David said as he pulled his sword from the rest.

"No matter the sorrow," Philip spoke, as he followed David's action.

"No matter how much we are hated," Alfonso pulled his sword off the table.

"No matter how many lies we have told," Louis spoke and held up his sword.

"No matter how marred our honor," Magnus did the same.

Edward laid his hand upon his sword. "No matter what suffering we must endure!" he held his sword high as all the other kings followed. All six swords held high above the table where the mark of seven swords now lay, branded into the oak wood of the table.

"This is the calling of the Brethren," I said. "This is the price we must pay. We must endure pain, suffering and sorrow. We must repent of our lies. We must be hated in this world. And our honor shall not be seen in the eyes of men, but in the eyes of God. This is our burden – this is our strength. We bring love to all men through Christ. We bring faith to the field of battle! We bring hope to the darkest hour! This hour we bring hope! This day! We have faith!"

Each King and every guard let out a battle cry at once and carried on until I raised my hand to silence them. "We must plan our attack." I said emphatically.

I sent one of the guards to summon Feargal, Piper and Luke to help develop the plan. The doors of the hall burst open as Luke entered. "Battle plan is it?" he exclaimed. "Let us hand those stench buckets…" Luke stopped short as he walked up to the table. He lay his hand upon it, feeling the details branded into the wood. He looked up from the emblem. The new emblem. The new sign of the Brethren. The emblem of hope. "Oh, I like this table."

Over the next hour, we developed the plan. There was nothing left to do but fight.

We decided that the Brethren would lead the frontal assault upon the ring of stone with the Scots, French, English and Castilians at our side. We would concentrate our greatest strength on the southern edge of the plain leading up to the stones. Once the southern front of the enemy was weakened, then Louis and Magnus with the Romans, Swedes and remnant of the Khans would charge upon the east flank and lay waste to that portion of the Varanus. Once that was taken, the Alliance would converge their troops upon the southeast center and concentrate the entire force as a wedge and fan to the south and east to provide passage through the horde to deliver the Brethren into the center of the stones – and to victory.

Humanity stood on the edge of destruction as we made our final preparations for the battle.

We arrived at the southern edge of the plain leading up to the ring. Midday was closing in quickly. All the world was assembled behind the Brethren this one last time – all mankind was unified against a single threat.

Edmond, Piper, Luke, Feargal and I rode at the head of the army. Lightening cracked the sky. I turned my horse to face the army.

"Here we are," I shouted. "We have all lost something, but through the pain, it has made us stronger. It has formed us. Shaped us," I turned my horse broadside to the host before and rode slowly down the ranks. "And do you know what has brought us here? Ask yourself. Why are you here? Hope! It is because of hope that we stand here this day. Our enemy said there was no hope! But if there was no hope, there would not be a host of men before me ready to die for their people, for their children, for all mankind!" I turned my horse and rode the other way down the ranks of the army. "Our hope brought us here and our hope, our faith in our Savior shall bring us through, no matter the cost! Today we cry - 'No more will darkness reign!'"

The men let out a collective cry of affirmation and resolve.

"But before the battle begins, before the blood starts running with the rain, I offer all of you a choice! A choice to stay and fight this war with us! To fight this final battle! So all you who wish not to be remembered in the pages of history, go now lest I enter you into the rage of battle! But all you men with hearts pure and devoted to God and your people, and full of love for those who went before us – stand with me this day! And if I am the only one, so be it! No more do I fight for myself, but I stand with Christ and His people! I stand for my brothers and my family, for my Father in heaven and earth! For my Savior!

"So onward men of courage! Onward men of God! Onward men of hope for this day we stand for Him! This day we stand for honor! This day we stand for hope! This day we stand for truth!" I drew my sword and reared my horse "This day!" my horse broke into a full gallop. "We stand. As. One!"

Wind blew in my hair and rain in my face. I dared not look back, and hardly to look forward. The stones rose higher into my sight, the sun nearly at the Alignment point. And a horde of Varanus swarmed around the ring.

"Look to their heads!" Edmond shouted. "Aim for their heads!"

I caught a glimpse of what was behind the Brethren. The entire army rode or ran behind me. The Varanus began to stir. As I closed my eyes, everything around seemed to stop. I felt the heartbeat of the horse and felt its hooves pounding on the ground. The wind whipped all around me, every raindrop felt more precious than my own blood. 'Jesus, for You, we stand.' I said to myself. 'Let Thy will be done!'

The lines of cavalry met the Varanus. The shrieks of dying men and Varanus instantly filled the air.

"The ring Brethren!" I shouted as I disappeared into the masses.

"To the stone ring!" I slashed the head off the first Varanus, and another came from my left and slashed the side of my horse. It reared up in pain, but I managed to stay on its back and stabbed my sword into the monster as it stepped back a few paces. Another Varanus attacked just as I withdrew my sword from the second. The Varanus slashed the head of my horse with its claw, killing it instantly and throwing me to the ground.

I landed on the back of another Varanus which grabbed my armour and slammed me into the muddy earth, holding me fast with both claws. It screeched as venom poured from its mouth and it prepared for the death blow.

Suddenly, the Varanus turned to stone with Piper's sword through its head. She leapt off its back and was about to help me out from under it when another Varanus gripped her back and carried her deeper into the battle.

"Piper!" I screamed as I watched her disappear into the chaos. I glared at the now stone Varanus pushing me into the mud. I pushed it with every ounce of strength I had and slowly began to work myself free. The sounds of battle rang in my ears. The screams of the dying and the burning filled the air. I thought of Piper and Andrew. I could barely breathe in the stench of searing flesh.

I continued to fight against my stone enemy for another few minutes. "I have been too late enough times!" I yelled with the final push from beneath the Varanus.

I hoisted myself out of the mud and vomited onto the ground. My head was light, and my hands were shaking. I fumbled around and finally found the blade of my sword in the mud. I winced as it cut into my palm and pulled it out by the hilt.

With my sword in hand, I climbed up onto the back of the statue of my former enemy to get a better view of the battle. The final ranks of the frontal assault tore their way into the horde and became intermixed with it. Thousands of statues littered the field. The smell of blood began to overwhelm the smell of the flesh burning. But there was another stench which filled my nostrils, the stench Luke always called the Varanus, the thick, deep smell of their venom. I did not notice it before, for it was so slight, but Luke must have experienced it like this when the Varanus attacked Château de Dourdan. And now with their numbers in the thousands, their deathly smell was so potent that it was almost overwhelming.

All around me men fought the beasts, and countless fires lit up the field – the fires of our brothers as they turned against us.

I looked toward the east. The forces of the Empire, the Swedes and the Khans crashed into the east flank. The east edge slowly gave way as the Varanus fled or were turned to stone. Finally, a line was formed around the south and east edges of the battle.

The wedge soon formed and began pushing toward the ring. But to my dismay our progress was halted. The two armies clashed, neither one moving forward or back.

I turned to the west and set the ring of stone in my sight. Resolve swept over me as I decided that the Brethren would have to go alone. I leapt off the Varanus and continued my fight in that direction.

Rain and sweat streaked my face. Blood and mud covered my body. I struck down one more Varanus and paused to take a breath. Noon was coming faster than I thought and I was only halfway to the ring. 'Had the others made it? Was Piper alive? Where was Edmond?' questions raced through my mind.

I climbed onto another statue and gazed to where the wedge should have been. Instead, I saw swarms of Varanus and the armies of men losing ground. I clenched my teeth and turned toward the ring.

Suddenly I caught sight of Luke fighting like a mad man. At least five statues were around him and many more Varanus closing in. I ran to his side and defended his flank as he laid waste to another Varanus.

"Good of you to show up!" he yelled over the sound of battle.

"I could not just leave you here, even as annoying as you are!" I yelled back. "Try to get to the ring!" I ordered and continued my advance after slaying another monster.

"Is that all you have?" the Adversary's voice boomed above the sounds of the battle. "Come on," he taunted, "show me your strength! Show me your God!"

Strength filled my heart. I cut the head off a Varanus and fought with even more vigor toward the ring and to the Adversary. The fight

I thought would end it all. The fight to free myself from my enemy.

I finally broke through the ranks of the Varanus and walked into the small clearing where the ring stood. Edmond ran to my side as I came near the stones.

"We are being overrun!" he yelled.

"I know!" I returned. "All we can do is fight to the end!"

"What do you think we have been doing?" Luke ran up next to us. "Oh, yes! I have been braiding my hair!"

"Get the Brethren here!" I ordered "It will take all of us," I began to walk toward the ring.

"Wait," Edmond stopped me.

"What?" I replied curtly.

He held his sword out to me. "Take it," he said, "you will need it."

"I cannot wield it," I said.

"Times have changed, and so have you Richard," he smiled. "I have had it long enough. It is time for a new man to carry it."

I reached out and took the sword. Its balance was perfect and the blade was sharper than a star in the sky. The wielding of it brought hope to my heart and I felt my strength renewed as I turned again to advance upon the ring.

As I advanced, the Adversary suddenly appeared from behind one of the stones. His grin was filled with hideous triumph as he raised his sword to her throat and held Piper's neck in his left hand. She was badly beaten and bloody, with a gash in her leg as well as across her cheek.

Rain poured from the sky like the weeping of a mother over her children. In horror, I stared at the Adversary's grinning face and Piper's dreadful gaze as his sword inched closer. I walked slowly across the clearing until I was within fifteen feet of them.

"Let her go," fear filled me and made my head even more

clouded than before.

"And why would I do that?" he replied pressing his sword harder onto her throat so that she could not speak. But her eyes screamed, 'run!'

"It is me you want," a righteous anger burned within me.

"Or I could just kill her and cause you more pain," he grinned as he pressed his sword to her neck. "Now would that not be an ending?"

"Let her go!" I demanded as I tightened my grip on the sword.

"Never. There is hate still in you," he smiled. "This should be amusing."

"I hate what you have done," I clenched my teeth. "And what has been done to you."

"I remember when I killed your father, how he pleaded for mercy. Perhaps you will do the same," he chuckled. "But her?" he looked at Piper. "No!" he turned back to me. "Her days are done."

"No!" I screamed as I ran toward him. Before I covered the distance between us, the Adversary threw Piper to the ground and swung his blade around to meet another. A deafening clang rang out as the two swords clashed.

"Let. Her. Go." Luke's rage caused the Adversary's face to shudder.

"You know you cannot win," the Adversary locked himself in a duel with Luke. "I have beaten you before, and I will beat you down again."

"I do not care!" Luke yelled as he advanced upon the Adversary with more fury than ever. "She shall see tomorrow! But you will not!"

"My words do not matter fool," he sliced Luke's leg and kicked him in the same place. Luke was kneeling yet still fought. "My sword is your concern now!" the black blade screeched down Luke's sword as the Adversary leaned forward into his face. "And after you, I will kill her too," his lips curled into a cruel grin, "and you will have saved no one!"

I ran to Luke's aid and deflected a death blow from the Adversary, while Luke regained his footing. The two of us, shoulder to shoulder, fought the Adversary and sent him into retreat.

"I will give you a choice before I kill you," the Adversary said calmly as though he had no fatigue. "You can join me and I will let her live. Or I will kill her as you watch."

"Never!" Luke advanced in fury again which clouded his thinking. The Adversary anticipated his attack and ran his sword through the right side of Luke's chest.

"You choose death?" he stared strangely at us. "You could have saved her and yourself, you fool, I offered you life!" he kicked Luke off his sword.

"Death is life for me," Luke collapsed with shallow breaths. Piper, who had been watching the entire engagement, limped to his side and applied pressure to his wound.

"You are a monster," Piper glared up at the Adversary.

"He is not dead," the Adversary sneered. "Yet."

"Let them go." I pleaded. "Please."

"Just like your father. Pleading for my mercy," he grinned. "Go! You will die another day!" Piper helped Luke up and stumbled away. "You are blinded, my mercy is death. Your parents did not die because of me. They died because of weakness."

"If my father truly pleaded for mercy, why do you try so hard to convince me? Do not forget that I too was there!"

"Then you would know," the Adversary stammered.

"Know what?" I demanded.

"That you have already felt doubt and dread," he smiled. "Next comes death!" he flew upon me. I raised my sword and deflected his blow and struck his right leg. He jumped over my blade and kicked my left leg causing me to fall to one knee.

He then swung his sword toward my left side aiming for my neck. I ducked under his blade and rolled out of range.

"I am surprised you have lasted this long," he crept closer to me ever grinning. Ever hating. "First you survived at Roger's house, then in France and Shrewton, but there is no one to save you now!" his brow furrowed and the grip on his sword loosened.

"I too am surprised," I said preparing for his next attack, "that you have not seen what you have done and what you are!" I spun for more momentum and slammed my sword into the Adversary's blade. It felt like I hit a pillar of iron.

"I see who I am! I see what I have become!" he raised his sword in his right hand and coiling the same arm. "Every day!" he struck my sword and then laid his fist into my clenched jaw. I fell back in a daze. "I see who I am," his voice changed. "I see the death I have caused," the hate left his eyes for a moment, but then returned stronger. "And I will cause your death! Just like your father!"

I glared up at him in confusion. "My father did what was right before God and man!" I stood up.

"What is that verse? Honor thy father and mother so that it may go well with you/ See how you have failed! By the words of your own faith, you have been condemned."

"You speak truth," I aimed at his shoulder, but he dodged and sliced my armour with his sword. I regained my footing. "Only, it is not too late! Even if I did not honor him then, I honor him now!"

"Thou shalt not murder! Search your heart and see oh murderous wretch!" he prepared his sword. "See that there is no place in heaven for one such as you!" his sword came crashing down upon mine.

"There is," I recovered and wiped the blood from my mouth. "And there can be for you too."

"My master forbids it!" as he brought his sword bearing down, I narrowly escaped and sliced upward with my sword, cutting through his armour. I then kicked him in the same spot, sending him tumbling into the mud.

"If your master forbids your salvation," I said, "he forbids your life, he forbids you! Your master is dead now. He no longer controls you. You are free! Let go of your hatred and violence! Feel the freedom Christ has wrought!"

"My master saved me!" the Adversary reached out, grasping my leg and pulling me down with him. "He gave me a new life! I shall never betray him!" my sword fell from my hand.

"A life of what? Murder?" I asked. "You are free!"

"If that is what he requires, my freedom is nothing!"

"My father loved you like a brother!" I pleaded. "How can you dismiss that? How can you forget that Norwood?"

He grabbed my throat and began to choke me. "If he loved me, then he should be glad I saved him from seeing what you have become!"

I reached for my sword and slammed the pummel into his temple. He tumbled back and rose on the muddy ground, grasping his bleeding head.

"You have become a killer. A murderer. You have not only murdered in your heart, but you have tried to murder me and you failed to save many more," the Adversary taunted me one last time.

"No!" I charged for him and ran my sword through his torso. He fell back into the mire with indescribable pain on his face.

"You cannot kill me just by the sword," he sputtered where he lay grasping his wound. "I will haunt you for eternity."

"I am not trying to kill you," I knelt down beside him with tears in my eyes "I am trying to save you! Norwood, you are free! You are free!" I stood up with sword in hand. I looked up at the sky "It is nearly time," I looked back on the battlefield "Soon," I said "the Brethren will rise," I turned back to the ring of stone.

"No," the Adversary stammered. I turned back to him.

"What?" I asked.

"I am not free," he replied.

"But Roger is dead," I exclaimed.

"My master ordered it," he pointed to the ring and lay his head into the mud, wincing in pain. "And he is waiting for you!"

A beam of light began to form above the ring and slowly began its descent to the center. I wearily walked into the ring and came to a sudden stop as every dark emotion swept over me.

XXII

THE BRETHREN RISE

My heart nearly stopped. As I took in the tall chilling form of a man standing in the center of the stones. His build was muscular and imposing, and was nearly clean shaven. His hair was black as soot and his countenance was dark. Just looking into his flaming eyes one could see that he was a clever, cunning leader. He was dressed in a black tunic and a long leather surcoat which came down to his shins. Engraved upon the surcoat were many designs which resembled the scepter he held in his hand – the same scepter I saw in my vision. Around his shoulders hung a large hooded cloak which billowed in the wind, and made him look even more imposing if that were possible.

Dread, greater than ever before, engulfed me.

"All this time," his voice shattered through the sounds of battle and the screams of agony. "All this time I have been planning, and now it is finally here. The day when I stand victorious. I can already see my triumph," he fixed his gaze upon me. My courage melted and my faith was pushed to the edge of breaking. "Richard," his demeanor was unlike the Adversary and far from Roger's madness. This man was fully in control of his mind, and his weapons were not only of steel but of also of word.

I staggered into the ring, staring in awe at the man before me. "You?"

"I am what?" he replied.

"But Roger?" I managed to say.

"I ordered his death. Do you not remember my servant asking for my permission?" his voice filled the air. "That moment of silence."

"Stop this now," I demanded.

"You do not see my vision yet. Someday though," the corner of his mouth lifted. "Someday, you will see why."

"End it!" I yelled.

"You do not understand – if I stop now then all the men you have sacrificed are worth nothing. It would only serve to show that they were too weak to survive."

"Those men were the strongest of them all," I retorted.

"You are right are you not? Because Bennet is dead," his voice made the Adversary's sound weak, "because of your anger."

"No," I tried to remain calm as his masterful tongue wagged. "It is not too late, no more people have to die."

He turned his face fully toward me. "Do you really want their deaths to be in vain?" his eyes were like cauldrons of pain and sorrow.

"Like Henry? He died for nothing. He died because of your ignorance and foolishness."

"No," I said through clenched teeth as my knees buckled.

He took a step closer. "Andrew is dead now too," he took another step closer, "because of your weakness."

I collapsed into the mud. The weight of every loss came upon me. My heart raced as it fell. I tried not to let my emotions take hold of me again, but it was excruciating. The death of Andrew and Bennet were on my head. The death of every man in this war was on my head.

Apollo knelt down next to me.

"Your mother is dead. Phillip is dead," I felt his eviscerating gaze as he whispered into my ear. "Because of you."

"No!" I screamed and lashed my sword to strike him but he simply stepped back. "They died for a reason!" I yelled as I stood up.

"Because of your doubt," he countered.

"No! They died because of you!" anger swelled within me. "They died to stop you! They laid down everything to stop you!"

"Your dread of me is why they died," fed by darkness and sorrow, his words burned like the hottest flame. "You could not face me yourself because of your dread. So they did, and paid the price."

"And whose fault is that?" I said as I tried to regain my wits after his soul striking blow. "It was not my fault that I feared you-"

"Feared?" Apollo interrupted. "The word fear is far too weak. A child fears the dark, and a man fears what looms in that darkness. But you do not fear me, no, you dread me, for I am more than the darkness that children fear, I am more than the horrors dwelling in the dark. I am the darkness.

"And now your dread remains, now in this time and in the past, and forevermore until the day you die. You will always dread me. You will always remember me and you will dread me."

"I do fear you, but there is no shame, for without fear - "

"There is no bravery - I know your consolations, and they are foolishness," he continued. "But even with it, you contradict yourself."

"How so?" I asked.

"You are claiming you are brave and yet you are not willing to die," he thrust deeper into me. "In the depths of your soul, you want to live. Deep down you want nothing more than to walk away from this alive."

"Yes," I replied. I struggled to find words to counter his. "I do want to live. But if I must die then so be it."

"So you would die to save all these people?" he gestured to the battle.

"I would," I returned this time without faltering.

"Then why did you not die when you could have? When Phillip fell and your mother screamed? Why did you not die for them?" he countered.

"Because I could not!" I returned.

"You were weak," Apollo hissed. "You were not strong enough to die. And you will not be now."

"No! I was not strong enough then, but Christ stands with me today," I pressed back, trying to regain my faith – my hope.

"He did then too. And He abandoned you then just as He will now. Death will come to all these men fighting here. You would crush their hope with your confidence, and their lives with your ambition," he spoke with dreadful soothing words which pierced deeper than the Adversary's ever did. "For when your God leaves you today, as He did so many years ago, you will run just as you did then," I took in his words while my grip on Edmond's sword loosened. "But this time, millions will die, not just your parents. The world will fall and only you will be left alive. Alone. To live out the rest of your life in torment. Remembering every time you look at the light of the sun that God left you again on the day of the Alignment. Is that really what you want Richard?"

"They will all die," I struggled to say. "Because of me?"

Apollo put his hand on my shoulder and gazed into my eyes. "It is your choice. I cannot make it for you. But make it soon and know this, whatever I did to hurt you was for your good. I want you to come with me Richard. This is why you were born – for something so much greater than humanity can offer."

Tears entered my eyes. "So either I run and live alone with the burden of death and loss? Or I surrender and they all live?"

"There is a third option. One that breaks you and me," he drew in a deep breath, "one I can never live with."

"What?"

"You die today."

Dread held me fast, 'I do not want to die,' I thought to myself.

"And I do not want to kill you," he replied. "But you would leave me with no choice," he stepped back. "If you surrender Richard, all these people will live. All these people will have a new life. All will be right. For if you surrender they will see it as the greatest victory. Phillip would be proud that you saved more than he ever imagined. You would save millions."

"Do you believe that?" I asked with tears streaking my face. "Do you really believe that my father would be proud? Of me? I have been filled with anger and hatred for so long – how could he be proud of that?"

"Because of your courage and hope. You hoped when no one would. You lead these men to war to save them. And you can end it to save them. You can save them all."

"Why do you not end it? You started it," I asked.

"I created something that was beyond humanity. I started this war because I needed to show you something."

"And what is that?"

"That you are worth it," he said. "That you have a purpose. To end what I started. I made you the man you are. Now take action. You are the final hope. If you let your pride rule, you destroy what I did for you. Be the man I never could be."

"Do you truly believe any of this?" with doubt creeping into my heart.

"I do," he said, putting his arm around my shoulder. "I do."

I thought hard. 'Should I surrender? He said it was the only way. Either I die and lose, I live alone and in torment, or I surrender, and they all live. Was it so bad to surrender?' I looked up at Apollo, 'But does God believe it?' I said to myself.

"He left me too," Apollo replied. "He left when I lost everything. He only cares about those who can bring Him more power, something I could never do. So He left me in unbearable pain, just like you."

"Is that why He left me when my family died, and not Andrew when he lost his wife and son? Andrew had the key to power and I did not?"

"Yes," Apollo returned. "He stayed with Andrew because he wanted Andrew. Now tell me, why did He leave you?"

"Because He did not want me," I wept. "He did not love me enough to keep me for I had nothing to offer Him!" I dropped Edmond's sword into the mud and collapsed with my head in my hands. Neither the rage of battle, nor the thunder, not even the power of the Alignment could sway me in my dreadful state. My hatred was gone, my anger was gone – the one thing that remained was my doubt. My dread. And the death of all those I fought for.

"Time is running out Richard," Apollo's voice broke the silence.

I picked up the sword and stood up, then held it out for Apollo to take. "I and the Brethren," I said through clenched teeth as I tried to hold back my tears. "S..." I stopped short and gazed at the blade of the sword. Upon it the words formed slowly like they were being burned in and soon revealed brightly – 'I love you. I am with you.'

My heart melted inside my chest and then reformed. My sadness turned to passion, my despair into hope and my agony into strength. I looked up at Apollo standing beside me. "Shall stand!" I brought the sword plunging around toward his chest. He leapt out of the way and let loose a wave of force from his scepter which threw both of us backwards.

"There is nothing you can do!" he thundered in rage, but with more remorse than hatred. It was the kind of rage that is the offspring of sorrow. "The end has come and there is nothing you can do to stop it!" he clenched his teeth as he tried to hold back.

I readied my sword, "You fear defeat. And that you fear it proves that there is a way! He will show me the way!"

"Enough," he waved his scepter in an ark in front of him, sending a wave of dark energy throwing me back against the stone. I gritted my teeth, trying not to show the pain, but it was no use. He walked over to me raising his scepter, "Doubt, dread," he spoke, "you have felt both. Now prepare for death my beloved one!" he brought the scepter down as I raised Edmond's sword and blocked the blow, throwing Apollo back to the other side of the ring by the force of the collision.

I gazed at the blade of Edmond's sword, "Where did you come from?"

"You have no idea what you are doing!" thundered Apollo as he stood up. "You have no idea what you have done!" black lightening leapt between his fingers and glistened in his eyes.

"As long as I am following Him," I raised the sword and held it in both hands and tried to steady myself, "knowing is of no consequence."

I blocked another hit, and sliced his leg. He stumbled a bit, then slammed his scepter into my chest thrusting me back into another stone. He came quickly to me, gripped my throat and brought my face near to his. The dark lightening stung my whole body like millions of burning needles.

"Such is the death of the Brethren," he wept as he squeezed my throat until I could no longer breathe "And everyone else."

"No!" I muttered as I raised my sword and stabbed his left

shoulder. "Such is yours."

He stepped back pulling the sword away from me. He wrenched it from his shoulder, and dropped it in pain as it burned his hand. "So long as the shadow lives," he extended both arms to the sky and exclaimed, "I live!" from the black orb came great bolts of the black lightening and the crack of thunder. "Such is my blessing," The darkness from the scepter struck me and cast me back against one of the stones again. "And my curse," My armour was charred black and smoke rose from where it was hit.

"Why are you holding back?" I stared up into his woeful eyes. "Why not kill me? I know you can!"

"Because," he gripped my armour and swung me into another nearby stone. "I want your hope to die slowly."

"We both know that is not why!" I yelled. "Who are you?"

"I am the one who hates," he pinned me up against one of the stones. But even as the pain coursed through me, I knew that I was not the one he hated. "I am doubt," he hissed as he punched me in the gut. "I am dread," he punched me again and still held back his power. "I am death." he released me to the ground with the final blow, yet even so I felt him holding back. Trying not to kill me. Trying to do something I could not understand.

"Why are you holding back?" I cried as I tried to stand, but all was in vain.

He gripped my throat again and lifted me into the air. His face was downcast and turned away. "Child, do you think I lied when I said your death would break me?" his voice was filled with neither rage nor hate, only sorrow could be heard in it. A sorrow that was beyond my comprehension.

"You are full of lies!" I whispered through the little breath I had left.

"Everything I did was for you," he released me to the ground. "I started this for you. I started it so that you could forgive me! Forgive my rage and hate!"

"I do not want your apology for the millions that you killed!" I replied. "I want you to surrender and face your judge!"

He looked at me in distress. "You do not want an apology?"

"Who are you?" I demanded again.

"You do not know me?" he replied.

"I asked, who are you?" my voice, along with my faith grew ever stronger.

"You have forgotten me," pain entered his eyes and the lightening in them became darker. "If you do not know who I am, then all I have done is pointless," he closed his eyes for a moment and a tear flowed down his cheek. He calmed himself slightly and opened them again, "Join me Richard. Forgive me. Ease my sorrow and pain."

"Who are you?" I gritted my teeth.

"I am doubt!" he wept and struck me with the scepter and I was thrown against the stone and slumped down. "I am dread! I am death! And that is all that matters to you, is it not?" he turned away from me. I no longer knew what I was fighting. "You can save them," he sighed. "Is that not what you want?"

In agony, I stared at Apollo's face. But something told me that he was in more pain than I. Perhaps it was the way he gazed up at the light, or the way it reflected off his tears. I heaved my head around and lay my eyes upon Edmond's sword.

"Lord God," I lifted my hand to my mouth, wiping away the blood and staring at my crimson hand. "Lord God!" I lurched my hand forward and dug my fingers into the mud. Raindrops stung my body and the mire tried to pull me in. I strained the muscles in my arm and dragged myself forward toward where the sword lay. "Please!" I gritted my teeth as I lifted my other arm and dragged myself a foot farther. "Show me the way!" I drew myself up and threw my hand upon the hilt, covered in mud, yet still shimmering. I lifted my eyes to gaze upon the blade. "Show me the way!" my voice broke and my head collapsed into the mud. And there I lay, listening to the sounds of battle and cries of death. The blood curdling screeches of the Varanus, and the rain beating down upon the bodies of the fallen.

But then another sound rang out that I could not identify. Like hope itself was burning its way into the battle. I lifted my head from the mud, and stared at the blade of the sword as it began to blaze. Letters began to appear upon it, burning away the filth, first one then another, they soon began to form words. Words that gave hope: 'Let the light shine.'

"The light?" I turned and gazed at the stone in the center of the ring. An ever-brightening light shone from within it. I looked further around the ring and now noticed that the other stones with the lesser lights were also brightening.

"Richard!" Edmond ran over to me and helped me up and out of the ring. "We are all here."

"We cannot kill him," I stammered. "He is holding back and he is beyond all of us."

"Then what?" Edmond asked.

"Stand behind the stones outside of Apollo's line of sight," I coughed. "See the glowing orbs on the stones?"

"Aye," Edmond replied.

"On my mark, remove them," I stood using Edmond's sword to steady myself. "We will have only a few minutes."

"And what are you doing?" he asked.

"What I have to," I said. "We have to remove the orbs from

their bonds."

"Right then," Edmond said. "I trust you," he ran back to Piper and Luke. Luke was trying to stand despite his wound and his face was pale with the loss of blood, but his spirit was bright. Feargal was with them too. It looked as if he had truly faced his greatest fears and come out alive. He was a new man.

I stumbled back into the ring and faced my enemy. "Apollo!" I yelled. "We are not finished!"

"But your time runs out Richard," he grinned, but not like the Adversary. Apollo's grin was in pain. The kind of grin you make when you are trying to see that all is not as bad as it seems. "Prepare to watch the world burn," The beam of the Alignment struck the center upon the main stone and split into four other beams just as Andrew had predicted. The beams hit the four other orbs and the light was blinding. Apollo reached for the center orb with his scepter and darkness slowly began covering the light.

I leapt forward in the way of the scepter, and it easily penetrated my armour as it soaked in the power of the central orb. Pain coursed through my entire body and I felt death creep in.

"No!" he screamed and yanked the scepter out. "No," his voice broke.

"Now!" I shouted as I reached for the center orb. My arm went numb and my body felt like it would explode, but I managed to pull out the orb of light and struggled to my feet. The orb entered my body as if it were my own flesh, and light coursed through my veins. I no longer felt pain but only strength and warmth, and a power beyond anything that I had ever felt before.

I reached forward toward Apollo, grabbed the scepter, and pulled it from his hand.

"No!" he scrambled trying to reclaim his possession. "You cannot destroy it!"

"Then," I stabbed Edmond sword into the ground and raised the scepter up above the center stone. "You have nothing to fear!" I brought the scepter crashing down with all my strength. As I did so, Apollo lurched forward and clasped his hand around the black orb. I held the scepter in place and glanced around at the four other stones. Luke was no longer pale and bleeding but stood strong examining his former wounds in bewilderment as an orange and blue light emanated from his hands. Piper too looked more alive and beautiful with radiant eyes and a confined wind blowing about her. The most changed was Feargal, his fear was gone completely and the ground moved around him. Edmond looked at me in peace as if to say again 'I trust you' while his eyes were flowing with tears of passion and strength.

Apollo struggled to pull the dark orb out of its place as the sun began to descend out of the Alignment. The four other beams reflected off the stones now that the orbs were removed and the light converged upon the scepter. Blinding light shone all around as the darkness slowly began to fade. "Tell the son of Freeman that I am coming back for him," Apollo thundered as the dark orb crept up his arms and leached into his body. He reeled back in pain. "It burns!" he screamed as the darkness of the orb consumed him. I closed my eyes as he screamed. "Remember me, Richard!" I could feel his woeful gaze upon me. "Remember who I am! Remember that I - "

The sun moved out of the Alignment, I opened my eyes and stared at my hands, the scepter was no longer there. I looked around at the ring. Apollo was gone as well.

"He is gone!" Edmond exclaimed.

"The Brethren have risen," I raised myself to full height and gazed up into the sky which was clear and did not bear any sign of what had just happened.

"The scepter is gone!" Luke exclaimed.

"Not exactly gone, but close enough," I replied.

"What do you mean?" Piper asked.

I knelt down next to the center stone and beckoned my friends to do the same. "Look in there," I pointed to where the orb of light once was – where now a dark sea of blackness swirled. "That is where it is."

"Could someone not just take it out?" Feargal asked.

"No," I replied. "The orbs were unable to be removed until the Alignment came."

"So at the next Alignment, it will be released?" Edmond inquired.

"That is my best guess," I said as I stood up and held out the sword to Edmond.

"No," he said.

"What?" I returned. "It is not mine."

"My time with it is done. I am a soldier, not a leader. The sword is yours now."

"I cannot accept this," I said.

Edmond smiled. "The Brethren needs a leader. And the sword needs a leader to wield it. Andrew led us through those years. You were like a son to him. It is your place to lead," he handed the sheath to me. "Wield it well."

I took the sheath and tied it onto my belt and took another long look at the sword before I sheathed it.

"Now what did those things do anyway?" Luke held his hand up to our view. It was glowing red and heat emitted from it. "Well, besides the fact that I am not dead and my hand is glowing?" Luke asked with a boyish grin.

I smiled. "I guess finding out will be the next adventure."

"Why is it that my hand is the only one glowing? Why could Feargal's face not be glowing?"

"I do not know!" I laughed as I looked at my own hands.

I felt empowered. I felt like I could shine brighter than the sun, run faster than any man alive. I felt strong.

"Let us not talk about it here," said Edmond. "We will have plenty of time to speak of the orbs later."

"The orbs?" Luke furrowed his brow and nodded. "I like that."

We walked triumphantly out of the ring. I stared across the battlefield. Countless statues littered the plain and thousands of men as well.

"We need to clean those up," Luke grumbled. "And my hand is glowing."

"That we do," I smiled.

We walked down into the ranks of the joyful men. Though many had not the good fortune to survive, a great number of them did. Yet even in the sadness and mourning of the millions lost in this war, relief and joy overcame the host that remained. The victory of that day was the greatest in history and would be for ages to come. Though no one could ever know the true nature of the war, it would remain forever in the hearts and minds of the men who made their stand that day.

"We did it," I said joyously. "We won by the Grace of God, we won!"

I looked back to where I had left Norwood. He was standing up now and walking toward me.

"Richard," he wept "I am so sorry!" he collapsed before me. "I am so sorry."

I helped him to his feet and met his familiar piercing eyes which were full of passion, wisdom and pain.

"It is over now!" I exclaimed and embraced him.

"He is coming back!" Norwood cried and pushed me away.

"No," I replied. "He lied. We are safe. The world is safe."

Norwood's eyes blazed. "Then why am I still afraid?"

XXIII

A HIGHER CALLING

"You did what?" Edward stared at me as I explained what happened in the ring while he and the army fought the Varanus.

"Aye, we bound the scepter in the rock until the next Alignment comes," I smiled as I realized he had no understanding of the mystery unveiled at the ring. "It is taken care of until then."

"And when will that be?" Edward queried.

"One thousand years," I promptly stated.

"So I need not worry about it?" he said.

"Nay - I think not," I felt the power of the orb coursing through me. "The Brethren have that responsibility."

"And what of the other kingdoms?" Edward asked, "France, Spain and the lot, are we at peace for now?"

"I have sent them back home," I explained. "Their land will be returned and their kingdoms as they were. They have all been ordered and you now as well, to tell no one of what happened at the ring. No one may know the truth of what happened so that we may protect the future. And as for peace, that is for you to decide, I am unable to make peace between you and the other nations. There is only One who sows perfect peace and you will need Him – especially with France."

"I know," The King sighed, "but I fear that our peace will be short lived. My meeting earlier at the Chateau de Dourdan with Phillip did not go as planned. Neither did he seem to change after what has happened."

"With all due respect Sire," I said, "nothing went as planned in France! We were attacked by monsters! That was not on my plan."

The King chuckled. "What are you calling it again?"

"The Black Death," I replied. "We are calling it a plague – not a war."

"Ah, yes!" he laughed. "Is that not a bit obvious though? Black Death?"

"Sire, the world does not believe in monsters. And I would like it to stay that way until this war ends for good."

"And this 'Norwood' character?" asked the King. "What will become of him?"

"He is better now. You need not worry about him either," I replied.

"How?" Edmond asked.

"He was controlled by the power of the scepter. Once we bound it in the Alignment he was set free," I answered.

"Is he still..." Edward's voice trailed off.

"Different?" I sighed. "Aye. But he will live with what he has done for the rest of his life."

"Where is he now?" Edward asked further.

"He has already been escorted to the town where our ship is moored. He will be kept there in custody until we set sail. Once we are established, we will determine his state and he will possibly be set free.

Once freed he has promised to atone for his actions and to serve the Brethren."

"Well done," the King commended. "Very well done."

I turned and walked to the door of the palace.

"And thank you Richard," he continued, "my thanks, and all England thanks you and all the Brethren. We owe you a debt today and for the ages."

"I would not have had it any other way," I smiled. "Tell England that we will be watching, waiting, until we are needed once more to defeat the enemies of this world."

"Will I ever see you again?" asked the King. "Before then?"

"We will be around," I said. "But wars, as you know them, can no longer be our concern. We now have a higher calling."

"And what is that?" Edward replied with more interest.

"Raising up new protectors to fight the unseen wars, to be there when the scepter returns and to stand if a darker night comes," I left the King's presence, mounted my horse and rode gallantly from London with a smile of pure contentment on my face.

***

I stared up at the ring. It had been a month and the battlefield was cleared, and the dead buried. Luke and I were the only two present.

I felt his hand on my shoulder. "So!" Luke exclaimed. "What are we going to call it?"

"Call what?" I asked.

"The battle? It needs a name does it not?" he replied.

"Well, yes," I thought for a moment then said. "Battle for the Alignment?"

"The Alignment is a secret though," Luke corrected me.

"True," I thought again. "War of the Ring?"

"Oh no! I did not fight in a war of the ring!" Luke voiced in disgust. "At least try to make it sound good!"

"Fine then," I grinned. "Battle of," I paused, lost in thought of what to call this historical battle. "Battle of lost time?"

"You are serious?" Luke laughed. "Battle of lost time? Are we running out of it?"

"Well – to later generations it will be lost in time!"

"No no no!" Luke protested.

"Battle of Amesbury!" I exclaimed.

"Does not hit me right," Luke frowned.

"Does it have to 'hit' you right?"

"Absolutely! I fought in that battle, therefore I get a say in naming it!" he seemed to forget that he was not the only man who fought. "And I say that Battle of Amesbury is not the right name."

"Fine," I said in resignation.

"What?" Luke asked.

"Fine," I crossed my arms. "You name it."

"Well then, finally some sense!" he crowed and I laughed aloud. "I will name it!" Luke crossed his arms and stared at the ring of stone. He stood there for several long minutes hardly blinking. He opened his mouth a few times as if he was going to say something, but he always kept silent.

"Name it already Redhill," I taunted as I began to lose my patience.

"Battle of Stonehenge," he pointed at the ring then spun on his heel and began walking toward Durrington.

"Stone, what?" I stammered.

"Stonehenge," Luke called back to me without turning around.

"What in the name of England is Stonehenge?" I exclaimed.

Luke turned with a beaming smile on his face and pointed toward the ring. "Now that is how you name a battle!"

"What is a henge?" I asked.

"Not a clue," he continued walking. "But it sounds better than the ring!"

"That is cheating!" I cried.

"No, it is not! Wait a few years! It will catch on!" he fired back with amusement filling his voice.

I looked back at 'Stonehenge' then at Luke as he strutted away.

"Where are you going?" I yelled.

"I want that table!" he shouted back.

"What table?" I yelled again.

"The burnt one! With the swords! I named it Septem Gladiis!"

"Septem what?" I asked.

"Seven swords!" he continued to walk away.

"How does he do that?" I said with a scowl. "Sure, yes, I will just call is Septem Gladiis! No one will ever wonder what in the name of England is Septem Gladiis! And oh look, that there is a henge!" I continued muttering to myself as I mounted my horse and set off in the opposite direction.

I arrived in Shrewton a little while later, dismounted my horse and entered the house – the one thing Apollo had not changed after himself. The windows were boarded over and webs hung in every corner. Aside from the disrepair, the room was the same as I had left it thirteen years before; the table in place and the chairs around the fireplace. I know not why but the bodies of my parents were not there. It would have been in Apollo's character to leave their bones, but by some mercy, they had been removed.

I lay my hand on the back of the chair. I could almost see that night again, but this time it was different. I saw it as the beginning of a better life for me, a new life. I fingered a ring in my pocket and felt the power of the orb course through me.

"It was all for my good," I said aloud. "All of it," I walked over to the table and looked at the rusted sword in the corner. "Even the pain and suffering, you always had a plan," I strolled over to one of the cabinets along the wall and opened it. A Bible once belonging to my father lay inside, so I pulled it out and let it open onto the table: 'For if you forgive men when they sin against you, your heavenly Father will also forgive you. But if you do not forgive men their sins, your Father will not forgive your sins.'

"Lord," I knelt down, "help me to forgive. As you have forgiven. Please strengthen my faith, and let me fight for you," I released the power of the Orb of Light, for each of us had named our gift, into my hand so much that it shone brightly. "Let me be a light in the world," I stood up and took one last look inside that old house, the old life. I took the Bible, walked outside and put it into my saddlebag. Then I turned back one last time to look at the house.

"My life here is over," I said raising my lighted hand, "I no longer exist in the known world," light like water flowed through my fingers and came to rest upon my palm, "I will become a legend," I held back the Orb's power with tears, "I am bringing the hope of my King in times of need for as long as I live," The burning ball of light shot forth and for a moment it seemed time had slowed down. The ball of light flew faster than I could comprehend, and for a split second, shadowy figures flashed across my view and fled. I jumped as the light crashed into the house. Shards of wood and stone flew everywhere as the house fell. I marveled at what I had seen and smiled. "Thank You, Father," I said "Thank You," A tear fell from my eye onto the ground. I turned, mounted, and rode out of Shrewton leaving it with its shadows gone and open to a new tomorrow.

***

I rode to Durrington and entered my other house there to get what little I had left. It had been three months since the Battle of Stonehenge. Europe had just begun restoring itself, but trade and communication would be absent for another few years. I packed up my bed and a few of my tools and the instructions for making my weapons and Valinium. As I did so, another horse rode up to the house and its rider dismounted. I faced the door as Piper came in. I had spent much time with her after the battle and our friendship had grown. Our experience in France and in the Battle of Stonehenge had brought us closer.

"We are ready to leave for Bristol," she said. "Feargal arranged a ship to take us to the island from there."

"Thank you Piper," I said.

"Do you need any help getting ready?" she asked.

I smiled as I put my hand in my pocket. "Well, you could do one thing," I said. "And I would really appreciate it."

"Right then," she said. "What is it?"

"I know I am no charmer and not much with money," my heart began to beat faster. "And I would fully understand your objection."

"What do you want me to do?" Piper interrupted with her eyes fixed on me.

I made a fist around the ring and pulled it out of my pocket. I took a deep breath and lay it in her hand. "I imagined this to be more formal, or at least to go smoother, but," I paused and shuffled about the room. "Ah, biscuit's blood!" I laughed. "Piper Redhill, will you marry me?" I gave an awkward smile which was meant to be dashing.

"See, people do not like those who flirt!" she smiled. "But that is Richard, fully human, no charm at all," her brow furrowed. "No really, none."

"What in the name of England does that mean?" I asked incredulously.

"It means yes – nitwit." Edmond shouted from the doorway.

I looked at Piper.

"He is right," she smiled.

"That I am a nitwit? Or that you are saying yes?" I blushed. "I have had enough riddles to supply a lifetime!"

"Both!" she hugged me and wind blew all around making my cloak fly and her hair sweep through the air. Light began to shine brighter than any I had yet seen. Tears of joy flowed as we embraced in a prolonged kiss.

"I know we have all the time in the world, but if you two are done," Edmond interrupted after a minute, "we have an island waiting and a man to recover."

"I hear you Edmond!" Piper yelled. "No need for the rush!" We left the house and I closed the door behind me.

"Are the weapons gone?" asked Edmond.

"I melted them and sold the metal to Edward," I replied.

"Are you sure you want to burn your home?" asked Piper.

"Forget his house!" Luke hollered as he walked up. "You sold my sword to Edward!"

"Correction Luke," said Feargal, "he melted it, and sold it."

"And it was my sword," I put in.

"Fair point. Back to your home then," Luke replied.

"It is not my home anymore." I smiled "It is just an old adventure I wish no one else to have."

I raised my hand to the house.

"Wait!" Luke threw his hand up. "I got this!" he laid his hand on the door frame. "Stand back," he smiled. As soon as we did, the house burst into flames.

We watched it for a while remembering the past times – the dark times. The house quickly collapsed sending up a myriad of sparks. I turned and began to mount my horse.

"Edmond," I said, "would you put out the fire before the King banishes us for burning the Kingdom?"

"My pleasure," Edmond motioned his hand through the air as a wave of water carried over the fire, instantly putting it out.

"Edmond you will ruin my maps!" Feargal yelled as he tried to keep his papers dry.

"Ha!" I laughed. "What does it matter? Today we begin anew!" I turned my horse, reared up yelling, "A new world awaits!" Then crashing down, broke into a gallop to the north, to Bristol, followed by the Brethren.

EPILOGUE

THE FUTURE TORMENTS

Off we rode into a new life. We would station ourselves on the island for quite some time. Edmond would later get married along with Feargal and Luke, their wives able to live with them in their long years from exposure to the Orbs just as Andrew did during the time of the Alignment. Time passed, but we were always young and strong, always fighting the unseen battles. Eventually, the children and children's children of the Brethren would form a multitude; however, none that Piper and I could call our own. Nonetheless, all these, as they came of age, protected the earth and all corners of it, the five Kingdoms of the Brethren, on every continent, from Europe, to Africa, to Asia to the New World and beyond.

We would spread far and wide, from sea to sea and from age to age. We lived in the shadows but not forever, the shadow would break into the light and all nations would know what the Brethren had done for them; how much the Brethren had sacrificed to save them. Hope sustained us all.

***

"So," I said with Piper by my side. We gazed off the bow of the ship upon the island. "Nearly there," I smiled.

Edmond came up and slapped me on the back. "Aye!" he laughed. "And we will be for a while!"

"Yes," Piper sighed. "Do you think it will hurt?"

"What?" I asked.

"Living so long and watching everyone else grow old."

"This is not the life we chose," said Edmond, "but it is the life we are called to live. The life we must live."

I sighed, "The worst is over now. Thankfully," I closed my eyes and drew in a deep breath. "It is finally over."

Suddenly I flew back in my mind – back before time began. Many colors swirled all around me like a tempest. I was thrown forward again. I watched the earth take its form, I watched the creation of man. I saw Adam's fall, the first murder and flooding of the world! I watched all people disperse throughout the planet. Shooting through all time and space I saw the beginning of the war and flew through time to places I have never seen and wish never to see again. All was a blur at the speed of light. I watched the end of humanity and the final battle of my brothers, the final fight for freedom.

And just as suddenly as I began I jolted to a stop. My head spun rapidly. I stood up and looked around. Edmond's sword was in my hand and I was wearing strange, unearthly clothing. Rain poured from the heavens and soaked the ground just like every other vision I had seen. A powerful voice pierced the silence. I turned to see who it was, at least I thought I turned, I did not think about it though. The man speaking was nearly a hundred yards away, standing and shouting up at a hill with Stonehenge fixed on the top.

'A hill again?' I thought.

But then it was not Stonehenge, something was different. The stones began morphing together as I focused upon them. They became one and then became larger.

My mouth dropped as I slowly realized what it was. There I stood, in the middle of a ruined city, staring at the great Temple mount. This was Jerusalem.

'What?' I asked myself in awe.

Surrounding the Temple was the largest battle I had every seen or the world would ever see, that had taken place just days before. Millions of bodies of men were piled up everywhere along with countless human-like forms which looked like they were made of metal. But what stood out more than these were the millions of statues.

'The Varanus' I said to myself.

I found myself walking toward the man as though I was unable to control my own body. He was giving a speech a few yards from the stones. As I came closer I could make out a few of the words, but could not understand them all. Something like he was sorry and that the other man was forgiven. I did not understand. The one thing that he kept saying was "Take me!" And "Let them live!"

I came up next to him. He yelled the last words of his speech, and whispered, "Take me instead."

I looked at him, then up at the ruin. A man in black stood at the top. I knew not who it was, nor did I look at him long enough to find out. I lay my hand on the speaker's shoulder and found myself handing the sword to him. He looked at me, all I could see was his eyes, blazing with passion, fear, love, and loss, pain and hope. He said something I could not understand, but his voice was familiar. It was the same voice I had when I fought Apollo at Stonehenge – it was the voice of hope. Final hope.

Suddenly another person stood before me. His face shined brighter than the sun and his hands were outstretched. He was my Savior.

"Were that these days be cut short. None would survive. The Brethren rise to the commission this day. The Culmination Day."

I opened my eyes, fell back and was caught by Edmond. My head spun. My mind was clouded. Shadows flashed before my vision.

"What is wrong! What happened?" Piper cried.

I could hardly speak, I know not why. All I could describe, all I could ever say about it was. "The hill," I gasped. "There was no hill..."

The Dream of Hope Will Come....

THE BRETHREN RISE

C. D. HULEN

COMING SUMMER 2019

BOOK 2

OF

THE DREAM OF HOPE

SERIES

CPSIA information can be obtained
at www.ICGtesting.com
Printed in the USA
FFOW02n1024230618
47181117-49865FF